Praise for *Dignity*

'*Dignity* is an exquisite novel: compassionate, beautiful and unflinching. I'm full of admiration for the skill with which it draws connections between the past and present, and manages to feel both timeless and achingly contemporary'
Fiona McFarlane, author of *The Night Guest*

'Through three women's distinct and wonderful voices Alys Conran explores the nature and meaning of home. The characters in this beautiful novel are fierce, compassionate, angry, but above all, heartbreakingly real. I was drawn in from the very first page'
Claire Fuller, author of *Our Endless Numbered Days* and *Bitter Orange*

'In Alys Conran's second novel, she tells the story of Magda, an elderly woman beset with memories of her childhood in India and her growing concern for Susheela, the young woman who works as her carer. As Magda's health fails and Susheela reveals struggles of her own, the women – difficult, complicated, sometimes unlikeable – draw closer in this surprising tale of the British Empire's long reach. This is a beguiling book with a fierce, uncompromising quality to it – a novel that continues to unfold its meaning after the story has ended'
Guinevere Glasfurd, author of *The Words in My Hand*

Dignity

Alys Conran, originally from North Wales, spent several years in Edinburgh and Barcelona before returning to the area to live and write. She speaks Welsh and English as first languages, and also speaks Spanish and Catalan. She has worked as a youth worker, teacher, and in community arts and is now Lecturer in Creative Writing at Bangor. Her late father, also a writer, was born in Kharagpur, Bengal.

Her poetry, short stories, creative non-fiction, creative essays and literary translations, and other work is to be found in numerous magazines and anthologies including *Stand* and the *Manchester Review*.

Also by Alys Conran

Pigeon

Dignity

Alys Conran

W&N

WEIDENFELD & NICOLSON

First published in Great Britain in 2019
by Weidenfeld & Nicolson
an imprint of The Orion Publishing Group Ltd
Carmelite House, 50 Victoria Embankment
London EC4Y 0DZ

An Hachette UK Company

1 3 5 7 9 10 8 6 4 2

'Dychwelyd' by T.H. Parry-Williams ©T.H. Parry-Williams Estate.
Reproduced through permission of Gomer Press.

Extract from *Culinary Reactions* by Simon Quellen Field on p352
reprinted by permission of Chicago Review Press.

This work was supported by the Arts and Humanities Research Council.

A CIP catalogue record for this book is
available from the British Library.

ISBN 978 1 4746 0943 2 (Hardback)
ISBN 978 1 4746 0944 9 (Export Trade Paperback)
ISBN 978 1 4746 0946 3 (eBook)

Typeset by Input Data Services Ltd, Somerset

Printed and bound in Great Britain by Clays Ltd, Elcograf S.p.A.

www.orionbooks.co.uk
www.weidenfeldandnicolson.co.uk

In memory of my father, Tony Conran,
poet and translator.

And for his friend, Shallu,
who came to care.

When the aristocracy of the great Olympian gods collapsed at the end of antiquity, it did not take down with it the mass of indigenous gods, the populace of gods that still possessed the immensity of fields, forests, woods, mountains, springs, intimately associated with the life of the country. These gods lived in the hearts of oaks, in the swift, deep waters and could not be driven out of them . . . where are they? In the desert, on the heath, in the forest? Yes, but also and especially in the home. They live on in the most intimate of domestic habits.

La Sorcière,
Jules Michelet

Book One

Chapter One

An Indian household can no more be governed peacefully without dignity and prestige, than an Indian Empire.

> *The Complete Indian Housekeeper and Cook,*
> Flora Annie Steel & Grace Gardiner

To my house at number three Victoria Drive the world outside is foreign. The gap between the inside of the house and what blurs past outside has been growing steadily throughout recent years until everything beyond the walls seems loud and staccato and completely out of time. Oh it is all whirring roads, fast-changing channels and quick shifts of sense so sudden there's not a hope of finding a meaning in any of it. Oh it is all people darting and quivering with busyness, leaving every sentence half finished. Oh it is all in pieces. It is all simply shards.

The house has to hold out against this small Britain, which has become so lax, and its unsteady world, which whirrs so. My house has to make a stand. It has to stand tall and upright with all its separate rooms. With its walls made of good brick from the days when brick was made right, its clean

3

sash windows over which blinds are perpetually hung, and its door, painted with black gloss, with which the house says, in its own way, *do not come in*. Although I barely ever use the door, I know that still, at the foot of it, a brush doormat lies. On the doormat it simply says 'Home' in small stern letters. And perhaps it's this that finally discourages the legions of those fidgeting people from the world outside to trespass up the path. For no one visits the house.

No one save the girls in their yellow uniforms. The house can't escape them; they come on professional business.

We're in the bathroom. The new girl, Susheela, tugs hard at my knickers to get them down over the thickened legs.

'Sorry, Magda,' she says.

'You should be.'

This is the first time we've been to the toilet together. I have tried, since she arrived on the scene, to avoid going with her. When I go with them, we must talk. I'm still unable to accustom myself to listening to the flow of urine in the presence of someone else, and so must make conversation.

'So you're Susheela, are you?'

'Yes, Su-shee-la,' the girl says now. A slight smile; she's surprised and perhaps pleased that I know her name at all, I can tell. We have exchanged few words on her previous visits.

'Did I say it incorrectly?' I know I didn't.

'No.'

'Then why choose to repeat it in that idiotic fashion?'

She laughs. Surprised, is she?

'Sorry,' she says. 'Didn't mean to offend.'

'Takes more than that, my girl.'

4

I cannot think of what she's presently doing, and so we must continue.

'Where are you from?' I ask. The other one was from Delhi, the other Indian girl, who lasted only one visit and was gone back out into the blur.

'Just down the road,' she says. 'Bay's Mouth.' Her soft voice fills the bathroom.

She has a North Indian look about her. Yes. I press it away, the longing, try to shut the door on it. But it's come in, settled down and put its feet up. Damn this girl. Ever since she turned up she's bothered me like a bite that won't settle.

Once she has me all back in order she wheels the chair out past the dressing table. I stroke the wood of it as we pass. When I could stand and walk alone, on my own path, I would linger here, beside it, the teak of the dressing table smooth and cool, like a young face. If you look into it for long enough, into the almost imperceptible grain, you can see it. The heat. And you can feel that this wood was once rooted. Touching it, you can watch white storks pick across a grove. Feel the dry air in your mouth. And hear it. The thick air. The sound of it. The hum and muster of Bengal.

The girl pushes my unlistening chair on and on through the house, at whoever's pace but mine. Into the living room. Under the clock.

Then she comes round to the front of my chair, and looks at me.

Damn it.

Damn it, I can't escape seeing the world in their expressions, the ones that come. That world in pieces. And them, in pieces. There's part of them here, with me, changing my

5

blouse, or running my stockings up the varicosed legs like pulling over a shroud. And part of them elsewhere, in several elsewheres: clocking in, clocking out, checking the messages on their small black phones, driving, braking, driving, making microwave dinners and watching the TV channels change. You can't help feeling sorry for them, the ones that come to care.

Sometimes I wonder where it is in them, that part of a person that needs to be separate and bounded, needs to be itself alone and set within its own confines.

I've even asked them. 'What do you do to come to yourself?' I asked the fat one last week, meaning *How do you wind all this down? How do you survive it?* And she looked at me and laughed, and then looked at me again, lost a demi-second before saying, 'This and that,' and some other obfuscating tattle.

What they do, I realise from hearing them talk to each other at the changing of the guard, is have a glass of wine, and then another and another, and sink into it. Forgetting. Their many parts sagging, and still apart.

I frighten them by asking these kinds of questions. Their only recourse is to behave as though I am as idiotic as I look.

'Oh, Magda,' says the short one almost every time she comes. 'Are you in one of your moods again?' Which is enough to make me want to belt her across the face.

Or, 'Oh, Magda. You do make me laugh.' The more reasonable, tall one.

Or – the most patronising square woman with the black hair – 'Magda, are you causing trouble again?'

Which I am. I most emphatically am.

★

'Coffee?'

I don't answer.

'Would you like coffee?'

'I should think you could check your chart and see if it's time,' I say.

She's looking at me in that incredulous, blank way.

'What do you mean?'

'A timetable for everything now, isn't there?' I smooth my skirt as I sit. 'Shouldn't think it matters if I want it; I shall have it.'

'But do you want it?'

'Does it matter?' I look up at her.

'It matters to me, Magda.' That small smile, as she says it, my Christian name.

My bones feel it, the way she's looking at me. Pity, is it? Is it? I look her in the eye, this new Indian girl, and make myself as upright as I can in the chair, stacking my vertebrae again, tall.

'And are you of any importance?' I say, as haughtily as my position allows.

She leaves me here, under the clock, and goes to the kitchen.

My name, I have tried to tell them, is Mrs Compton. I have a degree in Chemistry. I could once mix element with element and produce clouds of red vermilion, yellow cadmium, cobalt blue. I could write out a formula so correct that it sang. I could measure and weigh and make an equation balance, make it stand most properly to attention. I am all a balancing act, though lately I am having trouble, and my legs will no longer let me stand.

But my house stands.

My house has to stake its place against them. It has to hold out more stubbornly even than the old, declining hotels along the seafront at Bay's Mouth, hotels called the British, the Burlington, the Palace, the Imperial, which have none of my discipline, and whose bones are more crumbled by dry rot than mine. Sandwiched between the new, brash seafront, with its stark, freshly built guest house called the Colonial and the frightful tower blocks which rise to the back of me, wholly beyond the pale, my house is upright and still proper. I enjoy their discomfort at it, these women contracted to care. They're uncomfortable in my grand house, like peanuts in a chocolate box.

And then this one, Susheela, who I can sense pacing now, in my kitchen, like a flutter in my belly. She has that dignity about her that Anwar had. I value that. Dignity in a person who serves.

I wait a long time. There is the clock. There is me under it. Waiting under all that time.

Around me the furniture and ornaments and belongings tell a story, if any of them could be still enough to listen.

The beginning is this photograph of Mother, sitting, despite my anger at it, on the mantlepiece still. A sepia print, faded at the edges, and over-exposed to the bright Indian sun. Simply a wide expanse of lawn, blank canvas, and her at its centre. In the middle of the picture she sits, in a wicker chair, her feet tucked to the side, knees together, carefully,

carefully. If any of these girls that come could be bothered to look at the photograph for any length of time, they might feel how she smoothed out that skirt a split-second before the shutter opened, how she brushed any fragments of disarray from her shoulders, shooed the servants from the frame, shifted her posture, drew herself more upright and took on that accusatory look, taut around the anger that kept her in place. It keeps me in place still.

By the time I knew her she was either Mrs Benedict Worsal Compton or simply Memsahib. But on the back of the picture her name is written: Evelyn Roberts. My mother.

The story continues in this houseful of heavy wooden furniture, which were our packing cases once, to come Home with. On the back it still says our name, stamped on the chest of drawers, the underside of the dressing table, the underbelly of the wardrobe. It was the only way we were allowed to bring that much good wood Home. There were quotas. India was finally clawing back its assets. And wood was one. So you had to turn your exquisite furniture into cases for the ship, and then back into furniture for Home. I remember my blind rage when the furniture at the end, at Home, did not match what we'd had in our grand residence in Kharagpur. The furniture was not the only thing that didn't emerge from that journey intact.

See. The house tells a story, tells it through from beginning to end. This end. And over my dead body will there be anything after.

The girl doesn't come back. I listen for her. Has she left? She hasn't given me my pills. I need my pills. I listen for her. Yes.

In the kitchen I can hear her sniffling, and then the low sound of sobbing.

Already? I'll get rid of her soon enough, will I? Damn her, and damn this longing. I wait with the grandfather clock. Another thing that's whole. Its solid ticking keeps the house in order, keeps the presence of time here and keeps me sitting under it, under the pressure of the unifying tick and tock. Not the kind of time that separates, one minute from another, one hour, one shift, as time exists for these girls. No, this time is different; it binds, roots, links one second to the next, one age, one place to another. And the dead to the living.

Chapter Two

I stand on the deck, dressed in my new name. No longer Evelyn Roberts, but Mrs Benedict Worsal Compton, wife of Captain Benedict Worsal Compton. Beneath the chenille skirt of my new name, its silk blouse and new bob cut, my body is the same common, pale, permeable collection of skin and muscle and bone and memory, my feet within its patent shoes still bare, and between my thighs I still ache and want as Evelyn Roberts always did.

I am to wear his name wherever I go, like someone else's too-big shoes, or perhaps a nun's habit. But I stand on the deck, Evelyn, watching this strangely concrete India as we come into port, and thinking of that word he used for it: Frightful.

'We mustn't lose face in India, or it'll be frightful,' B had said, the last time I saw him, as we walked hand in hand along the seafront at Bay's Mouth, the cold wind lashing at us and battening me to him like a tethered bird. When I asked what he meant he didn't want to talk about it. And it's this not talking about it that makes it become a spectre. Standing on the deck, I find myself turning his words over in my head. Frightful. It. Will. Be. Frightful.

The ladies on board, once I had shared their table on the upper deck for several days, told me, over yet another milk and soda, of some of the dangers.

'They are terribly foul minded,' said the one called Eliza, who wears her grand dresses of beading as casually as if they were just kitchen pinnies. 'One look at a white woman's body, and they will never forget that we are flesh and blood.' She shivered. 'There are several recent tales of women dishonoured by a supposedly loyal Indian, though it's difficult to know if they're true. Who would ever admit to such a shameful thing?'

The shock of this sank into my spine. I have never met an Indian man, but I shall have to steer well clear. And yet isn't it inevitable that some of these copious servants we are to take on must be men?

'Oh nearly all,' Eliza told me. 'Though you may have yourself an ayah or a nursemaid if you have children. Otherwise it will be all men, and all for you to keep in line yourself.'

The manuals speak of the servants as infants, rather than as grown men. Standing on the deck, awaiting the first feelings of India, I think of my classroom of children in their short trousers shivering against the chills of early spring, their legs mottled like corned beef, and of how, in the schoolroom, little Jacob's face closed up as he stood at his desk with his hand out to receive the lashes.

I did give him the punishment, after a long moment of steeling myself against it: three sharp smacks with the cane across his little palm. I was meant to give him five. I can still feel the three hot stings on my own hand under this incongruous sun.

The ship is coming into a wide harbour. Concrete jetties are arms reaching for us as the ship is taken back in to shore. We pass several other big vessels. Things become dense and solid again, and so loud. Some of the noise you would expect from such a mingling port: the industrious clang of sails and chains, the men hollering back and forth, the sound of engines and the sashaying sea. But there are other, unfamiliar things drifting up to the ship once we are stationed in the dock. The calls of indecipherable men, like the crackle of insects I don't recognise. These intonations, strange in their vocabulary, rise from the portside, and gather to a low, swelling hubbub as we draw up to land. I begin to pick out individual faces on the dock, hieroglyphs in the crowd, as their voices become more pressing. Their opaque sounds twang and arpeggio at my gut. I look to the other women.

'That's the temple, dear,' says the old woman, whose name I can never remember, pointing at an oddly steepling roof between the other buildings, which on the whole are as flat roofed as the houses of Nazareth in our children's Bible.

'Oh how it does send shivers, to think what they're doing in there,' laughs the old woman, the beading of her blouse quivering slightly.

But I feel very sombre and stripped bare. I'm not a church-going type, but I hadn't much considered what it would mean to be so far from the God of my father's church, His familiar threats, His violent possibilities, His manuals and rules, His England.

The dream of this, in Bay's Mouth, was romantic, and I had originally thought it was all Kipling and elephants. B has got rid of some of these dreams of India, laughing them into little pieces, and saying how modern it all is now, but I'm not quite ready to have it be all about keeping up with the neighbours, and oiling 'the household machine' as it seems to be for these society women, their English peppered with words in Indian. *Sahib. Khitmugar. Musolchi.* Without any of the sights and sounds that must surely be the backdrop to its determined ordinariness, their world has seemed to me, on the ship, to be leached completely of interest. It has been all gossip and frippery in sharp splinters. Who is flirting with who and what dress is the right one for which occasion. Who has best control over her staff, or the most presentable garden.

At dinner last night, in the ballroom, as the Anglo-Indian girl sang and her pianist lover made waltzes and two-steps of her ribboning melodies, I looked around my table of ordered, married ladies and noticed the fierceness of their little white hands, how they all seemed to hold their fists closed as they spoke, gripping on to all their disapproval as if it was the only clothing they had. I hope to meet some women who are more like-minded once I am settled.

I think of Helen, who I have left so thoroughly behind; that expression on her face, what was it?

We wait at the dock for an hour or more before they begin disembarking. I go back to my cabin, where I am to await B.

'Don't, whatever you do, leave the ship alone,' B had said as he stroked my hair and kissed me gently, the grey Bay's Mouth sea raging to the right of us and his body firm and wanting against mine as we walked, B striding so surely, as only men from the best military families can, and me holding to him tightly as we moved towards this dream.

I sit in the easy chair in my cabin between one story and the next, waiting for him to take me finally from this unromantic, limited ship and into his India. I feel a kind of hunger. I've grown so weary of this ship.

'It's just as well. I always knew you'd go on to better things,' Helen had said, her voice a tight chord, twanging against the soft air with that sharp emphasis on 'better' and a bitter, dark look as she continued to knead the bread. The back and forth of her hands. The leavening smell around us. The faintness of the flour-tinged light. 'He's got real *panache*,' she said of B, bitterly.

And, although it was a bitterness she shared with my sister Lizzie and her husband, I can't help but think that unlike their grumpiness, which was mainly jealousy over how rich I was now to be, perhaps Helen's bitterness was more physical and violent, because B got to kiss me, and love me, while she did not — or not any more.

15

I miss her now, with the ache of an empty stomach. Helen whose hardened hands touched me so softly, who, more than anyone, cares that I have interests and learning, who gives me books and keeps each of the drawings I make under her bed like the kind of thoughts you keep in your belly and in deeper places.

On this ship any interest of mine is frowned upon. The very fact that I've brought from Home books that are not all romantic novels – and I have only five – is a source of great disapproval.

The first is a housekeeping manual which, of course, we all must have, and is acceptable, though it doesn't include a formula for my mother's tears, salting the air as she held me that last day. Oh how she held and held me against her round-nesses, her warm body, against her pinny smell of baking and soap.

The second is a romantic novel, which would be to their taste also, but that I chose because it seems thoughtful, and not overly sentimental for its type. Of the other three, one is a book on botany, for which I have scant use on board, and another is my father's Bible, which they would only look on with disgust, because it is rather small and old and poor-looking. The final book is a concise history of art, given to me by Helen, which has plain but beautiful illustrations I am fond to look at, and fond to touch.

In the event it is not B that comes to meet me, but Mr Bur-rows, a man of medium stature and wide girth who I have never before set eyes on, and who bursts in with great bluster, proceeding to introduce himself in that way military men have of speaking in half phrases, as if they are too thrifty and disciplined for ordinary grammar:

'Burrows. A colleague of your husband's. Come to take you safely in.'

'But he said he would come himself . . .'

'Ah, he's unable. Work, I'm afraid, as so often happens. Better get used to it, madam – pardon the impudence.'

I'm not sure that I do.

'Have you papers to prove that you know my husband?' I feel slightly afraid. My hands, which I now clasp tightly together, are shaking slightly.

He laughs, in a single short breath, and draws from his pocket a note in B's hand.

Darling. So sorry I could not come. Burrows is a friend of mine, he will bring you to our lodgings. Yours, B.

It takes a moment or two. I had been expecting an emotional reunion: my new husband, and I his new wife.

'You'll see him soon enough. Only a half-hour's journey to your place in town. Where's the cabin boy? Need him and several others to take all this in,' he says, gesturing to my three packing cases.

He ducks out of the cabin in search of hands. When he returns it is with my cabin boy and four other men with dark skin and eyes. My first close Indians. I try not to stare, and also not to smell. The ladies told me several times how they would smell. Suddenly my cabin feels very small and enclosed, just as the ship had struck me from the first, devoid of its expected romance, segmented and rigid against the fluid sea. In here with the ironwork windows, and surrounded by the railings of the decks, we women are birds in tiny cages. As is usual on all such ships, rank rises with level, and I am a pigeon making to be a monal pheasant. Every day as I've climbed the stairs to the first-class dining room, I've thought of what Helen calls my 'ambition'. The ship makes it too real.

Mr Burrows quickly has them all organised, bids them lift each of my cases and take them out on deck. I am to follow with only what I am wearing and my parasol. I feel for a second that it was silly to have worn my best dress since B is not to meet me after all, but within moments I'm glad of it, because the other women out on deck are so smart, and certainly not about to 'let the side down'. They look at me with slight disapproval – perhaps because I'm not wearing a jacket? As they shuffle in a tight little group, the thickness and heaviness of their layered clothes insupportable in the heat, they remind me of corn in a closed pan, shuddering to pop. I can see, by the blush of their faces and the perspiration on several foreheads, how these stocks and stays, bonnets and other armour only put their bodies under more pressure.

'Goodbye, dear,' says Eliza, cool as a glass of water, and I kiss her hot, metallic cheek, partly to test if she's real. On her skin I smell something human, and so smile at her before I step away.

The sound of the port is even louder now, as they begin the unloading. There are men shouting in what I presume to be Hindustani, and a great clatter of cars and carriages. There is a smell of something unspeakable. Cries of joy ring out from our deck as the ladies spy friends and relatives among the small crowd of white faces awaiting them. But my eyes are taken, not by the Englishmen and Englishwomen standing waiting so thickly untranslated, but by the fascinating new lexicon of the dockworkers in their strange nightshirts and pyjamas, their wrapped sarongs, their skin iron and deep rust under the sun.

We begin to bake now that the ship has been still so long. The women around me are gathering their handkerchiefs to their noses, like so many grieving widows.

'Oh it is a great trial, the smell. I had almost forgotten it,' says the old woman.

Mr Burrows offers me his arm and I take it, the ladies looking at me – no doubt wondering if this is my husband, and no doubt thinking what a gold-digger I truly am, for he's twice my age at least. I half wave to them, but they barely acknowledge our passing friendship as it recedes. They are almost all to be taken to Bombay station, and from there to board a special train to Calcutta – while I am to take a car to B's temporary residence in Bombay itself. It seems there will be several weeks when we are set up in temporary accommodation, and a great deal of moving of baggage, furniture and hearts before I can take root in a permanent Home of my own.

Land, when I step onto it, is solid, deeply still in a way that is strangely unsteadying. I almost fall with its disorientating thereness. Despite the seasickness, I had learned to rely on the swell and retreat of the sea. This solidity is a new rulebook.

Images slip and slide past as we make our way from the deck and down the staircase, beyond the waiting relatives and into it. Into *it*. Perhaps there are other bodies with us walking. And bodies walking the other way too. There is language everywhere, like a hundred bluebottles against a windowpane.

These things surge and fade their way past me over and over. Men. Skin like the best wood. Eyes averting. Eyes averting. Mud eyes. I am the frightful thing. Oh. I am the frightful thing.

A woman, passing, close enough for me to reach out and touch her brown arm. One of my wants for her, the softness of her skin beneath these fluttering fabrics. She passes wreathed in beautiful cloth, which hangs and drapes and winds, and her body leaves its imprint on my own beneath my prim clothes. I feel she has passed straight through me. *Helen*, I think suddenly, *Helen*. All at once there is a thin-looking white cow, of an unfamiliar, humped, camel-like breed, lounging in the middle of the crowded walkway. Is it really here? I feel sick with the confusion and onslaught, and with the impulse I felt for the woman, if she was actually there at all. But Mr Burrows has my arm and steers me through the crowd to where a line of cars and carriages are awaiting the new arrivals.

Opening the door of a grey, irrelevantly grand motor car, he deposits me inside and climbs in himself, shutting the door.

'There,' he says. 'That's the worst of it over.'

I can't see the driver's face, but by his dark neck, he is certainly an Indian. So they can drive.

Through streets full of such people, it is a good hour's slow creep in the sweltering car, the horn a constant refrain. I am feeling so unwell that I must sit with my eyes straight ahead, looking only at the cream fabric of the inner compartment, and not at what is outside which is so fleeting and confused I can't absorb it.

When Mr Burrows says, 'We are not far now from where you will be staying' – his first words of the journey – and opens the shutter on the window fully, it is to reveal things becoming focused again: a civilised and plain and English-looking drive, with planted trees lining its wide dusty avenue, clear and ordered and true. Surely enough, a minute or two later, the car stops and the door is opened and it is B!

B. Smiling.

'It's so good to see you,' I say, automatically. And I reach my hand, which is still my own hand, to his face, checking its contours, my breath slowing to steady again, and the line of his jaw becoming clearer by the second.

'You too, darling. You too,' he says. And he bends his head into the car and kisses me on the lips.

His lips, here, in the warmth of India, feel like something foreign. A man I barely know. My husband.

Chapter Three

*When the stomach is very irritable, a mustard leaf protected by muslin should
be put at the pit of the stomach.*

The Complete Indian Housekeeper and Cook,
Flora Annie Steel & Grace Gardiner

I've just got Henry, Mrs Jenkins and Magda to do before uni.
One breakfast (Henry), one cup of sweet, weak tea (Mrs Jenkins), and one of whatever the hell Magda wants today. In all,
there'll be twelve different-coloured tablets to be popped out
of their blister packs (six pills for Henry and three each for
little Mrs Jenkins and Magda), three trips to the toilet (if I'm
lucky), two little chats, one each with Henry and Mrs Jenkins
in their flats on the seafront, and then one stony silence in the
big house on the hill.

On the way to Henry's, along the promenade, I stop and
look out to sea: the wind turbines flailing their arms like
pissed girls in trouble, the oil rig, the Victorian pier stomping
out to sea on its black matchstick legs. Rain. Through the
rain, there's the far-away horizon. It tugs.

'Fuck.'

I say it to the horizon. To the big air. Salt. Memories.

I walk along the seafront, feeling Ewan's touch like tracings on my body: his hands stroking my back, my thighs, finding their way slowly to the places in me that wanted him back. I hold on to that, the want, but instead there's the feeling of trying to hold his hand, and of his fingers going loose round mine, and the knot of his hand slowly slipping.

And now, at sea level, in Bay's Mouth, the horizon's just empty and harsh with rain; and when I look down at my phone, yet again, there are no calls, no texts.

'Fuck.' I say it again. My mouth tastes of metal.

The walk to old Henry's helps my stomach settle. Henry lives by the park opposite the new marina. Usually, I like to stop and watch the kids mucking about, hurling themselves round the slides and roundabouts and see-saws in the park, skittles just made to fall over. But today I don't want to see any kids or mums or round bellies, no thank you, and I'm glad the park's dripping wet this morning and deserted. I'm relieved about that today.

I pass some blue-rinse tourists by the entrance to the marina, looking soggy and fed up while they get off their bus and grumble their way towards our old hotel: the British Hotel, on the front, which has flaking paint now and a boarded-up window top right. I can feel Mum, grumbling. *You've let the place go*, she says. *And you let yourself go too.* The shame is exactly balanced with the sore comfort of imagining her saying it, busybodying about with all her nagging and affection.

The old biddies getting off the bus are just a shade or two more spry than the ones I look after. A couple of them snoot at me, because *Bay's Mouth isn't what it used to be.* I read the thought in their looks when they shake their heads at each other like two bent old trees in the wind.

Before she got too sick to think, Mum was worried about it, all the bullshit lately about immigration and the way people've got slowly more free with their dirty looks. She'd seen it get worse before, in the eighties. Skinheads with *Sieg Heil* tattoos. Sick messages stuffed through people's letter boxes. Bricks through windows. She was right to worry. Last week two pissed guys shouted some fucked-up stuff at me from the pub doorway as I walked past. Their voices had that kind of hating that's wanting too. Both the hate and the want made my skin creep. No one tried to stop them. Not even Keith, the landlord, who knows me. Like this wasn't my town at all.

Fuck them. I think that about these two old biddies too, as hard as I can, and turn left towards Henry's. One day they'll lose that small-town, sure-of-themselves feeling, when they're old enough to need and need.

Up the stairwell, to the grey, closed door.

I let myself in. In the flat, the walls feel tight. Henry's cramped home, although it's on the fourth floor, always feels like being underground, and smells that way too. I stop trying to pull out the right words for it as soon as I hear him coming along the passageway from the bedroom to the kitchen, the only living space he has. They always take my full attention.

I focus on him while he inches along, one step at a time, gripped to the rail the council put in.

Henry can still get about, at least inside the flat,

furniture-walking, his arms trying to take a bit of the weight from his shivery legs as he shuffles along. Won't use a Zimmer. *Not that old*, he always says.

'Well hello, my dear!' he says in his cracked voice. 'What brings you here?'

I don't let him down by mentioning the council, or a rota or a shift. I just say, 'Oh, I was in town, thought I'd pop by.'

I don't mind the constant changing, the plain, repeated cooking – boiled egg, poached egg, boil-in-the-bag fish, fish fingers – and all the other dull rhythms of their lives, but I do mind when they're embarrassed of how their bodies wither like old roses, and when they're ashamed of the hell of needing us, sometimes so fucking desperately, by the time we arrive for our quick half-hour visits.

'Ah, what a treat!' he says. 'Can I trouble you to make me some breakfast, love?'

I'm a demon at porridge these days. And poached eggs. They often like a poached egg.

Henry likes scrambled. I break two eggs into a cup and whisk them up for his favourite. While I do this, I size him up. What kind of maintenance does he need? His hair looks greasy, and he gives off a whiff of something stale, but I haven't got time to shower him before Mrs Jenkins and Magda. I can flannel round his neckline, brush those few strands of grey hair back over his crown.

I can't count the times I've found them sitting in their own mess because we can't stay long enough or visit them often enough to properly keep them clean.

'The word "anger" isn't very vivid,' said my tutor at college,

'as an abstract noun.' But abstract nouns don't seem that fucking abstract when it's you feeling them.

I look in the fridge to see what else Henry has, but there's
nothing in there, nothing at all. I hold my breath for five
seconds and name it in my head. Anger.

It makes me want to be the kind of person who'd break
things. Riot.

Henry sits down hard, in the one comfy chair.

'Bloody knees,' he says. He's been on a waiting list for re-
placements ever since I've known him.

But despite the knees, and the legs that bow out now to
breaking point, he can do most things himself still; no need
for changing or getting him up. But he can't cook. His wife
always did that, and Henry's ninety and not about to learn
now. I give him a smile to say I'm sorry for his sore knees and
empty fridge, and he sighs and shakes his head, rubbing his
knee where it hurts.

Her picture's on the sideboard, his wife. The picture of the
two of them, getting married. One of those black and white
photos that's been coloured in – half a photo, half a painting.
She's a pretty brunette in a simple white dress with a bunch of
pink flowers and the unreal rosy cheeks the colourer's given
her; Henry, sixty-odd years ago, and in a nice suit, his hair in
a careful side parting, isn't so bad himself.

Looking at Henry's wedding photograph, and the way he
holds her, so gently, by the arm, I feel the gap in him where
she used to be, and the gap in me that makes the shape of
Ewan.

I look at Henry, and want to tell him about Ewan and
how he's disappeared for three days; three days of going to

his flat, three days of calling into the flat, and hearing it echo emptiness back. I want to tell Henry how I've only had one message, from his friend Darren, saying just *Ewan's safe.* Which is never really fucking true.

But today Henry's got the snooker repeats coming on at 9 and I've got to get out of here within the half-hour. I set him up with that, with the remote to hand, the eggs and a cup of tea steaming on the little table just within reach. As I leave, I stroke the back of his cool, freckled hand. He looks up at me, startled, and, when I turn at the door to check the room before I close it behind me, he's staring down at his own hand, resting on the remote, and it's like my touch has left some kind of lettering on it that he can't quite read.

The last time I held Ewan's hand, we walked up the bluff. Our palms were gripped together, like one of us was hanging off a cliff. We tried to walk each other straight, but the paths we took kept making us collide, and then pulling us apart.

We'd taken cheese slices, some thin ham, mayo, and bread rolls to put them in, a couple of beers to have on the top where we'd stopped with that wide view below us, the huge grey sea. From up there you see the Bay's Mouth seafront for what it is: a thin cover for the messier town that stretches behind it, thick with streets and buildings and growing almost by mistake. The hotels along the front are like a flimsy barricade keeping the town and the sea apart.

We'd eaten our rolls, cracked open the beers. Ewan put his arm round me then. He was warm, some scratchy stubble on his chin and the smell of the workshop on him. I didn't want the clouds gathering to mean rain.

But they did, and we put on our coats, and maybe it was the bad weather and the thick coat that took him off to that place where I can't get to him, but on the way down, we walked far apart. His eyes had that hooded, dark look.

Before Magda, there's Mrs Jenkins, just two floors down from Henry but as lonely as Pluto, who always talks to me in Welsh till I remind her again I don't speak it and she giggles and says, 'Oh yes, you're the Pakistani, aren't you?'

She's sweet, old Mrs Jenkins, and today she hasn't had any major mix-ups so I just sit with her for a few minutes and explain again that I've got family from West Bengal but I'm from just up the road.

'Fascinating. Fascinating,' she says, shaking her head in a bewildered way.

'*Desh*,' Mum used to say to me. 'That's something we all need.'

Mum'd been looking for the English for her beloved Bangla word for years, and not found it. She'd looked so pleased with herself as she said it. 'You need to connect with your *desh*,' she said.

Desh was belonging. The place you belong to. 'The *where* that's who you are,' Mum said once, smiling. *The where that's who you are.*

'I'm from Bay's Mouth,' I tell Mrs Jenkins again, in a bit of a pissed-off way now. 'Born here.'

She gets something, in my tone of voice, and nods. 'Yes,' she says. 'We have a word in Welsh for that. *Bro*.' The wide, open O at the end of the word opens a space for us in her kitchen.

'It's . . . what do you call it?' she says. 'Your square mile, but not quite.' She searches the countertops with her eyes. 'It's your place – you know?' She looks lost for a few seconds, far from her *bro*.

This is mine. Its pretend seafront with all its messed-up pomp, and then, when you burrow down, into the deep town, with the sound of the ship-ride tannoy and the sea fading, there's the messy, familiar streets, the bingo halls, closed cinemas, the pound shops and charity bazaars, the strange empty exits from the new roundabout – where they didn't build an industrial park – the new flats – which they did build but didn't manage to sell – the three bookies where people leak their money, and the working men's club where they drink it away. Bay's Mouth proper. My *desh*; my *bro*.

Without Bay's Mouth, I'd be free-floating, turning in zero gravity. Lying in bed last night, the voices of those idiots outside the pub last week played back their fucked-up insults, and I had what Mum'd call 'vertigo'.

It's a difficult thing for Mrs Jenkins, having a stranger in the house.

'Never had a servant in my life,' she says, trying to stop me from helping her with the dishes although she's not safe to stand for long. 'Embarrassing it is. Always knew how to do for myself.'

Standing at her sink, made into servant, I start to feel really sick. Even the clean, lemony scent of the washing-up liquid and the slosh of water in the sink make my insides curdle. I have to get out of here, away from sweet Mrs Jenkins and her closed-up smell.

Round the corner from the flats, I stop and stand and hold the railings, feeling the sick surge. I stand and wait for it to pass.

'I can't deal with this right now.' I say it out loud. *I can't bloody deal with this.*

I get to Magda's late. Bad start. Her house, as I'm walking up the driveway, stands looking out over Bay's Mouth, its hands practically on its hips. To get to her you have to pick your way up a path threatened by brambles, up to the black full stop of the door. You have to find the key between the cobwebs behind the empty flowerpots in the porch (she won't let us have our own), struggle with it in the old lock, and then shove and shove to get the stuck door open. The damp, autumn smell of her house swells out to you as the door creaks. You walk past the old boots and coats and through another door to a dark hallway, then another to the lounge, like peeling back the layers of a huge, dark fruit, until you find her, a seed in the middle of it all, small and uppity in her chair. As soon as I'm in her house, the sickness goes. She's the middle of it all here. You have to watch her carefully.

'Oh,' she says, brushing some crumbs off her lap and wrinkling her nose slightly as I walk into the lounge. '*You*, is it?'

I don't think she knows what time it is. She doesn't say anything about the lateness. But then she rarely does say much to me.

The house smells dead. Of old wood and polish and evaporated eau de cologne. The smell doesn't make me feel sick exactly; it's an empty feeling. What can she do in a big dead house except slowly die too?

The girls have been complaining that Magda can't get to her feet any more at all, not even to move between the seat and the wheelchair. They keep saying she'll need two people to come to her every time, she'll need a hoist, but the office keeps putting it off because it costs and everything's been cut back. Magda acts rich, but they say she hasn't got a penny to her name except this house.

We try the manoeuvre between her seat and the wheel-chair using the Zimmer as a rail. Holding it, she counts to three with crazy authority, but on three there's nothing but a slight impulse in her body upwards. A bird not managing to take off. I hold her, and I think *what's the weight like – stone, bone, sadness?* I lug her onto the frame. So tiny, and so fucking heavy. How do they get that way? My back groans. I can hear by her breath that she's still trying her best to use her own strength to stand but her legs are worse and worse. She sinks back to the same chair, failed. Her mood's like something under the earth, boiling. Eventually it's being so pissed off that stands her up and shifts her in a heap from one chair to the other. It takes us both a minute to get our breath.

I'm working her out, slowly, like doing some kind of foren-sics. How did she wash up like this? Like Henry, she wants to think she doesn't need us, but she's actually frantic with need, so she pretends harder and keeps us further away, like we're some kind of toxic chemical. If you try to talk to her, you just get peppery insults. Magda hates sympathy more than anything. She's not like Henry; she's not looking for a friend.

The other girls hate her:

'She's rude.'

'She's obnoxious.'

'She's a stupid old cow.'

But she isn't that. She's far from stupid, with her sharp tongue and don't-fuck-with-me eyes. Magda knows how to press their buttons. She runs rings round any of them. I like Magda. I fucking do.

Perhaps because we accomplished the first manoeuvre, she lets me take her to the loo. (No, to 'the lavatory', with its mosaic of royal blue tiles, its brass taps, its tall, elegant toilet, and its freestanding bath; even with the limescale, grime and the tap that drips and drips, left to fall apart like everything else around here, it's definitely a 'lavatory', not a loo.) I had the feeling she was desperate to go when I was here last time, but didn't want me to do it. I wouldn't want to go in front of someone else either. The girls say she sometimes wets herself instead of going with us, then she blames the wet clothes on the last one to be here.

Every small step is a tiny win with Magda, and this is a dangerous honour. In the loo, she asks my name for the first time.

Sure enough, afterwards she gets all stroppy about the coffee, and then throws one of her insults at me in a hot, angry splash:

'And are *you* of any importance?' Stuck-up as anything.

I breathe in, hold it for two seconds, like Mum taught me, *like water simmering down.*

I can take Magda's insult, from a woman the world's left to rot. So I just leave her to her own devices in the lounge for a bit, make myself a cheeky cup of tea in the kitchen, and wait for her to call and ask for whatever it is she wants next. Although my paid time's pretty much up already, I'm not in a rush; there are two hours until I have to be at college. I go through to the kitchen.

My phone buzzes in my back pocket. I reach for it, quick, like pulling a gun from its holster.

Ewan.

I read the words one by one.

I read them again.

A fucking text message?

The words float around me, detached, no sense to them.

I stand, watching the fear and anger of it rolling towards me, like a huge wave, barrelling.

When it arrives it throws my insides around until everything's unhinged, and I need to hold on to the counter, need to puke again. I'm retching at Magda's sink, and I don't care where I am. I don't care that this bloody house hasn't seen real feelings for years. I'm just crying and crying. Because I know. I just fucking know.

Chapter Four

For now hath time made me his numbering clock.

Richard II, William Shakespeare

Damn, where *is* the girl? Coffee, she said. She has to finish her shift at least, doesn't she? Give me my pills? A nagging, sinking feeling. No sound from the kitchen. Maybe she's left already. I thought there was more mettle to her than that. And I thought she was more of a woman than the other one.

I'm thirsty. And I need a drink anyway for these tablets. I see now, she's put them out, on the sideboard just beside me. A pink one for the angina, a white one for my digestion, and the big one, Valium, for the pain. The big one I want. I need it sharpish.

I'm not going to sit here bellowing for her like some kind of goat. Calling at my hollow house. Perfectly capable of getting myself to the kitchen. Of getting a drink.

Damn this deep-pile rug. Damn its fibres, which make the wheels so slow and heavy. Damn the corner of the doorway, which is so narrow it bruises my knuckles as I try to wheel myself through. I have to stop. The air is thick coming in and out of me. I can hear my own breath, like a slow gale. Across the hallway I turn the wheels an inch at a time. My right side is stronger than my left now so I start to swivel, and have to stop and just do left left left to get straight. Damn this chair, this body, this house, damn the girl. So breathless there's darkness closing in for a few seconds, but when I stop to rest, it lifts.

Through the doorway again. No bruising door-posts this time. I'm careful.

Damn it, she's drinking tea! In my kitchen. In my house. Who does she think she is? Sitting on the kitchen floor, leaning against the wall, her knees hunched up to her face and a cup of tea beside her.

She's so pale. Shaking. She's too pale, slumped against my wall. The house is uncomfortable with it, but it gives, it gives slightly for her.

'I'm pregnant.'

Her low voice trembles through the house.

Something real has come in.

Why is she telling me this? The old fear. Fear of wombs and bleeding and pain. It pulls at my guts. Damn it. We're both silent a long while.

'Is that a problem?' My voice is full of breath but it's steady. It is still steady.

'He's left me.' She says it in a bare way, looking at her phone. 'He's just left me. He just bloody sent me a message.' It's the pale disbelief of abandonment, the slow awful dawning of it. A cold recognition.

'Are you sure?'

Why am I even asking her? Why is she in my kitchen?

She shrugs dumbly. There's a long silence. She looks at me with raw eyes. So young.

'I meant the pregnancy. Have you tested?' The sound of my own voice, expressing such practical concerns, is a surprise – to me, to her, to the house.

Her head shakes. 'I just know,' she says.

'Well make me a coffee before you go to the chemist and get a test.' Best to be firm and directive on these occasions, although my voice is hoarse with breath now. 'I need a drink. My pains are back with a vengeance.'

That works. She nods. She slowly gets up, and collects herself enough to pour water from the kettle into the coffee pot. I sit and watch her from my chair. Her hands are shaking. I find myself wondering about her. What will she do? Oh the world is rushing in through the cracks in the windows. Oh the world is beckoning and drawing at me.

When she's given me my pills and three or four sips of hot, sweet coffee, I say it. Why on earth do I say it?

'Come back here to do the test, young lady, or I tell you right now, I'll be putting in a complaint.'

But she's already on her way out of the door.

'I'll do you for negligence!' Calling to the hollow house.

The house is the most important of all. Now Susheela's gone the house should begin to settle. What was I thinking, putting it in jeopardy like that? The walls will need weeks of steadying now.

Yes. The walls are uncertain again. Sitting in my chair, I'm holding on to the parameters of the room, but the walls begin to shrink back, and back. I try to hold them together, but my arms are too weak, too tenuous to be a scaffold. There's a window open here somewhere, letting the world in. I'm left open. The paraphernalia of the house is pouring into me: stamps, doilies, paperclips and other detritus mixing into my body, breaking me into pieces. The house mottles and crumbles too, carpets and blinds moth-eaten by the sky. Shards of blue cut me up. I've got on the wrong side of the house, come unstuck. I'm inside out. The world grows up and up from my floorboards, from behind my skirtings, architraves, the creases of my house, its elbows.

Hear the birds! The birds. They're calling down through the unbared roof. Yes. Perhaps the roof slates are peeling off? Perhaps there are fronds of growth poking through the floor? I have let the wildness in. There are insects crawling across my feet. Hear the birds! Oh! Hear the birds!

Turning my chair, turning in the house, forest walls around me. Can I find traces of plaster and mortar? Can I find the boundaries again, camouflaged by the trees? The songs of the white ghosts are playing from a gramophone somewhere in the wood, and yet I haven't wound it. Who's coiling me up and up until I unravel like a spool? I am unhappy. I am unhappy. I am unhappy.

I stagger from my chair, and fall against something that is a table, or a branch. I'm dancing my distress in the wood. I am unhappy. Tears are spooled up, and wound away from me into the wood like a string of pearls that I'm to follow. Follow the tears like stepping stones. *This tear is sadness. This tear is joy. And this tear is anger baked in a pie.*

The branches knot in a lattice around me. My skin is cross-hatched like a thicket. Veins are hard as twigs. Breath is forgotten in the wood and I'm caught by the net of my dead limbs. I must leave.

But where is the door in this forest house? Where is the door in this lattice of branches? I listen for the clock. The clock. The clock.

The clock. I hear it in the wood, listen until the walls settle again around me, grinding their heels into the earth and standing tall, listen to the regular tick and tock of it until the house has refound its axis and once again I am sitting in my chair, and impervious to change.

The sound of the door, the feeling of the door opening. She stands in front of me.

'You were afraid for your job?' It is my voice asking.

Susheela stands holding the paper bag. She's still pale. I can see the shape of the box in the bag, with the test in it.

'I didn't want to be on my own.'

She stands holding it, and starts to take it out of the bag. Then she stops. Puts it back in, and looks at me.

'Will you come in with me?' Her voice is small in the house.

'Come on then, if you want me in there. I'll keep my back turned.' My voice again. And the house is completely solid now. I have been clear and authoritative. I have made my wishes plain to her, and to all and sundry, and I have held it together. I'll keep my back turned while she does the test. Bracing and normal and matter of fact. No pity. No damned sympathy, and get it over with.

★

In the lavatory, sitting in my chair, facing the wall, I can hear her opening the packaging.

'Right. There's the control window,' she says, reading the instructions. 'That has a line if the test has worked. And then the test window. A cross for pregnant. A line for not pregnant.' She inhales deeply.

I nod, the wall in front of me blank.

'Fuck,' she says to herself before she begins. And then, 'Sorry.'

There's the sound of rustling. She's taking the test out of the box. Then, a silence. The sound of her grappling with her clothes. Then the sound of urination.

'So anyway,' I say. 'You're Susheela?'

She starts to laugh. The kind of laughter that only comes when things are this fragile. Despite myself, I laugh too. The indignity. The ridiculousness of sharing a toilet. The walls soften with it, and for a moment I don't mind. I can't remember the last time I felt this close to anyone.

Then, a silence. She comes round to the front of the chair and holds it for me to see. We're sobered now, watching the little test as it slowly turns: the little control window and that vital, indelible cross.

Chapter Five

Hyacinthus. HYACINTH

Of the bulbs that are imported, some only produce a few leaves, while others,
which appear to be forming for blossom, seem scarcely able to push themselves
above ground, and instead of opening all the flowers in the cluster at once,
open two or three first, which decay before the remainder expand.

Firmingers Manual of Gardening for India,
W. Burns

This B is perhaps more handsome even than the one before.
He is taller-seeming, and stands very upright and certain here
between all his staff. I feel dizzied by him, as if he were some
kind of a monument.

'You shouldn't try to do too much at first,' he says, stroking
my face. 'The heat won't be good for you. Take a half-hour or
so to settle in.' He is very clear in his mind, this B.

It's barely a minute before all my things are brought in by
what must be five or so of them in white clothes. They blur
past efficiently, and quietly enough. I am taken, on my request,
to the latrine, which, horror of horrors, is a commode. But I
shall get used to it, for that is all I have to do. Get used to all

this, according to B. Though he says we shall have a proper lavatory in Kharagpur.

Once I'm done, and have freshened up in the small wash-bowl brought by one of the servants, I go through to B.

He looks up as I walk in, watching me as if he is a cat and I am some sort of small, dancing thing that has caught his eye. I walk to him until I stand directly beside him, and stroke his fine face again, testing whether he is really here. He is. He has stubble, as always by this time of day. He begins to be real, to have volume and weight.

'So how was it, leaving the school?' he asks me.

'Not so bad.'

'Even little Jacob?' he asks with a smile.

'Oh, I did cry a little afterwards, but not for long,' I say (which is a lie as it was all night).

'And the ship?'

I roll my eyes, in a way that I hope is dismissive and haughty.

'Were they kind to you?' he asks me, with a look of concern.

'They were perfectly civil,' I say. And our eyes meet. I have already learned something of his India. He smiles grimly.

Something, maybe, but over the next three days every task brings a fresh lesson of my own ignorance. There are so many things to learn and I can't begin to feel I've absorbed them. We must check our shoes in the morning for insects or worse, before putting them on. We must not smile at the servants. We must remember what the individual role of each servant is, for the washerman won't cook, nor the latrine man wash the floors, and we must do absolutely nothing ourselves, though frequently it would seem so much easier to do so, for the language barrier is almost insurmountable, and I was given a pancake today rather than a fried egg. Still, it's not done to lift a finger, except to scold. Memories of Mother's industriousness, comely and limited, as she busied herself around our home with her washday, her baking day, her day for mending, her day for cleaning, leave me feeling guilty and idle.

B seems to have our plans all in hand from the conversations we've had so far, which haven't been many, nor of many words. He's so taken up with work. I'm uncertain when, in all these plans, he intends to sleep with me, as he makes clear I'm to keep to my own room in general until the church wedding, although we are married on paper already – which we did separately, me in Southhampton, before the passage, and he in a registry office in Calcutta.

Perhaps it's better to wait. Everything's so new, and that other new thing is perhaps best put off as long as possible. I've a kind of horror of it, which I know to be quite unusual and old-fashioned these days. B will be put off by my prudishness. He calls me a modern woman, but I know that I'm not. The touch of flesh to me is intimate. I can't imagine casual bareness, nakedness. There was only Helen. And that was different.

There's only B and I to share these huge rooms. B and I, and so many of these Indians. They seem to be everywhere I look, and behind every door. They walk into my bedroom without thinking to knock, and don't even apologise when I jump with fright, but simply say something in their language which B says is not Hindustani but Bengali, for they have come all the way here with B from that part of India. It's such a rigmarole of sounds. B appears to speak some himself, and I think him very expert. Therefore I assume at first that I must learn too, and am surprised when B resists my pressing him for little pieces of vocabulary.

'You shouldn't, you know.'

'What?'

'Bother with the language. It isn't proper that you'd have to. We have them learn English.'

'But you speak it with them.'

'And I'm a professional working man, which you're plainly not. We need it. Women don't.'

I'm stung. Partly because the description of me seems so idle, and at heart I still work, I am a teacher to my core. Also, it's not the attitude of the manuals.

'It seems a little presumptuous not to try at all.'

'Presumptuous of what?'

I'm only me, and these men seem to know more of where they are than I do, so who am I to make them learn my language? But it is as if he has heard my thoughts.

'You're my wife, Evelyn,' he says, smiling, 'and some of the servants are from the lowest castes in India. For you to stoop to change your tongue for them looks weak. We can't look weak.'

It's not the attitude of the manuals. But he takes my face then in his hands, and kisses me on the lips with such tenderness that I'm in a dream.

'Do you mind this place awfully?' he asks me, a note of timidity in his voice.

'Mind it, B? But I love it!'

'Good grief! Really?'

'It's so different. I'm exhilarated and full of . . . something. I'm unable to say it.' I laugh. 'I'm different and so are you. It's quite . . . quite . . .'

I feel my cheeks flush with the enthusiasm. And then I notice he's frowning.

'But what about the flies and the stench?'

'I've barely noticed it! There's so much to see. The other day, in town, when I was taken to the seamstress, I saw men forging chains right there on tiny hot fires, and there were women with their clothes put on in a way I can't even begin to understand yet.'

He's watching me. Something is not as he expected. I fall silent, hovering on the edge of saying other things that are wrong. I'm afraid I may have been out of place.

'Women need to be careful, dear Evelyn. The men, they lust after you.'

'Not these ones!' I say it with a laugh, for it seems ridiculous. The servant who walked into my room as I was changing had carried on his way as if my half-dressed body were no more than a piece of wood. And why would they look at a corpse like me when their women are so splendid?

He's stopped frowning and is smiling now.

'I should've known you'd make a dream of it.'

I'm laughing 'What else *should* I do?'

'And the latrine?'

'At least I don't have to empty it myself, and besides, I've seen worse. It's the grandest commode I've set eyes on. At home we had an outside latrine only, and the stench of it in the summer, the spiders in the darkness, the insects!'

'They have scorpions here,' he says, opening his eyes wide

to scare me. I laugh, and so he takes it as encouragement, putting a hand around my waist.

'We seem to have an army of servants to keep us safe,' I say, embarrassed that he'd be so affectionate in front of them.

He looks around at the men who are stationed by the window, the fan, the buffet trolley and the door. It's a look of almost blankness, as if he had forgotten there were other people present. And yet they have been standing for half an hour, and must have sore feet. He reaches for me again.

'Can we send them away to rest for a while?' I ask him.

'To rest? They have no need of it. These men work a whole day and night with no rest.'

Although they do not understand, I whisper to him: 'But we could have some privacy.' Part of me does not want to be alone with him. And yet, if intimacies are to happen, they had better happen without spectators.

He laughs.

'Privacy, I'm afraid, doesn't happen much in India. There's little hope of it. You must get used to that.' But as he says it he waves to them to leave us, in a fluent gesture that speaks of the several generations his family have spent in the colonies. The servants depart obediently and quietly, so perhaps there is some hope of privacy after all.

He follows them to close the door and then comes and sits so close that I have a flutter of fear in my stomach, which brings heat to my face. B takes my hand in his, and I'm over-whelmed by the feeling of his hand holding mine in its soft cage. The boy who was turning the fan has gone and the room is beginning to stew in the Indian air.

B is looking at my face, his eyes looking all around me, my eyes looking at his.

'We are to be married in two weeks,' he says gently, and he leans over to kiss my mouth again.

B is stroking my neck my face my hands my wrists my upper arms and now down the arch of my back. His hands are moving across me fearlessly because I'm his now. He unbuttons my blouse and begins to unhook my bodice. His hands, giving up that task for a moment while I take it over, trace their way up my legs under my skirts. It is so hot here. For a moment I feel his hands are snakes or spiders.

Suddenly he's up and across the other side of the room buttoning his trousers again.

He is pale. His hand is at his crotch. For a moment, he's ugly. I'm pulling down my skirt, and trying to recover some dignity; I'm a spilled vase, petals everywhere.

'We'd better not,' he says. 'Evelyn, we'd better not yet.'

I nod. It is better, oh yes, so much better to wait until the church wedding. The vice of my ribs relaxes slightly around my tight breath.

Later, I wonder, is it really the church wedding B's waiting for? Because he looks a little ill. He's been tracking this intimacy ravenously for months, as if following its scent, closing in on my body, only to be prevented, by something unfathomable, from feeding on it.

Chapter Six

'Will you get rid of it?'

My belly goes tight with the shock of Magda's question. *Getting rid of it*'s an idea that belongs to people my age, along with the morning-after pill, pot, and fucking around. While I sit with her, I feel her need weighing us both down to the house. God, she wants. She wants so much. I'm not sure what exactly, but I can feel this heavy pull from her. Needing. It holds this fucking house together.

'You're not the first in the world to be pregnant,' she snaps. 'Do you want it, or not?'

Opposite me, she's more real than before, neat in her blue cardigan and skirt. The shape of her shoulders is small against the square, canvas back of the wheelchair. Her wispy hair's bright and her skin's dull and crinkled. I remember that I used to feel sorry for her. How the hell did she fit into that feeling? Something like a laugh fizzes into my throat, some kind of bubbling muddiness, but it flattens like flat Pepsi while she sits, waiting for me to answer. The clock above us ticks. I sit, feeling desperate, racing on the inside in this still house.

I look at Magda and at her half-dead body. Did she ever get periods? Did she cramp and bleed? Was she ever pregnant, sick? I try to think of her hollowed chest swelling with hormones and milk. But her body says nothing. Instead, her question hangs in the air.

Abortion.

Marie, when I was at school, had an abortion, a late one, and she said they sucked it out. The muscles of my belly knot thinking about it. I remember Marie's pale face, how quiet she was for ages afterwards.

I try to remember when I had my last period, but all the periods just fade into one, and you can't remember when any of them started. Two months? Three?

'Will you keep it then?' She's looking at me, a schoolmarm.

A boiling feeling surges from my chest to my hands. I look at them, red from all the disinfectant handwash, and they're not mine any more. My body's a stranger. This must be *rage*. One hand starts to rise. It tingles with the smack it'll give Magda for what she's asking.

I drag myself back to my body, reach out and pat her arm, so fucking ashamed of that hot feeling that just almost overflowed to burn her across her flimsy cheek. I take a breath and look at her. Her practical question's like an anchor, dropping back to my belly. All I have to offer her as an answer is a stupid shrug.

'Better be going now, Magda,' is all I can say. My lips shake with all the other words. 'Is there anything else you'll be needing?'

'Scrambled eggs and a pot of peppermint tea,' she says, smoothing her hands over her skirt as she sits there, prim, like she's in some kind of restaurant.

Magda's notoriously particular, insists I wheel her to the kitchen so she can sit and watch me make the eggs, giving me instructions on how much salt, butter, pepper to add. Turn the heat up, turn it down. You'd think I'd never scrambled a bloody egg before. But the instructions keep my head with it, dabbing butter into the pan, breaking the eggs, adjusting the heat.

Apart from yes and no, I don't know what to say to her. Don't know where to start. I try to say sorry for what happened this morning: the tears, the stolen cup of tea, the test, and for letting my life leak into her house. But she just looks at me and I shut up, because I'm not sorry. And I think maybe neither is she.

'Were you married, Magda?' I ask her as I stir the scrambled eggs. It's not what she wants, to talk about herself. But she's muddled into my business and things aren't as clear-cut now.

'Yes. I was,' she says, in a small, hard voice.

I'm surprised she's answered me, and the answer leaves an open space that sucks me in, so I can't stop myself asking the next question, although I have a sick feeling I shouldn't.

'Did you have kids?'

The silence after it pulls the air tight.

'No,' like a dart.

49

She answers the next stupid question before I ask it. 'We didn't want one, OK? We didn't damn well want one.' Magda starts wheeling herself out. She's breathing frantically as she goes, in and out, in and out, furious.

'Oh. Right, I see. Sorry, didn't mean to pry.' It's a lie, and too late anyway. Shit.

'Those eggs will be burnt!' she shouts at me as she goes out in the chair, wheezing and wheezing, and hitting it several times against the door-post.

'Sorry. Sorry,' but I know better than to go and give her a hand. Some things you just have to handle yourself.

She's right. I have burnt the eggs. The burning smell makes the nausea rise again when I try to get all the egg off the bottom of the pan.

'Damned girl,' she says, when I put the plate in front of her. 'Damned stupid girl.'

'Magda!'

But she looks at me directly with those small, fuck-off grey eyes, and says it.

'Damned stupid Indian.'

I run down the driveway. Old cow didn't even fucking believe what she was saying. She said it to hurt, to get me to leave and it bloody worked. My guard was right down and she's played me like she plays us all. She found a soreness, and stuck in a knife.

I stop halfway down her drive.

'Shit.'

I forgot the test.

I'll lose my job. I won't be able to pay my fees. It all comes tumbling down, as I stand there, stock still in the middle of her leafy driveway, everything collapsing. One of the others'll see the test when they come, in a few hours, to make her tea. They'll go up to the bathroom, see it on the windowsill, sitting there with a story between its lines, and they'll know it was me, they'll tell Glenda and I'll be taken into the office for a talk. Worse. We need this money; since Dad's been off sick, we really fucking need it.

I consider going back to Magda, to her house, and serving her those eggs properly. Cleaning the kitchen afterwards and re-filling the china teapot with tea.

Fuck that.

I'm not going back in to her. Not now. Annette's in after me anyhow. Lovely, kind Annette. She'll just put all sign of it in the bin.

I stand there in the driveway. Slowly the worry about work, and the anger with Magda, fades into something sharper. That cold knowledge again. That being pregnant.

I take out my phone. It's so quiet and still and dead. I miss Mum.

I scroll through the list of names. Leah.

I've got a problem. Can you meet?

I stand, frozen, holding my still phone. I don't know how long I stand there, in the mouth of the driveway, where it joins the road. There are cars, a lorry, a little boy with red hair on a huge bike, three seagulls cawing overhead.

My phone purrs.

Three o'clock. Caffè Nero.

I text back. *Parliament instead?*

★

51

'Parliament' is actually a greasy spoon, cheap as chips and down to earth in a way I feel a need for right now. It's really called The Westminster Tearooms, and was probably quite a place once, but doesn't live up to its name any more – the tea's just builder's, and there are no scones or little sandwiches, only obscenely huge breakfasts for workmen. We call it Parliament because it's where all the important stuff gets an airing. All the stuff that makes either Leah or me hurt.

'FUCK!' She sits opposite me, her eyes saucers.

I sit with my milky, instant, one-pound coffee, staring into the cup. 'I know. I know.'

'Fuck.'

'Leah! Say something useful.'

'Shit.'

'C'mon, you can do better than that.'

But this is actually the best thing she could do. Leah sits opposite me, warm and frank and totally beside herself about me. There's no one else in Parliament today, except for a lone workman tucking into his full English. They've got the radio on in the kitchen. Top forty.

'Sorry. Give me a minute . . . oh fuck, Su! What the fuck're you going to do now?'

'I don't know.'

'Does Ewan know?'

'He left me.'

Silence.

'The fucking bastard!' It comes out full of breath from behind the hand that covers her mouth. Her hazel eyes are huge.

'He hadn't even found out, Leah. Told me by text an hour

before I did the test . . . See?' I show her Ewan's text.

'Fuck,' she says again, reading my phone. And then three more times. 'Fuck. Fuck. Fuck.' Her head in her hands. 'No. Sorry. I mean: *it'll be all right.* Fuck.'

'What d'you think I should do?'

She looks at me, looks at the phone. Looks at me again. 'I don't know. Shit. I really don't know.'

I'm actually laughing. 'Even Magda was more help!'

'Who's she?' she asks, a jealous look in her eye. Leah's insecure about the new people I meet at college, who she says are *a bit up themselves.* She means better off than she is.

'Just one of the old biddies I look after. She was with me when I did the test.' I keep my voice on a level. I don't want to talk about what Magda said.

'You did it with one of your old people? That's fucked up, Su!'

'Why? What's wrong with it?' My voice is thin, strung out.

'I dunno, professional standards . . . keeping your job?' she says, crinkling her nose and waving her hand vaguely.

'She was just there. I was upset. I got the test, and I didn't want to do it on my own.'

'Why didn't you call *me* then?'

I don't answer. How do you explain Magda to someone who's never met her? I shrug.

'Look, Su,' she says, grabbing my hand. Her nails are coral blue today. 'Call him. At least call him and talk to him. See what he says. He's been sick again, hasn't he? Maybe when he's well, he'll change his mind.'

'He's a mess, Leah. He left me by text for Chrissake!'

'I know. But . . .' She looks down. 'Honey,' she says softly, 'you might need him now.'

'Not if I get rid of it.'

She doesn't flinch. Just nods. 'Do you want to?'

'Don't know.' The milk in my coffee has a thin skin. I spoon at it, trying to lift it out whole, but it falls to bits and floats in the cup.

'So talk to him, Su. Want to use my phone?'

'He's not been answering for days.'

'Yeah, but now he's actually ended it, p'rhaps he'll talk?' She holds her pink phone for me to take. Leah has a contract since she started working at the estate agents, while I'm still on pay-as-you-go and always running out of credit. I nod, take her phone and press in the digits of his number, which I know by heart. I learned it, lovesick. In my hand the phone is tiny and cold, there's no life there.

He answers, surprisingly, after six rings. He doesn't say hello but the ringing stops and there he is, breathing.

We breathe.

'Hi,' I say, loudly. He'll have the volume turned up to full, but you still have to speak up. 'It's me.'

'Hi,' he says.

A long nothing.

'I was going to call this evening and check you're OK,' he says. The voice in my ear is far, far away. I can't pick out any detail in it.

My hot, cross words come boiling into the phone. 'Yeah, well, maybe it'd've been a good idea to call me in the first place, instead of just dumping me by text?' My voice is quick, high. Leah's making frantic motions with her hands for me to shut up. He'll just hang up. I stop.

Another long, empty time.

'I'm so sorry,' he says. Is there a slight break in his voice? I hold on to its rawness, a sore I can find my way through to get to him, to my Ewan. Some kind of apology plays into my ear. 'I didn't mean to hurt you. Sorry for disappearing. I just, I can't.' His voice is a broken instrument; it stutters until there're no more notes it can play.

There's a silence.

I break it by asking him to meet me in town. He agrees. This part of the conversation doesn't feel real. Phone conversations with Ewan never do, though.

Leah looks at me. She presses her lips together and sighs through her nose, then she orders herself a beer. They don't have a licence in Parliament, but they give her one anyway.

'Sorry, Su,' she says, 'I was gasping.'

I watch her as she slurps at the bottle with her pearly pink lips, Magda's words still echoing in the great big silence left by Ewan.

Damned stupid Indian.

Chapter Seven

Do not be alarmed at the dirty state of the house at the beginning of the season — it is English people's dirt, not entirely natives'.

The Complete Indian Housekeeper and Cook,
Flora Annie Steel & Grace Gardiner

The church wedding is to be in Darjeeling. Until then I make Bombay a temporary Home.

B has determined to stay away from me, in *that* way, until our big day. This is made easier for him by some malady that means he takes to his bed for several days, leaving me to unpack and make Home as well as I can. Making Home in this India will be like climbing a mountain. And making a home to the standards of Home perhaps an impossible mission?

And yet it's not uncharted territory. I've already seen it done. We've spent endless nights already at the sumptuous houses of B's friends playing backgammon and sipping lemonade and cream soda. At Lynne Mason's house we were served real custard and, before it, Yorkshire pudding that would have put even my mother to shame. And Mrs Mason did not even seem to break a sweat, although her attire bore no concession to the forever encroaching heat. When I looked at Mrs Mason even I felt utterly convinced of it: her complete steadiness, and the honour of her Empire.

Unlike my mother's fluent, practised housekeeping in Bay's Mouth, with her self-taught cheats and recipes, her pinnies, her rolled-up sleeves and the round-stomached comfort of her improvised home, unlike her kitchen sprung with cinnamon and clove smells, the speckle of the floured light, the chopping boards cut from old furniture, the clothes darned and re-dyed in spontaneous shades of newness, this kind of housekeeping, the Raj kind, happens by rule. It is fixed. It is a measure of civility. It is a crusade.

Still, Mrs Mason drops a visiting card round, and I make an arrangement to visit her the following Thursday.

I see something different, more fragile. When Sajid drops me there in the car I find her completely alone except for the servants, who even I sometimes forget to notice now. They are almost like ghosts, moving in a different world as they do, but all around us. They're certainly not any kind of company for her.

'Ah, Evelyn,' she says. And her smile is warm, relieved. She's pleased that I've come. I wonder, is she lonely here in this grand, perfect house? Her husband works, like mine will, so frequently away.

'Make us some tea,' she says to the tall servant. The butler. I still can't remember the Indian names for the different kinds of servants. He slips out. There's only the sound of the fans now. Whirring. Perhaps the one who's operating them is outside the door? I mustn't think of it too much. B says I'm still too distracted by them. It makes him impatient that I insist upon commenting on it constantly, all the backstage activity of the servants and of the real India, which keeps the Raj ticking over. He's lived with it forever, that other life happening in the wings of his, and the best way to live with it, it seems, is to pretend it isn't there.

'So when do you plan to go up to the hills? Have you decided?' Mrs Mason asks me, passing me a cigarette from her purse. It's all they talk about at the moment. Which hill station is the best to spend the summer in? With the hot season fast approaching, soon none of the wives will be left here. I am no exception.

'Yes. Next week in fact,' I say, bending to let one of the footmen light my cigarette. I notice he smells of an English garden before he retreats quickly to his station by the wall, like a dream that fades on waking.

'Very wise. And you will be married there then?' with a smile.

'Yes. In a church in Darjeeling. Will you be coming to the hills?'

'Shimla,' she says. 'Another of the hill stations. So I'm afraid I won't be near you. Though I would very much like to be.' She smiles warmly.

I feel unexpectedly sad. Although I've only known Mrs Mason these few weeks, and only in company until now, I should have liked at least one person I know to be at our wedding, however brief our acquaintance. Someone to make it a little more real.

'You said the other night that you made botanical drawings?' she asks.

'Sometimes. They're not very good.'

'I'd love to see your sketches, if you wouldn't mind.'

I nod. 'Do you draw yourself?'

'No, but I like to look at a craft like that. I respect it. You'll find it very helpful up in the hills where sometimes there's little to do but keep house, keep house and keep house.' Her laugh is bitter.

I nod. I'm already getting a sense of how boredom weighs on the women out here. And loneliness, too, as the men are so often away on the railway or out at the club. I feel a tenderness towards her, and straighten my back. I must be careful with this kind of feeling for other women. Helen taught me that.

'Do you like to garden?'

'Oh yes. Very much. I had a patch of my own at home – I grew rhododendrons, and roses, and ferns.'

She looks delighted, her face flushes and she springs up: 'I haven't shown you around ours yet, have I? Come on. We can have a walk. Have my spare parasol.'

Mrs Mason's garden is marvellously English. You wouldn't have thought so many honeysuckle and roses and pansies and other such flowers, that like a wet soil, would manage here.

'Doesn't it take an awful lot of water?'

She nods. 'When it's hot they water them twice during the day, and once after sundown.'

They're lovely. I look at them and feel a throb for Home. Beside our house there was a meadow. I should like to grow some wildflowers. Or perhaps some tulips.

There are several big pots. I'm surprised she uses pots, as they will get dry so quickly.

'The pots make it easy to transport the garden when we

move,' she says, seeing the way I look at them.

'You take all these with you?'

'Yes,' she says with a laugh, 'I'll take them up to Shimla, and bring them down again when the hot season's over. Many of us do. It helps you to feel at home. You'll see. I can even give you a pot or two to take.'

I'm stunned at the willingness of this practical woman to bear such a complication. Fancy transporting your garden on a train! Life out here is so endlessly pernickety. Just to serve a basic breakfast you need several servants and a week's planning. I kiss her cheek when we say goodbye. We are both flushed. I may not see her again.

I take the car back home feeling once more alone. Sajid is a good driver, but I do wish we could speak to each other, whatever B says. It's odd for me to be trailed by these spectral beings, who do not communicate. Or perhaps I am the spectre? The one trailing? Certainly I am tight-lipped around them.

When we arrive there's a gentleman leaving with a briefcase. He sees me coming and seems to hurry to his car.

'Who was that man?' I ask B as I walk in.

B is reclining on the couch. 'What m . . .' he starts, his shoulders lifting as if in defence. Then he changes tack. 'Oh, just someone from work.'

It isn't until I see the man again, when I'm taken by Sajid in the car to pick up my quinine from the doctor's surgery, that I know there's something wrong. The man is Dr Hammond himself. I see him, going into his room. His name is written up on the door. I don't press B, however. It must surely be a small matter, and we're not yet so intimate as to know all the details of each other's health. I tell myself sternly not to worry. But sternness doesn't come easily to me, and never did have much effect.

B has me go up to the hills first with three of our men and a lot of our things, which we pack into huge wicker baskets, leather cases and wooden chests. He has reserved a whole carriage for me and all our paraphernalia. We're taking everything up there for the hot season, including furniture and plants, just as Mrs Mason said. It seems absurd at first, and from what I hear is only done by the best families these days. But what I see through the windows of the train on our way into the Bengali hills makes me glad to be taking these things, as a kind of blunt arsenal against the unfurling complications of the detailed world outside.

India, the tapered droplet to which I have pointed on the yellowed globe of my classroom, and of which I have reeled off primary characteristics (rivers, mountains, capital city) to be learned by rote by small, pale boys standing meekly at their desks, is, as I see it passing through the windows of my carriage, now intangible and impossible to digest. It is the varying perfumes that come through the window from outside. It is how they linger and penetrate. It is everywhere I look and will not form itself into a pattern.

I struggle to fathom the scenes beyond the window of the train. I had thought, having read my Kipling and my Diver, that it would be somehow romantic and therefore somehow always remote and distant. Perhaps I lack the right approach? All I see is dust and poor people living their poor lives. Is that a house? Is that a real dwelling? Are these real people living on this dry ground? How do their bodies fold so neatly as they squat by the brown river to wash their things?

I've never seen so many thin and half-starved children in my life, despite the mining towns, and although, during my teacher training in Liverpool, we had children at school who came regularly without breakfast, and even in Bay's Mouth I used to take Jacob some biscuits, slipping them into his hand before we started the lesson. Those needs now seem so tiny. Thinking of that small effort for Jacob's breakfast against the scale of the Indian undertaking, I'm dizzy and appalled. Our small island pitched against the attempt to breakfast and teach an immense land like this when we don't even know how to feed little Jacob. I find myself wondering why B never really described the poverty, and wondering slightly if it is like the servants, something he disregards and therefore doesn't see. The thought has an unfamiliar sourness about it. A pickled taste. I ask Sajid for water.

As we pass a long heap of uncollected rubbish where more white, humped cows stand to their supper, there's a sour smell which permeates the carriage when I open the window to smoke. A smell of things putrefying in the heat. Keeping all this from our home will be hard work. The walls of my carriage are very thin against all this India. We will need a house with a thick skin.

The servants, as a matter of course, avoid my eyes still, and so I'm completely alone, although they do everything I ask and keep me in the greatest physical comfort possible, as if I am some kind of delicate fruit tree which blossoms unreliably and only when subjected to impeccable and idiosyncratic treatment. I am to be given air at the right moment, and watered regularly; fed cucumber sandwiches for my distressed roots.

The servants also treat me as some kind of dangerous specimen. On this journey they spring away from me whenever it seems we might come within sniffing distance of each other, and I swear they would wear gloves to touch my clothing and my food if it were proper. My attempts to reach beyond the remote planet that is my body, even by small expressions of warmth or gestures of vague affection, seem to occasion them to recoil like burnt moths. They have, after all, been schooled by B, who is vehemently protective and believes a wan smile between me and a servant to be a perversion of propriety. A little less propriety and a little more warmth wouldn't go amiss now that I'm speeding away from B among all this equipage in my private carriage, my body deadened and comfortable to the point of being completely extinguished by their dedicated service.

Now, parted from B, I begin to long for the steadiness of Home, the smallness and familiarity of Bay's Mouth. I haven't stopped moving, or the world hasn't stopped, ever since we left shore at Southampton. Compared to the ruddy ground outside, and the dry air, and the constant unruliness of every scene that flits by, the ship was a bastion of groundedness. On this journey, which lasts only days but which seems to extend endlessly, I am constantly swimming in unfamiliar things, with no coordinates for which way is up. And it is not like reading of it in a book, not so much exotic as assaulting.

It's only when we change trains at Siliguri to take the famous mountain railway up to Darjeeling that I feel we're finally

63

travelling through the high dream-world of those stories I'd previously heard of India. The landscape outside has changed, and now we curl upwards on our own steam through the most lush and dramatic scenes. It's quite a feat of engineering that takes our steam train up into the steep Darjeeling hills. A system of pulleys and pumps drags the train through and up the gullies and embankments, and I know, if B were here, he would point to each of the carefully engineered contraptions outside on the rails.

But he is not, so I focus on the dream-world beyond the tracks. It is far colder, and I must ask Sajid to bring me my woollen coat. I sit and watch as the hills gather and pleat around and below us, with little wooden houses perched perilously on their slopes between plantations. It grows greener, and I feel I swell lush again too. I see several species of ferns that I recognise, and many, many that I do not. There are a number of the trees of Home, and others I don't find even in my book of botany. I shall have to get a volume that explains the local flora and fauna, for my own will not suffice in all this exoticism. I find myself smiling at the greenness of it all, and at the wide, more oriental faces that I see at the sides of the track as we pull through mountain villages and up and up towards Darjeeling.

The lady who gets on the train to greet me after we finally come to a halt at a station bustling and wild, is the wife of a colleague of B's. Mrs McPherson has brought her servants to help with our luggage and, as she ushers me out of the carriage and along the platform, driving the servants and the luggage ahead of us, she tells me briskly that, 'The ladies of Darjeeling are already in preparation for the wedding. They have a dress in mind and have decided on the cake and the catering. The church is booked, and the drink is bought.'

How strange that they should throw themselves into it when I've never met them. How strange that there should be no one I know at my own wedding. Mrs McPherson seems much taken with the whole occasion, though she doesn't seem to be interested enough in me to ask me anything about myself. In the car that takes us up to the house, she talks end-lessly about the wedding as though I was nothing whatsoever to do with it. I have no sense of who she is at all.

She is, I suppose, kind to come to get me, and kind to follow me around our new bungalow, although I could happily do without her sighs of mock exasperation as we open each of the rooms and see its state of staleness and dust. Afterwards, when she finally leaves, having ordered her servants and my own around for a fair half-hour, I find, standing in my new, empty dining room, that I struggle to remember what Mrs McPherson looked like. Unusually, her presence has left no physical impression on me at all, and has not called to me in the deep and soft tones that most women's bodies do, as if she was entirely empty, a mannequin of the Raj.

After a night's vertiginous sleeplessness, in a camp bed that stands alone in the only bedroom that Sajid has yet managed to make presentable, I finally find a pivot to turn around, by thinking of B, my fulcrum in this disorientation. The know-ledge that I'm to be married in just a few days rises frothily to the top of my thoughts, and thrills me, because marriage is to make of me something else. Following the thrill, there is the terrible fear at the prospect of making a home amid all this.

I am to make it tidy. We are to have three servants here, as well as Sajid, who has come with us from Bombay, and I quickly set them all to work on the house as if they were small pupils, to be caned if they are lazy. We've beaten out the curtains and soft furnishings and polished the windows, and I've had them brush and scour the carpet – for one portion, which was badly stained by damp, we have had to make a special detergent from scratch, a recipe I found in *The Complete*, to scrub it with until it comes clean. We've polished what is to be polished, and supplemented the soft chairs with several new cushions and throws, and I've had Sajid go to the bazaar to buy a birdcage and three little birds, which sing from their cage in the sweetest way. Our home is taking shape, and though there is still something distinctively Indian about it, which I can't root out, I fancy I've done my portion to create a little bit of Home on this hillside so far away.

Within days I begin to like Darjeeling. I like the town itself with its little square and promenading ladies, I like the tennis club, the gymnasium, I like the restaurants, the shops, the hotel, which stands guard over the town, and most importantly, the bookshop, which has as fine a selection of English books as anyone could ask for – quite a miracle, really. Most of all I like the mountains floating in the sky.

Generally they appear in the morning, before the humidity settles in and makes them invisible, hanging above the clouds, like some kind of dream kingdom. The Himalayas are sublime. Sublime. And I am both a grand lady and newly tiny.

Things are settling into a kind of neatness, at least within the boundary of our home. Our sitting room is comfortable enough and Sajid sits me down each morning, and serves tea with remarkable efficiency. Looking out at the garden, at the servants organising our plants on the veranda, I find myself perturbed by the approach of a wedding that seems not to belong to me at all. The yearning for my parents is heavy and sinking.

My dress needs some small alterations, which are done by a local seamstress remarkably quickly and, I'm assured by Mrs McPherson, at a negligible rate. There seems very little else to do, for the women here have taken care of it. I don't need bridesmaids, and B isn't to have a best man. Just him and me and a church full of strangers who seem to delight in the whole affair in a way that's quite odd, if rather generous. I'm beginning to assume that the various women who make friendly overtures here will not become lifelong friends. Life in India is so transitory. People move on and on from season to season, and with their husbands' work. I should have liked to have made friends with Mrs Mason, in Bombay, but who knows when our paths will cross again? Yet strangers here act as if I, barely an acquaintance of theirs, am a lifelong friend, and should hang on their approval or lack thereof.

So I'm embarrassed, walking into the church on Mr Burrows' arm, with everyone staring at my dress and discussing the cut of it and the arrangement of the little clutch of flowers I hold, as if I myself were just a doll and this marriage just play-acting in which they can delight.

It is worth the discomfort to see B's face. He does love me. I can see it by his looks. We repeat after the minister our 'I do's. The minister is rather stern. He's a missionary, and therefore,

I'm told, rather overzealous. But we don't mind. Because we are getting married, and for love. Sweet heaven, for love! I'll never forget the brazen feeling of our first kiss in public.

The wedding feast is laid on at the McPhersons' house, whose servants have really put their backs into the work, so that I should like to thank them personally if it were proper. But instead, of course, I thank Mr and Mrs McPherson themselves – who, to be fair, have been very generous in donating their immense garden and parlour to the occasion. There is even a string quartet playing. Our very own brown string quartet.

Everyone speaks to me of my dress, and the wedding, and so far no one has so much as asked me where I'm from, or about how B and I came to meet. Which is as well, because it was not really overly romantic. We met several times before we took note of each other in particular. I had thought him far too grand to notice me, and I still don't know what made me take his fancy.

Luckily B is impatient for us to go home, and so we leave promptly, amid knowing looks. As we get into the car I can hear the wedding party, for which we were only really an excuse, getting into full swing. Now that the musicians have gone, a gramophone is being set up. There will be dancing.

B has his arm round me as we sit in the back of the grand car that we have borrowed from the McPhersons. And then he begins to kiss me, with hot, demanding lips, although Sajid is sitting in the front.

'B,' I whisper. 'It isn't decent.'

'Why?' he asks, as though genuinely confused.

'What about Sajid?'

'Oh,' he says, as if he'd simply forgotten the man was there. Having remembered, he waits until we're in the house, and in our room, and then he begins to undress me, baring one part of me after another to the cool air, and then moving towards the bed, touching me, and telling me to lie down. He unbuttons his trousers. I don't look. Then he pushes himself heavily onto and into me. He doesn't take too long, and, although it hurts in a bruising, smarting way, it's not as bad as I was afraid it might be, though I still bleed, and feel very sad somehow, perhaps because it is my wedding day and the dreaming is over.

Chapter Eight

Do what you will, this life's a fiction,
And is made up of contradiction.

William Blake

A few weeks after Mum died, and months after I met Ewan, Dad and me were sitting in the kitchen over two cups of undrunk tea, having one of those days when time going on without her was like catching a train we couldn't bear to board.

On these kinds of days it felt impossible to drink, or to eat either. Bread turned to cardboard, all butter tasted rancid; even the pizzas we occasionally ordered smelled of a kind of life we were miles away from.

Neither me nor Dad could bear to talk to Mrs Marsden next door, who peered at us over the slatted fence and popped by with jars of jam or pots of soup, worried because our garden had turned into a tangle of brambles; because Dad's car had been towed away; because our bins hadn't been brought back in and our post gathered in worrying piles against the PVC door. The days when Mum was here, nagging Dad to get his model train sets and heavy-metal memorabilia cleared into boxes in the shed, or telling me to get off my phone and look her in the eye, seemed to move away from us more quickly if we took part in the smallest rituals of daily life, even opening a letter or answering the phone. We wanted to stay put, do nothing and nothing and nothing.

On the few occasions that we switched on the telly in those hazy weeks, the news just talked about cuts again; more cuts. Neither of us ever mentioned the bigger things that tied us to time: the shifts he was missing at the hotel, the classes I wasn't going to at college.

This was one of the many days Dad had taken off, because he *was* ill, with grief, before the American company that really owned the British Hotel finally put him on long-term sick leave.

Dad was particularly bad that day. When I called up to him to ask if he wanted a cuppa, he'd not answered, and I'd gone into his room to find him curled up on his bed, a hurt bird, plucked and defenceless. He didn't answer when I said, 'Dad. Dad!'

As Mum'd lost weight he'd got thinner and thinner too. And in the weeks since she'd died he'd gone from being my wide-shouldered, heavyset, booming Dad, with his big grin and his rough affection, to being something almost flimsy. There'd been no music in the house for months. No fucking noise. No air guitar and no trains.

Enough. Mum, in me, saying it. *Enough!* I ripped the blanket off him, stepping into my mum's place. She was a pretty fearsome wife sometimes.

★

Mum wanted me to marry well.

'I'm not into arranged marriages and all that stuff,' she said to me, looking up from her *Homes & Gardens* magazine as she sat opposite me at the kitchen table, her hair still thin from the last round of chemo, 'but a good match. A nice young man.' She reached across the table to stroke my cheek. I smiled along. Early on in the cancer, we'd all realised that any worry over me or Dad made her worse. Little lies just crept in slowly, to keep her safe. Now she's gone, they're still there, between Dad and me, lots and lots of little lies. On my cheek there's the feeling of her cool hand, stroking it, the slight scratch of her callouses from all the cleaning.

'That one's gone cold, Dad,' I said now. 'Shall I make you another one?'

'No, it hasn't,' he said. And then, after trying a sip, 'Yes, it has.'

He's always been full of contradictions, Dad.

On the one hand, he's a massive metal fan. Took me to see Iron Maiden as a teenager. I was one of the youngest in there between the old headbangers. Dad was pretty much the only bloke with a brown face, not that you could see most of their faces for the hair. Headbanging when you're going bald on top doesn't really work and they all looked pretty funny, but he bloody loved it. We had kebabs afterwards on the esplanade, and between bites he lectured me on the difference between American and British heavy metal.

'Dad, you've got sauce dribbling down your chin,' I said, totally bored.

He shook his head to himself. 'Metal's wasted on the young,' he said.

True. I think it's bloody awful.

The other side of the coin is that he used to dress up in tails and act the butler better than anyone else at the hotel. He used to do a kind of silver service where the punters paid a bit more per night. Dad had a way of making all the blue-rinse guests feel like empresses of half the world again. He could give them back their glory, just with his voice. Steady.

'I presume madam would like another Lambrini?' he'd say, and deliver it with a flourish from his tray. 'And perhaps some sausage rolls?'

They'd not pick up on the irony at all. It was his tongue-in-cheek elegance, not theirs, but it gave them a sense of borrowed dignity and they'd feel great, sip their Lambrinis and their cheap gin and own-brand tonics and *have a really royal time at the British Hotel*. He'd chuckle about it at home. 'No skin off my nose,' he'd say, kicking off his shoes.

Since he loves anything old-fashioned and British, he's got a weird thing about narrow-gauge railways. Trains, for fuck's sake – trains. Before Mum got sick, he'd be up in the attic with his train sets most weekends, playing air guitar to himself, with that Iron Maiden song 'Run to the Hills' blaring as the little trains wiggled their way along the tracks through the green rolling countryside and little picture-postcard villages he'd made for them. The soundtrack made it fucking mental. That's Dad through and through. Those trains on the one hand and that soundtrack on the other.

Now he looked old, though, all the contradictions smoothed away. They'd been a team, Mum and Dad, running the hotel together. He did everything official, and the front-of-house work, and she was behind the scenes, keeping the housekeeping going, keeping an eye on the chefs. 'Spic and span,' was her favourite expression. 'Keep it spic and span,' she'd say, which always made me laugh because she sounded so bloody cut-glass Bengali. She also loved to say 'As clean as a whistle' a lot.

He'd take off the butler stuff and stick on his Black Sabbath T-shirt to walk home in. Dad in work and Dad outside were two different men.

Leah thought it was bloody hilarious.

'Su,' she said to me once, 'you do know your Dad's a fucking legend?'

But it was Mum that let him carry on with the whole thing really. She genuinely wanted the hotel to be the best of British and wanted British to mean something that wasn't fucking skinheads and all that. Something old-fashioned and reliable. The reason her folks had wanted to come here in the first place. Mum still had their high hopes of the UK. Somehow the hotel had healed some of the disappointment: her genuine belief in the insanely civilised project that was the British Hotel, and Dad's ability to support her, however ironically, in the dream. He loved to tease Mum about her hopes for 'an old-fashioned way of life' in a Britain that never fucking existed in the first place. But he played along, because what she was making bloody worked, and it made her happy. The hotel raked it in, right up till she got sick.

She'd be so ashamed of the way the place looks now, the B of BRITISH hanging at an angle, the S missing some paint.

Today I got him downstairs by telling him off in a voice as close to Mum's as I could get it, full of her sayings and cleaned-up swear words. But opposite me he was still in his boxers, like the husk of something.

'She was my bloody life, Su.' He shook his head, tearless and lost.

There was a long silence.

'D'you know what, Dad? She wouldn't want you sitting here like this. She'd want you getting this place together. Getting yourself together. I'm not having it. I'm not bloody having it.' I'd sprung up from my seat, a cobra looking down at him, sitting at the table. It was the first time I'd ever spoken to him like this. For all his sense of humour, Dad's tradition-al that way. You don't cross him. You don't answer back. He stared at me. Then he got up and left the room. I sat in the kitchen, trying to imagine that we ever fucking laughed.

When I came home next day, he had supper ready in two pots. Dad had always been pretty much barred from the kitchen by Mum, so this was a shock. It wasn't much. Just some boiled veg and some chicken stew made with ready-made stock from the shop, but it tasted of food and of home, and he looked pretty proud.

'So, how're things at college?' he asked, sitting down awk-wardly in Mum's apron and shaking out a napkin to lie it across his lap. Such a simple thing, his question, but it let in life. I looked into his face, and for the first time in a while, there was a bit of his old odd wholeness.

'Not bad you know, not bad,' I said.

'Liar,' he said, with almost a grin. He came round the table and gave me a hug. It was the first time I thought it. *We'll be all right. Eventually we'll be all right.*

So I told him my problem as honestly as I could, while we sat there.

'I'm behind, Dad, really behind. I'm only just holding on.' I was almost crying, pushing bits of his stew around my plate. I needed to eat it. I needed to show him this was good.

He steadied me, with an arm round my shoulders. 'Right, well, we'd better get you back on track,' he said briskly. 'From tomorrow onwards, I cook, you work, every evening,' in that firm voice he used to put on for porters and groundsmen and hotel maids, and also for the haughtiest of the old women who'd visit the hotel for *a bit of that imperial charm*. I'd not heard that voice since Mum died.

Next day he started going through Mum's recipe books and over the next few weeks he learned to make practically everything Mum'd ever cooked for us: shepherd's pie, dahl, Yorkshire puddings, mutta paneer, chapatis and lobscouse, marinades, pies, rarebit, pickles and home-made custard. Mum wouldn't have believed it. He filled our house with smells and memories of her, to nourish me. He started playing his records again as he cooked. That's when I realised home for me was Iron Maiden and roast dinner with fucking pickles.

I passed the term with decent grades in the end and they let me through into second year. Dad was so proud when he heard that. He made me and Leah a three-course meal, topped off with apple pie and custard.

'Bloomin heck,' Leah said, tucking into pudding. 'This is like flippin' Windsor.' She always tried not to swear around Mum and Dad, although Dad himself could swear like a trooper.

I felt awful. Neither Leah nor I mentioned that the degree I was actually doing wasn't the one he thought it was. Education was one of the things Dad was traditional about. And neither of us mentioned Ewan, because boyfriends was another.

I'd met Ewan in Journalism class in the first semester. His first subject; my second.

He turned up alone, standing outside the lecture theatre with the rest of us while we waited for them to open the doors like a gullet and let us all be swallowed in. He was older than the rest. Mid-twenties, maybe. In the foyer, he didn't chat to anyone in particular. The other students were nervy compared to him. Overcharged. Their conversations clattered against the walls of the foyer, which was shaped like an ear. He was still. He smiled at the conversation of the two girls next to him who were going on, in an insecure, grasping kind of a way, about the bits they hated in the new *Star Wars* film.

'I thought he was crap.'

'Yeah. She was pretty amazing though.'

'The cinematography was awesome.'

'Yeah, but the fighting was lame.'

He smiled, looking settled into himself in a way the others weren't.

I followed him in, and sat next to him in the lecture theatre and then regretted it because he wrote notes on his phone the whole way through the class. He had the clicks on, so every time he pressed a key on the touchscreen it made a sound. I leaned over halfway through and grabbed it out of his hand.

'Thanks mate,' I whispered. 'That's confiscated.'

He looked at me, shocked. Then he smiled again. His eyes were so soft.

'Sorry,' he said, and there was something in the way he said it, too loud and a bit off key, that made me think, for the first time, was he deaf? His hair was over his ears, so you couldn't see if he had a hearing aid or whatever.

At the end of the lecture he turned to me.

'Can I have my phone back, please?' with a fresh smile. And again, there was a separateness, between the sound of his words and the shapes his mouth made, almost like he was marking the words out, mouthing them like old Henry does, and Henry's pretty much stone deaf without his hearing aid.

'OK,' I said. 'But can I turn them off first?'

'What?'

He didn't have a clue.

'The clicks. Your phone . . .' I could feel my face flushing. 'It makes a noise every time you press the buttons.'

'Shit!' he said, so loudly that the students shuffling out of the lecture theatre turned round. 'Yes, fuck yes, turn them off.' He laughed, but he looked embarrassed, or perhaps more than that, ashamed. 'Sorry. You stop noticing them after a while, you know?'

'Yeah,' I said.

I looked through the menu of his phone for him, found the right icon, selected off, and then handed it back. I'm good with stuff like that. Our hands touched as I passed it over. Heat flooded my face. He was looking at me, carefully.

'Hey, look,' he said, 'I really am sorry I ruined your class. What's your name?'

I didn't answer. But I did say, 'Don't worry. It was boring as hell anyway.'

'I know, right?' he said. 'I thought it'd be interesting. Sex and crime. But turns out it's totally not for me.' His hazelnut eyes lit up, warm. And now I was laughing. I couldn't help laughing.

Although there was an age gap, we shared a lot of things. One of them was that both of us seemed to be making it work at uni without the maximum loan. And not from being rich either. Me with the care work, a smaller loan for the fees, and living at home, and Ewan with what he called 'the discharge cash', and his work at the garage where he fixed carburettors, exhausts and wheel bearings, with a skill that seemed to come from nowhere. He was mercury quick at it.

All the other students have a cut-loose feeling that gives me chills, something to do with the debt they push to the back of their minds all the time, and the big nothing we all might have to go on to after college. A few weeks into uni I realised slowly that almost none of the other students can bloody sleep; the student counselling service has a waiting list weeks long. Midway through semester, a girl from my Lit Theory class ended up in A&E. She'd taken a load of tablets, left a note for her flatmates that said she *couldn't face the future*. The first time in a while I'd heard any of them mention that word that's been taken over by sci-fi and dystopian programmes on the TV until it's just a fucking cliché. *Future*. I remember now how back then, even with Mum and everything, I'd never really felt the way that girl did about it. But right now, I don't know if I can face it either.

'She might find in the future that her liver's been fucked by those pills,' Anna, one of the other girls in that class told me outside the lecture theatre, from behind her black, asymmetrical fringe, 'but at least they pumped her stomach in time so she'll still be alive to pay back her loan.' She looked at her phone for reassurance. 'Fuck,' she said to herself, shaking her head.

When the girl who almost killed herself finally came back to class, she was stick thin, and there were bandages round her wrists. I tried to smile at her, but my smile was too sad, and she turned her pooly eyes quickly down to the hand-out the lecturer'd passed round to us all.

Ewan was different from the others. There was something quiet and clever about him that I liked, and that kind of gentle kindness that only people who've known real harshness have. I know now that he was afraid of the past, not the future.

Ewan was the only person I knew who understood the way I felt about writing and the course, who understood how I held on to it. Three years of pure learning. It felt like looking out over a big bright sea. Fresh. Glimmering. Alive. We'd hunch over course texts together, reading out the best bits, which sounded almost electric in the gloom of his kitchen. We worried for hours together over two lines of my first attempt at writing a poem, trying to get the words singing together just right. He had the same need to make the words sit tight, packed in, checked and checked again, and the same anxiety that they might not say what they were meant to.

He'd come in, waving his latest marked assignment, saying, 'You're not going to bloody believe it!' And he'd have got an A again. He couldn't take it in when he got a good mark, as if it belonged to someone else. His smile had that fear in it that he couldn't really own it, the course, or how peaceful things were with me, in Bay's Mouth.

He'd not come the usual route to uni. He'd had a whole life first.

A whole life, and, as it turned out, a whole lot of death too.

Despite his hearing problems, Ewan liked me to read him the poems I was set for my course. T. S. Eliot. Federico García Lorca. Siegfried Sassoon. He'd watch me as I tried to speak my way smoothly along the lines and stanzas of them, and we walked the tricky paths of those lines together.

He only reacted badly when I read that war poem. We were sitting together, at the small table in his flat. I'd read the words and was whirling in how sad it was. Distant and close. I took a breath for the next poem.

'Stop, please,' he said suddenly. 'Please, no more of these.' And there was something in his voice, a rough place, a soreness his words caught on. So I closed the book, and put it away quietly. His hands, lifting his beer to his lips, were shaking.

He'd lost his hearing in the army.

We were in bed, for the first time, in his small flat, curled softly into each other, when he told me.

'It was an IED. I was lucky. Some of the others weren't,' he said, looking away from me, out of the window.

And just like that, it came into our peaceful room. It came in, and I could almost smell it, with us in the bed, its sick fury. And I realised it'd been there, in Ewan, right from the first time I met him. The shape of it, the shadow, of what we'd learn – much later – to call trauma. I was freaked out by it, and not prepared at all. Afghanistan, Libya, Iraq were just places on the news where a few lads from school might've ended up, the ones school couldn't handle, or the ones who didn't manage to find another job. None of them were quiet and steady like Ewan, none of them had that ability he had to pick out the right word and say it gently.

Tender. That was the word for him, and the way he was with me.

He sat up in bed, with a sharp in-breath, separate from me suddenly. A dry laugh.

'D'you know what's funny,' he said, 'I didn't even hear that thing go off. Or I can't remember it. Everything just went muffled and quiet, and it's been like that ever since.' He shook his head, sitting there on the edge of the bed, but somewhere else completely. 'The only thing I can remember about the biggest sound I ever heard is the deathly silence of it.'

The silence he couldn't hear was loud in the room. I didn't know what to say.

'Our CO told me to use my brain for a while,' he said then, turning again, a pale smile, and reaching out to stroke my shoulder. 'I figured if Dad had a brain, maybe I did too. I got a medical discharge, but they pay me for the rest of my enlistment. I'm putting that towards the fees.'

His mate Darren, when I called round at his one of the times Ewan disappeared, to see if he was there, told me Ewan'd joined up out of desperation, when he was only just eighteen.

'He was a bright kid,' Darren said, 'but he'd missed too much school because he looked after his dad.'

Ewan rarely mentions his dad, who was a teacher before he got motor neurone disease. He doesn't talk about how difficult it was for him at seventeen when his dad died and their benefit was stopped overnight. But Darren's told me.

Ewan had nothing left. No job, no qualifications. The army was good money. A quick way out of a fix.

'In a way,' said Darren, sitting in his living room, surrounded by empty bottles and full ashtrays, 'it sorted him out. Look how he's just powered through that fucking access course — sharp as a tack, he is. Army showed him what he could do; saw he was clever pretty quick. But the army's messed him up too,' taking several quick swigs of his beer, although it was only eleven in the morning. 'Him, and the rest of us.' Darren's eyes were clouded.

Darren always seemed to understand what Ewan was going through, although he didn't see him sweating through the nights, didn't wake to find him half conscious and staring into the dark, catatonic with fear, didn't see how he cowered at home for days on end when things were bad, nor how he sometimes lashed out if you touched his shoulder when he didn't know you were there. These things, between Darren, Ewan and the rest of them, are just there in the background, assumed. When I asked Darren if it was PTSD, he said nothing. Turns out Darren had problems for a while after his second tour, and the doc said it was 'anxiety'.

'You get less money for that,' Darren tells me. 'And anyway it sounds fucking weak. Post-combat PTSD's what you want them to say, if you've got to have a fucking condition. You can't tell your mates you've got fucking anxiety.'

That first night together, before the other nights full of nightmares, I'd pretended that I was at Leah's, for the first time of many. I sat up in bed with Ewan, a hand on his shoulder and down his back, brushing his hair away from his hearing aid with the other hand. I kissed his ear. I'd learn that he could hear me with it. Some. But not the high notes, he couldn't catch at the songs of birds except for pigeons and crows, nor quiet sounds, not my breathing now. I'd learn that his hearing was a wrecked landscape, very few landmarks left, high places, peaks, troughs, and no perspective, no depth. Sounds couldn't soar and they couldn't sink. I'd learn he still liked to listen to music, with me, and watch me for the way it moved, feel its plain beat through his body.

But knowing all that was for later. My questions, then, were the simple ones.

'How d'you manage at college, in lectures?' I asked him, bringing his face round to mine with my hands. 'Dr Madison 'specially; her voice is tiny. Even I miss half of what she says.'

He nodded. 'I can't follow much of her sessions at all,' he said. Then, suddenly, he brightened, and there was that laughter across his face again. 'Have you noticed there's a middle-aged woman who sits in the front row taking notes like crazy every time?' He was grinning, holding up the question, knowing something I didn't.

'Yep – is she deaf too?'

His belly laugh was dark chocolate, delicious.

'No, no! She's mine. She's my note-taker.'

'Seriously?'

'Seriously. Look.' He got up, naked and beautiful from the bed, went to his rucksack, pulled out the notes from the lecture, and brought them to me. Perfect. Neat. Complete.

'Wow,' I said, poring over them. 'Can I make a copy?'

'No way!' He grabbed them and held them away, laughing. 'Strictly needs must only.'

'I have needs,' I said.

'I know,' he said, putting the notes on the floor and kissing me, my neck, my shoulders, then tracing butterflies slowly down my body with his soft lips.

I introduced Ewan to Dad just as a friend, although we all knew what he was. Ewan stood, hopping about on the doorstep in Darren's old suit. It didn't fit him, so he just looked like faulty goods in new packaging. Dad, being a professional bullshitter, has pretty good bullshit censors.

Dad took one look at him and decided he wasn't good enough. But he invited him in anyway. Gave him a cup of tea and some hard flapjacks he'd made. Frowned at him while he ate them, sitting all awkward on our sofa.

'What's your job, young man?' he said, like some kind of fucking town councillor.

'I'm a student at the moment. Journalism. But I'm a mechanic too.'

Dad's eyes were scanners. 'Journalism?' His voice was that arch, ironic voice he used with the guests at the hotel. He looked to me quickly, and then back to Ewan. 'Did you do an apprenticeship before college?' Dad was looking at him in a strange way. 'How did you learn to be a mechanic?'

'I was in the army.'

A silence. 'And what happened?'

'I left.'

I looked at Ewan sharply. He had a ban on talking about his hearing to anyone else. But this wasn't good. Fuck.

'Did they sack him?' Dad asked, after Ewan left. It's not that he cares about the army. But he cares about people hiding stuff.

I just looked at him, and said nothing. I didn't want to tell Dad about Ewan's hearing yet, nor about the dreams.

'I can't get the measure of him, Su,' Dad said. 'I just can't get the measure of him.'

I didn't call Ewan straight away after he left. And although I did eventually, and we carried on like before, it had set something off inside me, that heavy silence at the kitchen table between them. I should've been the thing they had in common, but the version of me each of them wanted was so different, I was pulled two ways by different kinds of love, stretched tight between them:

Oh our Susheela's a great girl. She's got such brains. Her mum'd be so proud. Studying business at university – she'll go on to great things, you can see it. I tease her, tell her she'll be bloody well keeping me one day.

No, not my Susheela. She couldn't care less about business, or money. Susheela loves swimming in the cold fresh sea, oh look how she lies back and dips her toes out and up into the air. She read a poem to me last week, recited bits of it over and over. Said fuck twice because it was so delicious. She loves what she does so much, it's like breathing to her now.

Our Susheela, above all, has always been as honest as the day. She was such a rock during her mum's illness. Through everything, we've always known we could trust her, and she had our back. Watch how she held us all together. I look at her, now, a young woman. She keeps me going. My girl. There's so much of her mother in her. Honesty, kindness, strength.

But my Susheela lies. She tells her dad she's studying business.
Covers all her books with fake skin. The Norton Anthology
comes with a cover saying The Principles of Profit. *Steinbeck hides*
beneath a red one, Business in Today's World.

And neither of them completely false or completely true. I
started keeping Ewan a secret. And it worked, for a long time;
it worked like a false skin will, until it breaks.

I sit, waiting for Ewan in the pub. I don't put anything on
the jukebox, so eventually Keith at the bar puts on his own
choice. Nirvana.

'That man of yours coming, is he?' he asks me, with a grin.

'Think so,' I say.

He rolls his eyes. 'Not sure, are you?' Keith can be such a
fucking busybody. Ewan's never liked him, says he's a creep.

I say nothing, get myself a half-pint and sit waiting in a
corner, with a view of the door, so I can see him when he
comes in. I will it to happen: he'll come in, smelling of the
garage, as if this is a normal day. I'll tell him. He'll make it OK.

My phone rings.

Ewan.

'Hi,' I say.

'Hi,' he says.

There's a silence. The sound of him breathing.

'I'm sorry, Su,' he says. 'I just can't. I can't come.'

I say nothing.

We sit together, in the silence. And then I say it, quietly.

'I'm pregnant.'

For a second we hold the silence, me at the table, in our
local, and he somewhere lost, far away, but still holding on.

And then the flat tone sounds, the smell of oil trailing after it, memories of touch leaching into the mottled carpet of the pub.

I sit. Nirvana blares slowly.

Eventually Keith comes over. 'Your fella not coming?' Motioning to the seat beside me.

'Nope. Looks like.'

Keith pulls a face. 'If you want my opinion . . .'

'I d—'

'I think he's a prick,' he says, picking up my half and taking a swig from it. 'You can do much better.'

'Cheers, Keith,' I say.

'Never liked him.' He says it proudly, although it's not true. He's always bloody loved Ewan. 'You're not pregnant, are you?' he asks me, looking at my undrunk half-pint. I don't say anything. My heart thrums a fuzzy beat in my ears.

'Christ!' he says.

'No. No, I'm not,' I say then.

'Good bloody job,' says Keith. He grins. 'D'you fancy a drink with me then? No one in, could have another.'

I can't compute what he's saying. I just sit there, still, still, and so he leans towards me. 'I've always liked South Asian girls,' he says, reaching a hand up to my hair. 'Lovely hair. Lovely skin. Lovely eyes.' He shakes his head. 'I'm not one of those men who don't like them. Not at all.'

I stare at him. His words land finally, hot and disgusting. 'What the fuck, Keith?'

'What?' Both his hands held open now, palms to the sky, shoulders shrugging. 'Just saying: I'm not racist, that's all.'

I feel sick. 'Fuck,' I say, staring at his red, stupid face. 'You total fuck.'

I grab my phone, my bag, throw my coat on, snatch my arm away from him when he tries to hold my wrist to say something else, some dickhead thing, and I run out through the pub's heavy door. My breath's too fast in and out of my throat, the door's heavy. My eyes are hot. I taste salt.

'No harm trying, is there?' he calls after me as the door swings shut. 'No harm having a go?'

Outside I retch into a bin. *Keep Britain Tidy*, it says on the side. Except someone's scribbled out 'Tidy', and replaced it with 'White'.

Chapter Nine

Where the world has not
been broken up into
fragments

By narrow domestic walls.
                  'Where the Mind Is Without Fear', *Gitanjali*,
                                Rabindranath Tagore

When number three Victoria Drive was abandoned and un-loved, after I was left here alone, I made Home from scratch just as my mother had, according to the specifications of *The Complete*. I did my laundry meticulously, and on a strict rota-tion. I wasted nothing. I kept accounts of kitchen expenditure. I preserved and did not waste and kept the Empire's place within my four walls. And I kept those walls standing strong and imperious. The only components missing from the house were servants. And by some cruel twist, I now have those. Except these subjugate rather than serve.

The girl, Susheela, doesn't come the next day, or the one after that. The whole week it's just Annette and Gemma and

Clare and the others with their unending procession of dull, anaesthetic names. It's going from one toilet visit to the next and being fed by rote and being patronised until you almost forget you're a human being. I nearly let my house of cards topple between all this fuss of women. She doesn't come.

There's nothing unusual in it, necessarily. Often I won't see one of them for a long time. You never know who'll come when. Like this Annette, who's just shaking the rain from her brolly in the dark hallway.

Annette went off on maternity last year. No one told me if she'd had the baby, was it a boy, was it a girl, was she all right? She was a kindly, plump sort of girl, and I did miss her quietness, and the habit she had, when she had fully dressed me, of patting my right shoulder briefly, gently, with almost-affection.

I didn't ask after her, so no one said anything. Then she just walked back in last week, a few hours after Susheela had left. Must have been a year or more since I'd seen her.

'Hello, Magda. Gosh, it's been a long time,' said Annette with a grin. She was much slimmer than when I'd last seen her, and looked a damned sight more drawn, because of the little one at home probably. God knows what she thought of the state of me by now. My limbs have less and less connection to me these days. I forget about my body, except when the girls come to move, dress, wash, feed it, and make me remember.

'It's time for my tea,' I said to Annette, as tartly as I could. She laughed.

Later, when we were in the bathroom, Annette found Susheela's test on the floor, just left there, silly girl.

'Oh gosh,' she said, to herself. 'Gosh.'

'Don't gawp at it. Put it in the bin,' I said quickly. And she did. A good girl. She put it in the bin. I restart my habit of slipping her some extra money. She restarts her habit of accepting it, despite what the company would say. I've a small, dwindling stash of notes, between the mattress and the underlay, enough for a few more tips before I'm done, but not enough to mend much about this house if it continues to come apart at the seams.

Over the week, the pieces of my house turn slightly, but they're still wrongly aligned. Like that puzzle brought by the little boy who came. What did he call it? A Rubik's Cube. My house is like that. Pieces of the house are in the wrong place, and I can't find a way to line them up again.

He walked right in yesterday, right through the door without knocking, the boy. One of them had left it open, must have, or he came in through the gaps in the house that Susheela made when she walked out.

He was small. Must've been eight? Or seven, perhaps. Their ages have become difficult to match up. He had bright pumps on. They had very thick plastic soles, which were also very bright. Perhaps lime green? Perhaps. He had a jacket that must have been made of polyester, or another modern excuse for a fabric, because it shone dimly in the light from the window. He had red hair. In he walked, into my sitting room, and stood opposite me.

'Hello,' he said.

'Hello,' I said.

He walked towards me. He looked at me for a few long moments. Big, January eyes, dark lashes. In his eyes I saw myself as he did, sitting in my chair, the tartan blanket over my lap.

'How old are you?' he asked me.

'You're not supposed to ask my age,' I said. 'And besides, I'm not entirely sure.'

'What? You don't know?' he said. He whistled. 'You must be well old then.'

I did smile. I smiled. And I nodded. I don't do birthdays any more, and no one else does my birthday either, so there is no grand measuring of age each year. But the boy was undoubtedly right. I am becoming extremely ancient. That very morning I had looked at my own hand and could not think how to move it.

'What's that?' I asked him, pointing at the brightly coloured shape he held in his hand.

He passed it to me. A coloured cube. Plastic again.

'It's a Rubik's Cube,' he said. He whistled again. 'Haven't you ever seen one? You must be well, well old! Even my mum had one!' He looked pretty excited about it, my great age.

'What's it for?' I turned the cube over in my hands, its bright, improbable colours.

He came and sat on the arm of my chair.

'It's for making perfect again,' he said. 'You make it all one colour on every side. So this side will be yellow and this side will be green and this side will be red and this side will be blue, see?'

It was hard and cold and awkward in my thin, thin hands. I couldn't hold it properly to turn it. He took it from me and turned one of its cogs a couple of times to show me. Then he said, quite kindly, 'You can have it, if you want.'

'Don't you want it?'

'Nah. My sister gave it me yesterday. She said they used to play with them when she was a kid. It's a bit boring. I like PlayStation and stuff.' He turned away.

'But you haven't solved it.'

'What's the point?' turning back to me, shrugging his slight shoulders.

'But that is the point!' I said. 'To make it perfect, you said.' I tried to smile at him.

'So?' He left the Rubik's Cube on my lap. 'Anyway,' he said, 'I'd better go,' sounding bored with me already.

I wanted to ask him where he was going to, or where he came from, or would he come back, but I just nodded, weakly.

'Bye bye,' he said. And I lifted an arm to wave with my limp, limp hand, as he walked out of my Rubik's Cube house, into all that future.

Annette, who they keep sending, gets me breakfast this morning. I drink it, for it's one of these dreadful energy shakes, and then it's upstairs to the lavatory, and to rest in my easy chair in the bedroom.

We have trouble, getting from the wheelchair to the chair. I'm unable. Even with support I am unable to use my legs enough to stand and hold the frame for several minutes and have my chairs swapped beneath me. My breath is short, and then shorter.

When Annette says, 'I'll have to call it in, Magda. You're a two-person job. They shouldn't send me on my own,' I get frantic.

A two-person job means there'll be two of these nitwits at any one time, and they'll talk to each other over my head about what's going on outside the house. The senselessness. And I will not tolerate it. I heave myself onto the frame.

'Do it!' I say. And within a few seconds she's changed the seats beneath me and I'm settled in the easy chair. My chest is as heavy as plumb. When I look at the room, the corners of it are darkened, as if I was looking through a spyhole, as if I wasn't in the room at all, but standing outside peering in through a crack in the wall.

As Annette stands at my china sink in the bedroom washing her hands, I can hear static in the room, which must have come in from outside. And when I look at her again, from my chair, she's broken into little squares. Annette's coming apart. The room is becoming more diffuse, making the space between me and Annette big and vacuous, so that when her lips move, and I can see her speaking, I can barely hear what it is she's saying over and over, though I think instantly that it must be my name, Magda. My name, Magda, repeated and repeated, Magda, quicker and quicker until it becomes a vibration that disappears into the little squares.

Somehow I manage to tell her to leave.

'Get out of here, you stupid woman,' I say. I say it again and again into the bleak room until I'm sure she is gone. And now I'm alone, and, when I lift the sheet to look at my own legs, they're disintegrating too, my thighs coming apart into a thousand tiny squares of flesh and bone and blood.

Chapter Ten

If you look into any snake's eyes you will see that it knows all and more of the mystery of man's fall.

'The Return of Imray',
Rudyard Kipling

We are only married two weeks when I become ill. I don't tell anyone at first, saying I have stomach pains and taking to my bed. But soon it is impossible to hide. My pelvis aches and I have such an unpleasant stinging pain on urination that I'm afraid to go at all. B has the doctor called, and I am prescribed some medication. They talk quietly about me outside the door.

'What's wrong with me?' I ask B, when the doctor has gone.

'It's just a urinary infection. They're common here, it should be gone in a few days,' says B.

But I notice that the pills I have been given are the same ones I saw him take in Bombay, and I can't help wondering about it. Have we caught something Indian? I quieten myself, knowing that whatever it is, B will have it made well.

★

Mrs McPherson comes to see me, on the third day, when I am much better. When we are finally left alone by the servants, at her request, she is bold enough to ask me my symptoms.

'You mustn't be squeamish about talking to me,' she says. 'I've had every single thing going. Most of us have. That's the way it is in India – one thing after another. If it isn't typhoid, it's malaria. If it isn't malaria, it's the clap.' I start when she says this last. 'Oh,' she says, 'we mustn't be naive. Generally our men have been out here for a long time before we arrive.' She busies her hands around the flowers the servants have brought in, and set, rather tunelessly in vases. 'Men have needs, Evelyn,' she says as if she were speaking of the characteristics of a cat, 'and unfortunately there are plenty of loose women around, white and otherwise, and they are none too clean. None too clean at all.'

I feel sick at the thought of it. And at the thought that this is what she thinks of B. Luckily she leaves fairly quickly, having delivered her serving of spite.

The pain is gone within a few days, and although I feel weak and feverish, I start back at my homemaking.

I do ask B. We're sitting together on the big chair in the day room. I'm curled into him like a bird in a nest. I listen to his even breathing as he reads over my shoulder from one of his engineering annuals. I try to breathe with him. Three, four breaths. I have adhered myself to him and cannot come unstuck so I endeavour to feel that our bodies make a duet, not a duel. But in our shared breath, no peace. Slowly his body, around me, seems to change from a nest to a vice. I must escape it. I sit up.

'How many women did you have before me, B?'

'Why do you have to ask such things?' he says, and I feel his body stiffen further. He gestures annoyance by motioning to the side with the engineering text in his hand. The gesture says get off, and feels imperative as he is so used to being obeyed, but I stay seated on his lap, more upright now.

'No reason. I should just like to know.'

'It will only make you jealous,' he says, pushing me to my feet, and standing up himself.

'So it's many, many then?'

He begins to pace. There is something unsettled in him, some fragility or brittleness. He walks to the window, his back to me.

'Evie, there's no need for you to think of this. Men have needs, for women. That's the way it is. You know that.'

In his voice, the slight tremor of fear. Of losing me perhaps? Of losing our dream?

I nod; I don't want to lose it either. It's a long while before he comes back to sit with me. We sit together again, our breath making discords, and I wonder how many, and what kind of women, and whether they were healthy or not, these women whose cells are now part of mine, whose story is a prologue to my own.

The next morning I find a snake in our bedroom. It's there, lying across the floor between the dressing table and the bed. I've never seen one before. The long muscle of it reminds me of the tubes of hot iron I saw at the smelting plant where my father worked. Men threw the iron around as they hammered at it, and this snake could writhe and flick like those tubes of hot metal if it wanted to. For a moment I'm as solid as cold iron watching the tube of the snake, coiling on the floor. I am as silent as lead too for that moment, and then the tearing sound begins. My own scream.

It's Sajid, not B, who rushes in. He sees it and stops still. 'Still,' he says to me firmly. 'Be still.'

I didn't know he spoke English. I'm silenced by my own language, so swift from his lips.

Sajid grabs one of B's guns from the wall, cocks it, deftly, and shoots the snake in the neck. It is hurt and tries to slither away, but too slow. He goes close, and shoots its flat head, blasting its eyes apart so that something dirty splurts out onto the clean floor. It writhes once and is dead, lying both impossible and mundane against the dark wood. Sajid comes to me then.

'Shh,' he says. 'Shh,' and I realise that I'm shaking. I fling myself on him, and cry and cry. He doesn't step away, although I'm untouchable.

The next minute B has sprung between us, and is shouting at Sajid, and smacking him across the face. Sajid's saying something in Bengali and, cowering, he leaves by the door. B is about to dive after him, but I grab him, shouting, 'B. He saved me! That snake . . .'

B turns to me, and then looks to where I'm pointing, at the snake's carcass, its slow blood on our pristine floor. He looks at the snake. Turns to me.

'Are you all right?'

'Yes. He killed it before it got to me.'

B nods. But doesn't move to go after Sajid and apologise or thank him. He kisses me on the head, his body warm, comforting, but still taut with the tension of his anger. I'm shaking, cold with the shock.

'Come and sit down, I'll have one of them bring in tea.' He takes me to the chaise longue and has me lie down, placing a blanket over me as if I'm a small child. And I feel that I *am* a child here. I know and understand so little. I close my eyes. There's the muffled sound of servants organising themselves around carrying out the snake, and cleaning up. When they've gone, I open my eyes and sit up to take the tea.

B's very quiet, tight-lipped.

'He shouldn't have touched you,' he says, as he pours the tea himself.

'It was my fault, B,' I say. 'I was so grateful, I went to him. He couldn't avoid it.' Surely that is understandable? Surely Sajid was in the right?

B's look is black. 'They're not supposed to touch.'

'Oh B, really that is silly.'

'Their code forbids it, as well as ours. Perhaps we should let him go.' B is like a small child, sulking.

'B! He just saved my life, for God's sake!'

He looks at me. Thinks about it. And nods. So Sajid is safe.

I look over to the space where the snake was, on the floor we had polished assiduously just days before, and which has been quickly cleaned by the servants again. It looks freshly polished, empty.

I try to thank Sajid next time B is out.

'Thank you,' I say. 'I am very grateful.'

He looks at me briefly.

'Not poisonous, Memsahib,' he says, with a half-smile, and walks away.

Oh I am such a fool!

It is several weeks after B and I are married that I first realise I am pregnant.

We have, with great difficulty, finally settled into our house in Darjeeling, having got rid of a positive infestation of mice and having installed bars on the lower windows and stationed a servant outside on the veranda at night ever since thieves came in and stole some of our best ornaments. The house finally feels safe. In fact, with the new window pots and our flowers from Bombay, it's actually very pleasant. I don't mention to B that it sometimes feels like an ornate cage, a cage in which his rather relentless passion for me makes me a tortured bird. He would be hurt, if he knew I felt this way. Indeed, I believe he does know, and, perhaps does hurt. I have turned my face away from his wanting lips rather too often, and have once or twice even recoiled at his touch. Occasionally I spy, beneath his dignified comportment, a faint faultline of self-doubt, a hairline crack which will let in trouble. I can feel it, how trouble stands in the wings, as if waiting to serve us tea, guarding its fury.

Every day I leave the cage for a walk. Usually with Mrs McPherson or some other of the society ladies, though I should like to walk much further than they're able. Today Mrs McPherson and I are accompanied by Sajid because it is not such an established path and he must beat away the undergrowth so that we can walk freely. It is a relief to be out of the house.

I take my botany book on these walks, and have acquired another from the bookstore. The Oxford Bookstore really is at least as good as any bookshop in England. It's astonishing the number of plants and insects that I've never come across. I'm so happy, identifying them, taking cuttings to be pressed and set in my scrapbook.

This must be the most beautiful place on earth. The hills, at this time of year, are splendidly lush with pasture and wood-land, and flowers of all sorts. The land pleats and ribbons its way down into valleys dotted with the small, vivid houses of Nepali farmers, flowerpots set at each door. There are lush rivers too, laced with a rainbow of prayer flags, and even I can see that the water that springs out from these mountains is holy. It's like Eden here. Eden with bars on the windows, and Mrs McPherson, unfortunately, for company.

Mrs McPherson begins to talk about Sajid, although he's walking just a pace ahead, can hear and, from what the snake incident taught me, understand fairly well.

'Is he loyal, this man?'

'Who? Sajid? I should think so. B has trusted him for many years.'

'Only I've heard bad things of Bengalis.'

'Really? I'm sure they're as honest as any other men.' I say it quietly.

'I believe the Bengali is given to lying, far more than the Nepali, who is by nature very honest.'

I'm embarrassed that she'd say such a thing, straight out of one of the old guidebooks, but Sajid must not have under-stood, because he just keeps walking, and doesn't change his gait.

'Women are advised against having them as servants, you know. They cause no end of trouble, fiddling the accounts and what have you, and are very lustful besides. Oh! It isn't *their* fault. It's in the blood.' She looks at me meaningfully.

I can't listen to any more. 'Sajid!' I say. 'This path is impossible. Let's turn back.' And I turn on my heel, without waiting for either my companion or my servant, leaving Mrs McPherson and Sajid behind. I can't believe the woman would be so rude as to talk of a man like that in his presence! And imagine if Sajid did understand. My cheeks are hot at the thought.

Sajid does make me uncomfortable, though I don't know why. He seems so intelligent. And some of what Mrs McPherson says about him being of a lying type is true, for he doesn't own to knowing any English, and yet I know, as fact, that he does. Still, I don't care what Mrs McPherson says, I'm no attractive prospect to Sajid. He never so much as looks at me. Perhaps it's worse than she thinks. I have a feeling that he views us with disdain. Looks down on us. Finds us lacking. And I can't blame him. For I'm as useless here as an axe in summer.

It's what happens on the day of B's birthday that makes B decide he no longer wants Sajid. We are all at the McPhersons, having lunch. Sandwiches and salads and pickles and drinks. It is pleasantly warm. B is telling tales of his exploits in hunting, his favourite tale being the story of how he was once accidentally shot in the arm by his hunting partner. He still has a shallow scar just above his elbow from the incident, and the scar, with its silver, angry bite, is about to be shown to the party. I've heard the story many times already, and besides, suddenly I feel unbearably hot and unwell. B's voice is saying, 'I was just running through the wood, after the stag, when a searing . . .' but I hear nothing more, because the scene's gone quiet and begins to darken inwards from the edges.

I don't know I've fallen, but when I come round I'm being cradled to the ground, safely in someone's arms. My vision doesn't clear immediately, although I hear voices around me, and am aware that there's a scene. When it does become in-telligible I realise that it isn't B looking down at me, but Sajid. I'm in Sajid's arms.

B's rushing across the grass towards us. He pushes Sajid away.

'What's wrong, Evie darling?'

'I don't know,' I say tiredly. And then, after a silence, 'I've never done that before.'

'It must be the drink. You're not used to it.'

'But I haven't had any!'

Mrs McPherson's saying, 'Just sit there a moment, my dear, and we'll get you some water,' but already I'm getting to my feet. Telling them I'm all right.

'I'll go home in the car with Sajid,' I say.

I am surprised at B's vehemence that I should not. He makes me stay with the party, although I can't manage to be lively, and so I just sit, all afternoon, on their chaise longue, feeling rather ill and trying to count the days since I last bled, which, I'm certain now, have been too many. Eventually I fall asleep right there, and only wake in the morning, covered in blankets. The McPhersons evidently decided that I should sleep here. B has gone home without me and will come to get me in the car himself.

'Himself? Why not just send Sajid?'

I don't know the answer until we're home. Sajid has already packed and left. I try to ask B what happened, but he's dismissive, and won't speak of it.

I ask for the doctor, and when he comes it is confirmed.

We are so very delighted.

Chapter Eleven

Even if collapse sets in, and apparent death, hope should not be given up. Every effort to keep up circulation should be continued, many people having literally been brought back to life by devoted nursing. Hand-rubbing, hot bottles, mustard, turpentine, everything should be tried; stimulants and opium avoided, and ice given liberally; and also beef-tea iced to a solid.

The Complete Indian Housekeeper and Cook,
Flora Annie Steel & Grace Gardiner

At the family planning clinic, I sit under the chlamydia poster and wait to be called.

'Susheela . . . Gupta? Room 3, round the corner.'

I walk down the corridor, the walls filled with noticeboards and health posters, push open the door. It's a woman, thank god. She has short grey hair, glasses. She looks a bit school-marm, and I find myself thinking of Magda.

'How can I help you?' she asks.

'I'm pregnant,' I say, sitting down. The word sounds made up. A language I've just invented. The word doesn't attach to the feeling.

'OK,' she says. I'm glad she doesn't smile, or say congratu-
lations. 'How do you know?' She looks at me over her glasses.
I feel thick and young.

'I did a test.'

She nods.

'Was it planned?'

I laugh. Then stop laughing and shake my head. She smiles
grimly.

'How're you feeling?'

'Sick. Tired.' Desperate, I want to say. Fucking desperate.

'Yep, afraid that's normal,' she smiles. 'No pain?'

'Sometimes. Just indigestion. My boobs are sore.'

'That's normal too,' she nods. 'Right then. Those tests
are pretty accurate, so I'll give you some information
to go home with and book you in for a scan and blood
tests.'

It's all so quick.

'Can you give me information about an abortion?' I hear
myself say it. The room gets hollow and big.

'Yes,' she says, 'it'll be in the pack. Would you like to talk it
through?'

'No, it's fine.'

'And you're feeling OK?'

I shrug.

She starts writing something. 'So,' she says, 'even if you think
you might not carry to full term, you should take these.' She
passes me the prescription. 'Folic acid. And stay away from
shellfish, prawns, eat tuna only once a week, don't drink or
smoke. Cut down on tea and coffee.' She reels off the list of
detailed instructions. I nod, with half an ear open.

'All right then,' she says. 'Anything else?'

I hesitate. I want to tell her about Mum, about Dad, about Ewan. But she looks in a hurry, and shifts impatiently in her seat, so I just get up and walk out.

I've managed to get out of two shifts at Magda's, but now I find myself walking towards her house with the pack from the doctor in my hand. Her house reels me in. I think of it, the way she said it: *damned stupid Indian*. Like most of the old people I work with, Magda's territorial as hell about her heart. Perhaps that's what makes her a fucking bigot. I didn't tell the office about it, because she could just as well tell them about me. And she hasn't. I can tell she's not said anything.

Her overgrown garden. Brambles across the path. They grab at me and hook into me as I walk past and I have to detach my tunic from them a couple of times. I should bring some cutters for those. Get at least the path cleared for her, and for us girls for that matter. She wouldn't want it like this if she could come out here and see it. I correct myself. She *could* come out here. It's not her body stopping her. Her chair has wheels. We've been told not to try. Just the thought of leaving the house makes her ill.

I go into the galley kitchen, and boil the kettle ready to take her a cup of Darjeeling tea upstairs, which is what she prefers. The kettle here is slow, like everything else except Magda. As it boils grumpily, I clean some plates left by the last girl. We're supposed to clean up after every meal, but the company only allows us half an hour to give breakfast, and often there's no time left before the next person. I see from the tick list on the wall that it was Annette who was here this morning anyway. She's barely coping with being back at work after the baby, so it's no surprise to find the odd job half done.

Magda'll have had her breakfast and will be sitting reading a gardening manual or a book about exotic wildlife for hours. Painful to keep reading about something you can't do any more and places you can't go to. Or you'd think so. She reads *National Geographic*, but never goes past her front step.

I walk up the stairs with a cup for her and a cup for myself. I wouldn't normally have one myself. We don't have time. And anyhow we don't like them to see us eat and drink. We don't like them to be reminded that we have bodies too, that might get old, although at Magda's, I've broken those rules that keep me safe and private and cold already. There's a pull in me, right from the belly, to see her. To take the information the doctor's given me, and show it to her.

She's there, in the cruel chair. Her back to me.

'Hello, Magda,' I say. 'It's me. Susheela.'

She doesn't answer.

I put the tea down on the table and slide its little wheels under her chair so that the tabletop can be moved right under her nose, and it's only then, as I'm getting myself into position to start holding the cup to her lips that I realise her eyes are closed.

'Magda?' I say. 'Magda?'

The eyelids don't move. Is she breathing? The house feels unsteady. I watch her chest. A barely there shift, a flutter at her wrist; yes, the tiniest flutter of breath and pulse. Her cheeks are very pale.

'Magda!' I say, louder this time. I take a hand to her shoulder. Her eyelids move slightly, but nothing more – or was that flutter the house itself, moving with my high voice?

Chapter Twelve

Dirt, illimitable, inconceivable dirt must be expected, until a generation of mistresses has rooted out the habits of immemorial years.

The Complete Indian Housekeeper and Cook,
Flora Annie Steel & Grace Gardiner

As soon as I am pregnant it is open house. Mrs McPherson comes almost every day and bosses the servants, telling them *it should be this way* and *it should be that way. This is how you make lemon curd. This is the best way to make gravy. Don't be dirty. Your trousers are badly made, these linens are not properly pressed, keep your eyes down, and have some respect.* She says these things to the servants in my house. It's improper to stop her.

'You must keep an eye on them,' she says. 'You must keep them in line.'

What line? I don't even know the parameters of correct behaviour here myself. Polite society closes around us all like the cover of a manual, and we line up, numbered pages, obedient and limited, each in turn.

She seems to use the chance to get closer to me, or rather to approach the delicate issue of my wardrobe. Today she comes in, and asks if she might arrange my closet, and then proceeds to take out every garment I own and examine the cut, asking what style it is based on, where I obtained it, and whether this is the cut the girls are wearing at Home. Thinking at first that she's here to criticise my style, a slow understanding comes that she is, in fact, poaching ideas for her own closet. I begin to wonder how long it is since she has been to England because she seems to know so little of fashion as to think that I am up to date. The very next time she comes she wears a dress identical to one of mine which she has had made up by a seamstress in town. I notice that a couple of other women, since I arrived, have also changed the fit of their dresses to match my own. It seems I am the latest arrival, and so the bastion of fashion, at least for this season.

It is odd how these women think of Home. But I am beginning to understand it. As Home gets further and further away, the memories seem to sweeten, to refine, their backdrop becomes more brilliantly clean, more fresh and more luscious. And against that backdrop I myself begin to dull. I feel less and less the person that I was, the schoolteacher with her class of children. I try to remember how awful the English winters are, and that the summers themselves can be so glum. But still I find myself dreaming of sitting in my mother's kitchen, shelling peas, with light flowing in through her net curtains and the sound of children playing outside, or of being with Helen, sitting in the back of the bakery, watching her stir or mix or knead. It is always that kind of thing. Some idealistic vision of Home which I know can't really exist. I'm aware, as Mrs McPherson is, of how my skin and my clothes and the very guts of me are being worked on by this India, how it's in my bones, and how in my bones I am slowly less and less of what I was. So that I can understand how Mrs McPherson grasps at straws, would be so excited by a dress pattern that is current at Home, current in a place present and now and yet a part of what we once were.

Partly because of her eagerness to poach, I still can't encourage her to have a real conversation with me. I have barely found out where she's from, though I believe it's somewhere in Kent. She has no family worth speaking of, and seems to prefer me to think that she had no life before this, which is clearly untrue. Mr McPherson is ugly and not the type to marry far beneath him, so she must have been something already, but will not say. Instead, she likes to talk of fashion and recipes and my health, which she guards lavishly with home-made medicines from *The Complete*, the time-honoured manual she swears by. She has her female servant make these potions from the recipes, and insists that I take them although they make me feel even sicker than before.

Finally, as we sit in our sitting room one day, she does tell me something. She tells me that she is a mother.

'Goodness! But I didn't know!' I'm quite taken aback. 'How old is the child?'

'He is six. No, seven,' she says, her fingers working urgently at the pleat in her skirt.

I'm a little surprised that she is unsure.

'He's at school?'

'Yes.'

'So you will see him in a few weeks' time?' The schools in Calcutta break up a little late, and so the children do not come up into the hills until later in the season.

'No,' she says. 'We shall see him some time next year.'

'Next year! Why so long?'

'He's in England, Evelyn. It is not so easy to get to them.' Her voice is a little sharp, pinned down at the edges.

'England!' My voice is high. Too high. It sounds judgemental, I can't help it.

'Of course.' She has become cold and aloof.

I'm staring at her. I can't stop. Seven is so young. I knew that the children were sent Home eventually. But seven!

'It's the best thing, and entirely normal,' she says, her voice cracking as she says it. After an awkward silence, she gets up and takes her leave. Now I understand why she doesn't like to talk of her life. Better to talk of nice frocks and keeping house than of a child across the sea who is missing his mama. I could never do what she has done, no matter how customary it is. I know too much of how children can suffer with bad parenting, or parents who are absent. At my school we had several little bastard children who came from the Barnardo's home, and, although we were as kind as possible, they never thrived without the individual care of a parent.

I find myself quite uncharacteristically sentimental, when I think of the children at Home. Indeed any matter where feelings are involved seems to have an amplified effect on me at the moment. Perhaps it's not surprising that I feel a different person. I have noticed other changes, for which I feel embarrassment, though I know them to be expected. My stomach hardens and distends. My breasts are paperweight heavy and full. My mouth doesn't taste anything the same, as though it's no longer my own. My usually nimble legs, which have always been relatively strong from all my walks across moorland and Welsh hills, are torpid when I take even the tamest of my customary strolls around Darjeeling. And as for my sense of smell, even Darjeeling's flowers are now acrid. Yesterday I peeled a lychee and it smelled of copper coins. Mrs McPherson assures me this is normal. Normal? It's not normal to me.

B has also changed towards me. Though perhaps that too is unsurprising. After several weeks of horrific passion, he's now sunk into his shell, and takes little interest. When I ask if he's excited about becoming a father, he says, 'Yes of course,' a little too quickly. Mrs McPherson says that the nine months of gestation are a strange time for men.

'For women do change shape and become different, and therefore can't raise the same level of desire or love.'

I'm a little shocked that she said this so directly. But I feel she's right, perhaps. He's less loving, less adoring, and I realise that he begins not to notice me, as if I were merely one of the servants. The other day I brought him tea myself, and he didn't so much as look up from his paper. I don't mention this to Mrs McPherson, for she would only make me feel more insignificant than I do already, and probably berate me besides for the very act of making the tea myself. But B's waning attention, though I had pushed it away when it was at its height, does make me feel so alone, as if all the spaces of the house have stretched out vastly, and my voice and my body have become tiny, tiny in the house. I begin to write Home every day, and to await the replies with painful eagerness. But the letters take so very long. I would give anything for a conversation. I write to my parents, and I write to Helen, but have heard nothing back from her.

My father, in his latest letter, tells me that he has given up work. With the money that B has sent and his pension, he has enough to allow him to finally stop. This is a great relief. His fingers were so knotted by arthritis he had trouble holding a hammer at all, and I winced at the thought of him beating metal with one.

'When do you suppose we might think of a visit Home?' I ask B.

He looks up from his reading.

'But you've only just arrived. You're surely not wanting to leave yet, Evie? I thought you loved India.'

'I do,' I answer, for it's still true that I'm exhilarated by what I see here, by everything that is not our life. 'But I should so like to see my family.'

'You can't travel like this anyway,' he says then, gesturing to my stomach.

'No. But it might be nice to know when I could go with the baby.'

B comes to me then, for the first time in days, and holds my shoulders.

'You must get through the initial homesickness, Evie. It's only a phase. You must learn to tolerate it, or it'll win out.'

I nod. He's right, of course. But 'Perhaps it would help to know that we are going, even if it is in a year's time or more.'

'Well then, let's say we'll go in a year,' he says, sitting back down. But his assurances seem so provisional that they are un-convincing, and certainly do not stifle my longing. Longing has become my bedfellow already, for I keep to my quarters and B to his. The few words of endearment at the end of my father's letters are rare gems now. I read them, the simple expressions of love, 'our dearest', 'with love', 'dearest daughter', I read them over and over, and hear them sing into the echo of the house. I lie at night waiting for these nine months to pass so that I can have my little baby companion. Someone to love and be loved by.

Chapter Thirteen

Rather, ten times, die in the surf, heralding the way to a new world, than stand idly on the shore.

Suggestions for Thought to the Searchers After Truth Among the Artizans of England,

Florence Nightingale

Walls tumbling in the house, and an opening door. I am being wheeled out. There is a slot of sky, and another between green leaves, the sky winking. I wink back. What is this gale? It's my breath. In and out. Close it out, the sky. Close out the breath. The girl, Susheela, is walking beside me as I am wheeled out.

Out.

Vertigo of roads. Something moves around my face, clasps my nose and mouth and fills them with cool, liquid air. An oxygen mask. I inhale. The gales slow, a cool breeze into my lungs. I'll be kept alive again. I am surprised that I don't struggle more, bury myself more deeply in the earth. The girl sits beside me. She pulls at me.

When I start wanting to remain here, lying here beside her as she sits, is when I begin to lose it, the world, I begin to fall backwards into it after all. The sea. The thick sea. I'm sinking downwards, downwards into it, the thickening clouds, into the silt at the bottom, the earth.

I hear her voice. Aashi's voice. She sings to me, under her breath. It's the sound of the wind, something elemental. And I want it. She is beckoning me back. *Don't leave me*, says the girl. *Don't leave me*, says Aashi, standing on our veranda, her eyes melting in hot tears. *Don't leave.*

I move towards her through the malarial sea, sinking and rising, rising again to the surface and air, and then, heavy once more, I sink.

Chapter Fourteen

To Raise a Weak Patient. Take 1 ¼ yards stout canvas or calico. Sew a runner at each end. Slip this under the patient; run a stout bamboo in each runner. Then with a person at each side the patient can be raised easily.

The Complete Indian Housekeeper and Cook,
Flora Annie Steel & Grace Gardiner

What's she had to eat, love? D'you know what medication she's on? While the ambulance shudders, I look frantically through the file I've brought from the house, the one we all use which tells us how to care for Magda as if that's all she is, a timetable, a set of notes. I read out to them the long strange names of the different-coloured tablets we serve up to her at regular intervals. They shake their heads. *She shouldn't be on all that, not all at once,* one says to the other. *She shouldn't be on all that.* I notice then that in the medication schedule, someone has written over some of the numbers with a thick black pen, diazepam has been upped to four from what looks like a faded one. I look at Magda buried beneath the blankets, an oxygen mask covering most of her face.

'Fuck,' I say.

'She's stopped breathing,' the man says. 'She's stopped breathing.'

An impulse in my gut. *C'mon, Magda. C'mon.* I'm holding her papery thin hand. Stroking it in a way she'd never allow. *C'mon, Magda, don't leave me. Don't fucking leave me now.* He gives her an injection. The needle's so definite and strong going into her delicate bird's arm. I feel it myself. 'Breathing's back', he says. And the ambulance starts up again, its sirens screaming. I feel the man putting a blanket around me. 'All right, love,' he says. 'All right.' And I realise I'm breathing for Magda, the breath coming in and out of me in choppy waves. 'All right,' he says, his hand on my shoulder, until my breath and Magda's are slow and steady, slow and steady as the ambulance pulls up outside the hospital and she's wheeled in.

'Family?' asks a nurse, as they wheel her into triage.

I shake my head.

'I'm afraid you'll have to wait then, love.' She says it kindly. 'Have a cup of tea; we'll keep you informed. Come and ask in an hour or so.'

A long time. I can't sit still, so I go off, wandering the corridors and around the hollow stairwells. The hospital echoes with those last few months with Mum, the illness that was a foreign land we all had to set up camp in, like refugees. It all feels so familiar: the dowdy mobility aids, the adjustable cot beds, the repeating forms, the retro piles of still-not-digitised medical notes, the controlled violence of treatment plans and operations. And the other things, the warm things you don't expect: the sudden gentleness of porters with their great bad breezy jokes, the precious candour of nurses, the feeling of watching doctors trying their best to think through the exhaustion. These tired, tired people pulling together like a bloody miracle to keep a badly funded hospital together by the skin of its teeth. I feel it, filling my chest and throat as I sit in one of the empty stairwells, my knees up to my chest: the intensity of that love we lived then, with Mum, on the edge. My body aches with it. She's got to bloody well get through this. My fists are closed so tightly my nails dig red gouges in my palms. She's got to.

My phone rings. Glenda. I let it ring out, but I do get up, and start one step at a time down the stairwell.

I go out of the turning doors and across to a grassy bit where a few old men are standing in their dressing gowns, smoking. I phone in.

Glenda, on the phone, is so matter of fact.

'Oh right. Right,' she says. 'Are you supposed to be going anywhere else now?' she asks me. 'To Mrs Jenkins?'

'I've missed that already.'

'Why?' she snaps down the phone.

'I came in with Magda ... Mrs Jenkins will be OK. She usually insists on making her own lunch anyway.' I realise how lame it sounds, as soon as it's out of my mouth.

'There's no need for you to stay *now*, is there?'

'I don't know if she's all right yet ...'

'That's the family's job.' Glenda's voice is tight and in its box.

'Magda hasn't got any, has she?'

There's a silence, the sound of papers rustling. 'We've got a contact number here somewhere,' she says. 'She has to have a next of kin.' She hangs up.

★

I sit in the relatives' room, sometimes staring at the wall full of posters, sometimes looking out of the window. You can just see houses, and the top of the big wheel, with no tourists in it. No wonder. No one fancies looking down on the marvel of Bay's Mouth and its forgotten seaside extravaganza on this grey day. My nails have worked red sores into my palms from clenching. I open them and look at the marks, not taking them in.

A young doctor comes out into the corridor.

'I've got a Magda Roberts.'

I leap up. 'Yes?'

'Are you her next of kin?' he says, looking me up and down. I can see him computing whether or not that might be, in any genetic way, possible. I want to say *Yes*.

'No. I'm her carer. Her friend. I brought her in.'

'Right. We shouldn't really talk to people who aren't family, but she's asked us not to call anyone.'

She's alive to give orders!

'Is she all right?'

'Yes, and no.' He looks at me. Perhaps it's the worry he must see on my face that convinces him I fit with his confidentiality rules, because he decides to keep talking. 'Her heart's been a little irregular but seems to be settling. There were some contraindications in the medication she's been on. Some of it shouldn't be taken together. We're sorting that out. And she also took far too much of it. Any idea how that happened?' There's almost a suspicion there. He isn't much older than me.

'I think she changed the amounts on the chart we use.'

He raises an eyebrow because we should have been checking

the right amounts on the packet, not just on the chart. 'She'll need to come off the diazepam, gradually,' he says. 'We'll need to keep her in until she's settled. Is there a number for us to call?'

'I'll give you my number.' I reel it off. 'Can I see her?'

'If you let her rest for an hour or so, you could come back then if she's awake. She'll be in the high-dependency ward.'

He strides off down the corridor, on to the next person, and the one after that.

The hospital canteen is a mishmash of staff, patients, people looking happy – probably about a birth, I realise with a kind of off-note in my belly – and other people crying and sharing tissues, probably because someone's dying – which makes my throat tighten up again. A strange, hyper-living place. I get a watery instant coffee and settle down next to the window. Outside there's a gravel rockery, a few sad-looking plants, more smokers standing there. I decide to go through the door into the pale sunlight and phone Glenda again.

'Have you found anyone?'

'What d'you mean?' Glenda sounds bored. Sometimes I wonder if she even knows people's names.

'Magda's family.'

'No. Tried, but the number's not right. Doesn't even ring.' There's a bit of a silence. I realise that Magda's probably just fobbed them off with some made-up number. 'Magda's getting too difficult for us, and she's got no family around worth speaking of,' she says in a flat, empty kind of way. 'Social services might decide to put her in residential care.'

I try to imagine this for a few seconds. Magda leaving her

house and swapping it for a room in one of those places. I can't. It'd bloody kill her. When I worked in The Seaview, some of the residents barely seemed real. They just sagged all empty inside their clothes, which half the time were actually somebody else's skirt and blouse the laundry'd mixed up. You got complaints from visiting relatives every time you came on shift. 'You've not given Mum breakfast,' or 'Dad says he's not had a drink all day,' or 'Poor thing's been sitting there in his own urine all morning. Can you imagine?' And you knew these things were true. They told me not to say sorry because it acknowledged that we were at fault. But I was sorry. I was sorry about the short-staffed shithole we worked in.

She needs her house. Caught in one of those places, she'd just give up, like a fish on a hook that's done with struggling.

'I'll talk to her,' I say. And hang up before Glenda can kick up a fuss.

On the ward, Magda lies on the bed. Her small body barely makes a lump under the blank hospital sheets. She's still wearing the oxygen mask but her grey eyes are bright again. She pulls off the mask when I walk in.

'Hi, Magda,' I say. 'How're you feeling?'

She doesn't really answer. Too knackered. She's still floundering, you can see that. Too tired even to send me away. She motions for me to sit down. I see her glance towards my belly. The pregnancy's between us, holding me to Magda, and holding Magda to me.

'You look better anyway,' I say.

Her eyes almost roll. She makes a huge effort to say something.

'Stop the silly chit-chat,' she whispers, then lies back on the pillow, breathing heavily with the effort.

I almost laugh. She's going to be fine.

'Right,' I say. 'Thing is, Magda, we need to call your family.'

She just shakes her head without lifting it from the pillow.

'They *need* to speak to someone.'

I don't want to tell her what Glenda said, about the home. Not yet.

There's a long silence. Then she half lifts her head and tries to say something again. I crane my head forward to hear her whisper it:

'Over my dead body,' she says, into my ear.

It will be, I think. That's the sad thing.

I give her a kiss before I leave. Her cheek is softer than you'd think, and warmer too. She still smells of eau de cologne, even here.

'I'll come back in the morning,' I tell her. Magda reaches for my hand. She grips it, looks at me with those firm grey eyes of hers.

'Get some rest, woman,' she tells me, fiercely.

'Ah! *You* get some rest.'

She lets go of my hand and waves me away, like she's swatting a fly.

When I call the office, Glenda's all in a fuss about it.

'The next of kin she gave us was just a random number. I'll get the hospital to call in social services in the morning. This isn't in our remit. We don't do hospital visits.'

'I don't mind, and someone needs to keep tabs on her.'

'They'll do that. We need to hand over now.' Like a robot.

I say it quietly: 'Give her twenty-four hours.'

Glenda sniffs. 'It's Saturday tomorrow anyway,' she says. 'They're not around over the weekend.' She puts the phone down.

In the silence afterwards, I listen to my own quick breathing. One weekend, and then they'll tear her from her house like a baby from a womb. She isn't ready. I'm not ready for that.

Chapter Fifteen

Scouring drops. Mix 2 oz. rectified spirits of turpentine with 2 drachms essential oil of lemon or cloves. Rub on with a clean rag until the stain disappears.

The Complete Indian Housekeeper and Cook,

Flora Annie Steel & Grace Gardiner

When I have surfaced through my opening eyes, coming up for air, I take in the small ward with its four bays, its four armchairs, its four standing bed tables, its jugs of water, its drips and tubes and machines, its two female nurses and the male nurse, and its transient, fleetingly important doctors. I lie blinking and monitored.

When the male nurse comes by, I ask for Susheela.

She comes.

When I try to speak, and cannot, Susheela holds my hand. Her hand is firm. Her hand is Aashi's hand. I close my eyes. Am I, momentarily, loved?

'They'll try to call your family,' Susheela says. There's a moment when I hope for it. And then I remember.

★

When Susheela leaves, I lie on my side, watching the wall, and the shadows of the nurses dancing.

Slowly, I become aware of her. She sits, my mother, Evelyn Roberts, at the end of my bed. Her brow is furrowed as it always was. She smells of lemon soap. My bed is covered in picked flowers. Cowslips and dandelion clocks, daisies. She has her *Book of British Flora* out, and is comparing them to the pictures.

The nurses clip past, oblivious, as we always are to other people's truths. They close the curtains around the bay opposite, and talk to the aged lady there, encouraging her onto the commode. Their tones are practised, reassuring. I can't hear what the lady is saying, but her voice is tight with the fear of indignity. The ward darkens away again.

When I wake, the ward sister is there, standing, checking my chart. She smiles at me briefly and continues to scribble. She comes around, holds my wrist, feels for the ebb and flow of me, and measures it by her wristwatch, the old-fashioned way. A trolley comes up the corridor, with smells of breakfast.

I push the plate they put on my bed table, upsetting it. Scrambled egg and cooked tomato and toast make a broken stain across the bedclothes, the floor. I'm calling her, 'Mother, Mother,' into the dark ward. 'Mother.' But she isn't there. They hold me down with their uniformed bodies, placate me with stifling words.

'It's all right, Magda. Calm down, love. It's all right.'

But it isn't all right. This place is so empty. Only pollen stains remain on the white sheets, where the flowers were. Only my ragged breath, slowing again.

★

Since I am the main guest, the main event in the quiet single bay where they've put me since the breakfast incident, they play me classical music through little speakers in the wall, and have made my bed as I like it (two sheets, two blankets, only the sheets turned down). I expect that tomorrow they will allow me to make selective alterations to the menu. Despite these conveniences, it is all still empty here. They will only give me coffee with a terrible thickening agent in it, to make sure I swallow it correctly and do not choke.

Susheela comes, sits beside my bed. She holds my hand again, as no one has held it for so long. I keep my eyes closed, and feel the softness of her palm wrapped around my fingers. Her hand whispers to me, bringing me into the beckoning world.

I need to grow, to grow in the bed. I need to take control.

I take my hand away, and try to sit up. I fail.

'Bring me coffee,' I shout to the nurse. 'Bring me coffee without that awful stuff.' And when she refuses, shaking her head and offering the thickened slew instead, 'Bring me real coffee. Coffee.'

The nurse ignores me. But the girl, Susheela, she brings it secretly, wet and bitter and sweet to my lips. I take a long drink. I cough. I drink. I cough.

'Good coffee,' I say, my voice trailing after Susheela as she leaves me here, alone again among all this automatic nursing.

My house is battling against the ward, and tries to draw its walls around me even here, its walls of memories and Mother. I don't want to see her. It hurts to see Mother polishing the windows in the ward. Muttering about how to make my bed correctly (two sheets, two blankets, only the sheet turned down). Her drawn face, her anger and her fear. She doesn't look at me as she speaks into the empty air of the ward.

You'll have to go, Magda, she's saying, sitting beside me craning over her work, which she's placed on a small table, and has lit with a small tassel lamp. *You'll have to go Home like the other children.* She's doesn't look up from her copying, copying and copying the flowers in her book of British botany. The flowers, cowslips, dandelion clocks and daisies are pinned down and accurate in Mother's book, and no longer like live flowers at all. I'm crying. I'm a child again crying, because I don't want to go Home.

'Calm down, Magda,' the nurses say, pinning me to the bed. 'It's just the withdrawal. It'll pass.'

I don't want to leave. I don't want to leave India, the servants, Aashi. I hear it echoing from the other beds. Susheela's voice. I hear her voice, saying it. *They'll put you in a home, Magda. They'll put you in a home.*

How dare they. I hear my mother saying it. *How dare they call it Home.*

Home is my big, unchanging house. It is my clock, my chair.

On my lap, as I sit, propped up in my perfectly turned-down bed, is a book. I open it. *The Complete*, its yellowed pages. A recipe for scouring a stain.

Chapter Sixteen

After the first home, the second one seems draughty and strangely sexed.
'Eighth Duino Elegy',
Rainer Maria Rilke

It's the same with all the women of class. The children are sent Home. And why do the mothers not go with them? Why do they stay? To begin with I couldn't fathom it. But I begin, I think, to understand. Ever since I saw B with that woman.

I was in the back of the car, leaving Mrs McPherson's and passing across the square when I saw him. He was standing beside her on the street, a pretty girl with slim legs, wearing one of those tauntingly short flapper dresses popular with the faster girls at home, its shapelessness tempered by how it slunk from one of her shoulders and was gathered to her small waist by a patent belt. She was turning a curl of her short hair in her hand. He was smiling at her, and then he stepped towards her. He stepped, and as he did the distance between them closed beyond propriety. The sickness rose up my spine. My husband B held her half-bared shoulder and kissed her neck.

The way he kissed her, full of lust and wanting, wasn't love,

I could tell that. He was a man who'd stray for lust. B fell right then from the stage of my dream. And I fell, quietly, out of any kind of love, if it ever was love that I was in.

I didn't challenge him on the matter. It seemed hopeless. If he'd stray now, in public, when I was with child and at my most needful, there'd be no reasoning with him, for he'd simply tell me lies as he evidently had already: he was working late, he was tired because of work, he loved me. I simply allowed myself to hate him quietly, and he paid me so little attention I barely think he noticed the difference, and won't, I think, until a few months after the baby comes when he may begin to come to me with that needful pressure. I'll not then be so forthcoming. My boundaries stiffen around me. My skin is terracotta hard. I think of it, of what Helen called 'my ambition', and feel frequently very sick.

Mrs McPherson brings up the matter of infidelity suddenly, on one of our walks around the small shopping bazaar.

'They all do it, you know,' she says. 'Well, perhaps not all. Henrietta's husband is rather good. But many at least.'

'What?'

'Stray, my dear. Stray.' She corrects the angle of the parasol she holds, resting like a hunter's gun against her shoulder, the frills of its canopy hanging around her face. 'There are just so many parties in the hills. So many opportunities for frivolity.' She says this as though this particular frivolity, of the flesh, were just a delicious extra cocktail.

I bite my lip. I've no urge to talk to her about it.

We keep walking past the other ladies, doing their turns, and past the shopfronts, uncannily familiar and English. After a while I summon the courage to ask her something terrible.

'Does anyone ever get divorced out here?' My voice is high, desperate.

'Keep your voice down!' she says, grabbing my elbow. 'Good lord no,' she whispers fiercely. 'Not in India. Can you imagine how we'd all bear the indignity.' The spit-filled blast of that last word lands on my face. Cold aluminium. 'No, even when a marriage is beyond redemption, there's none of that kind of thing. Oh, the woman might get shipped Home, of course. But her husband out here will just carry on as before, or worse, and she'll be left to her own devices in England.' She turns to me. 'We don't *do* divorce. Can you imagine how it might be perceived? Weakness, my dear. We must put up and shut up.' She pats me on the arm, in a businesslike way, and then stops me to view some rather pretty blouses in the window of the English draper's.

As we stand there she says, 'You'd better stay in India and bear it. A woman like you could be left entirely abandoned in England with her children. And even if you did, somehow, have a divorce, you couldn't then find a good position in any self-respecting school. And could your family afford to keep you, dear?' She shakes her head. 'Could you even bear the shame of return under those circumstances?' She humphs dryly. 'The guilt of needing your family's money for the passage? Their house for a home, possibly forever? Would you be taken back as a schoolteacher? Surely not with a private life in tatters. No. In India it's our lot to work hard to hold on to our husbands, whether we love them or not.' She takes my elbow and we continue our walk in silence. I hate her.

I can feel the baby now, turning inside me. And as I wake,

move, eat, sleep, I imagine myself turning around it with no thought for any Indian day's horizon, only looking inwards towards my child. It becomes a pivot. It's the only thing about me that's still touched by love, at my belly, under my heart, its gravity tugging me inwards, and I make myself a nest for it, cradling my belly day and night, touching my child's horizons with my hands, listening to its movements, waiting for the pull of its homecoming.

Chapter Seventeen

In this body, in this town of Spirit, there is a little house shaped like a lotus,
and in that house there is a little space. One should know what is there.
'The Doctrine of the Chhāndôgyas (Chhāndôgya-Upanishad)',
The Ten Principal Upanishads,
Translated by Shree Purohit Swāmi and W. B. Yeats

'Fuck it,' I'd said out loud at the coffee machine in the corridor, and pressed the button for black coffee twice. I'd decanted the plastic cup into a blue hospital one, with a spout, which I'd smuggled from the ward. 'Just fuck it,' pressing the lid on tight.

I'm sitting by her bedside, holding the plastic hospital-issue cup to her lips and feeding her strong coffee, despite what the nurses say.

But my body's less brave than my mouth and my hands shake a bit as they raise the cup to her lips. The nurses stopped me on my way in to tell me again not to give her coffee, so I told them it was juice. They couldn't tell because of the lid.

'Good stuff,' she says, totally spent by the effort of sipping, and lets her head fall back to the pillow. She'd not have accepted anything less.

I'm not sure how to broach the subject. The hospital, when I asked them again, said they couldn't contact a relative against the patient's wishes even if they had a number, and every sinew and varicose vein of Magda's body's is set against it.

I tell her straight. 'They're determined to put you in residential care, Magda, unless we can argue against it.' I'm too tired, too fucking stressed out to lie.

Her lips make a tight zip. She'd been half expecting it, you can tell. Magda's many things: stubborn, rude, aggressive, a bloody bigot, but she's really not thick.

'I shall argue against it myself,' she says, all prim, bending her head to take up the straw again, and sucking more of the warm, rich coffee from the cup I'm holding.

I sigh. 'Not sure they'll listen to you, Magda.'

'I have money,' she says.

I wonder if this is true after all. 'Not sure even your money can keep you at home any more, Magda, not without someone to keep tabs on it all. Your house is a bloody mess.'

She turns slightly pale. 'It is *not*!'

'Magda, when was the last time you saw the inside of any of the rooms except your bedroom, the bathroom, the kitchen and the living room?' I say it gently, but still it's like shining a searchlight into her dusty rooms.

She stews over this so darkly that I feel guilty for bringing the house into it at all.

'Why are you picking on me in such a way?' she says eventually, sulkily.

'You need to understand the situation.' I sound like my mother.

'I understand my situation perfectly well.'

'So what're you going to do about it?' As if she was Leah. As if we were in Parliament together, over a bad coffee.

'Stay at home!' she says.

I sigh. 'Magda, they just won't let you.'

'They can't stop me.' She purses her lips.

'They can refuse to care for you there.'

'I shall care for myself.'

'You can't. You know that.'

'I should manage perfectly well,' she says and reaches for the cup again. This time she coughs for so long it scares me. 'Good coffee,' she says after it's over, and then closes her eyes and lies her head back on the pillow, exhausted. I look at her weary face. Not even she believes what she's saying.

'Is there no one at all in your family who can come, Magda?'

Silence.

I'll let her sleep on it, have a think. I get up to leave, but before I stand, her hand grips my wrist.

'There's no one,' she says, in a fierce, sad voice, and then she falls back on the pillow. 'That's the truth.'

I stand, looking down at her, not knowing what to say.

'Go to the house,' she says, 'and get me my bank book. I'll show you how much money I have.'

The dark garden circles the house like armour. The door stands hard. I get the key. I turn it. It clicks. The house seems to breathe in quickly, getting itself ready for what's about to happen: an invasion by part of the sudden world. I feel for it. I know what it's like to have your body invaded by something alien. This time the gatekeeper isn't here in her rigid chair, keeping watch and keeping me out. I let myself into Magda's house. A thief. In college, they told us to build a character by describing the things they keep: letters, photographs, ornaments, keepsakes. Magda keeps this house. My hand shakes as I place it on the door, and push.

I turn on the light in the small entrance hall. As it pours its odd brightness into the dusty space, my eyes fall on things that I've not noticed before: the coat stand filled with a surprising number of coats – several of them right for a tall man, not for a small, white-haired woman – and the umbrellas gathering dust: two umbrellas, one short with a paisley print, and one black, wooden-handled; and then the big boots, beside the little ones. Men's boots.

The possibility of Magda having relationships, affection or love, is like summer sun in midwinter.

My heart's counting down to something, and I can hear that steady tick and tock, the heartbeat of the house, way before I arrive in the lounge. The switch, when I press it, floods the room with a light that's too refreshing, inappropriate, like opening a window in an old museum. The dark, exotic furniture, the tired upholstery, the cobwebs, the murk, things I know as Magda, light up electric and wrong.

I turn around, back into the entrance hall. A breath. Two breaths. Up the long staircase this time, climbing the spine of the house, Magda's backbone, vertebra by vertebra. I push the door to one of the closed rooms carefully. The house shudders with it. Disapproves. This door hasn't been opened in years. Inside has that untouched, musty, silent smell. A few moths flutter, and there are cobwebs draping the door.

I'm surprised that the bare bulb lights at all when I switch it on, but it spreads naked light to show an old study, bookcases around the walls and a bureau standing centre-floor. I wonder what Magda did in here. Did she sit at the desk? Did she study or write or keep accounts?

I go to the bureau, open it carefully. They fall out. Letters. Piles and piles of them, shut away here.

She's carefully put the letters into sets, placed them back in their envelopes and circled each set with cord, like old-fashioned presents. If I take off the carefully tied string I'll never be able to re-tie them right. Magda's from before Sellotape and knows how to use string. My mum did too.

She'll never make it back in here anyway. I begin to take the old string off, to open the crumbling envelopes.

Dear Magda, it says at the beginning of the first letter, and above it, a date: 1941. On the front is a stamp, which says Calcutta, and the letter is signed *Mummy*.

I don't read it. The stern house is telling me not to. I just grab her bank book from the drawer in the lounge like she told me to.

I'm leaving; I do intend to leave.

I find myself in the bedroom. Anything that matters, she'll keep here, close, so that in the night, when the sound of cars and the light from the streetlamps outside can't be shut away, she'll know the pieces of herself are all around her. I want to know her. Raw Magda. I feel hungry for it.

I open several drawers. Old stockings. Pale, old-fashioned underwear. Cotton buds. Curlers. Her scent bottles.

Then, a drawer full of the pills, the blister packs heaped up inside, and tied with elastic bands. Where on earth she'll have got so much from I don't know. Must have been stockpiling for years. I start heaping it out of the drawer into my bag. This stuff'll kill her. When I've finished, the drawer looks empty. I look at the brown paper lining briefly, and then just close it.

I'm about to leave the room, when something suddenly makes me open the next drawer down.

Nostalgia. I reach into it, tear memories out of the drawer and chuck them on the bed.

Magda.

The first photograph I lift from the pile is of a young girl. Must be, what, thirteen? Done up 1940s style. She's pretty handsome, a jaunt to the way she dresses. Her cheeky knee-length skirt. Laughing, she looks a bit to the right of the camera. Someone's making her laugh and then pointing and clicking the shutter.

I turn it over. *Magda*, it says on the back in fountain pen. I've never seen Magda laugh before. I heard her, that day in the toilet, but she had her back to me. It was a stifled sound, out of practice.

There's a name after Magda, which has been crossed out. A double-barrel? Someone's deleted it, and above it written just *Roberts*. Magda tells us to call her Compton, and that's what they've got down for her, at the hospital.

A heap of very old photographs. A black and white world. A couple with their dogs sitting on the veranda of a posh house. Parasols. Shade. A whole set of people in smart clothes, sitting on a lawn beneath a white, white sun, the table beside them all laid up with dainty little cakes, sandwiches and fruit, and two perfectly groomed grey dogs at their feet. It's only when I look to the edge of the picture and see a line of three men standing in white tunics, their faces dark, dark below the white hats on their heads, that I realise it. My mum's country stares back at me in Magda's bony house.

The next photograph is even older, faded and weak. A grand-looking lady is bouncing a baby on her knee. Beside her stands a woman in a pale sari, whose face could be North Indian. Like Mum's, like mine. But there's a shrouded look about her. She shouldn't even be in the photograph, you can tell. I turn the photograph over. *Magda and Mummy*, it says on the back. The woman isn't given a name.

I only see one more: of men standing in a street somewhere, minding their own business, midway through their lives, with its label on the bottom left-hand corner in that thick, faded scrawl.

The Natives.

'Damned stupid Indian,' says her big, rigid house pushing me back out, down its grumpy staircase, out through its rigid hallway and into the garden with its brambles digging, shooting their claws at me as I pass. Magda's words play back to me, more serious, more fucking heartfelt each time, until every inch of me tightens up against them. I leave it, shed Magda's house, my pale baby churning in my belly. I half walk, half run back into town, along the streets where the cars are backed up because of some funfair, trying to feel it as hard as I can: the *desh*ness of Bay's Mouth. But I pass The

Crown, and it's there, stronger than ever, the feeling of what happened when I met Ewan's mates there for a pint the first time; a smothering feeling, and I can't get it off me, like a zipped-up body bag. I sit on a bench, looking out to sea. Vertigo.

That night, Keith, behind the bar at The Crown, had looked a bit nervous when we all walked in, twitching his eyes along the line of them. Some of Ewan's mates looked pretty hard.

'Mind if we sit in front of the telly, mate?' one of them, Darren I think it was, asked him.

'No, no problem,' he said, although the cricket was on and he'd been watching it.

We sat down on the leather sofas, in front of the telly.

Ewan introduced me as Su.

'Good to meet you, Sue,' said the one Ewan introduced as Nathan. And he reached out a hand. Ewan'd told me he had trouble with his eyes after being in service, and I could tell he couldn't see much. I put my hand in his, and squeezed. He smiled. A nice smile, into the dark.

The other one, Darren, was OK too. He made some joke about where on earth had Ewan found me.

But the third, Giles, said nothing, just looked me up and down like some kind of a horse at market.

He seemed in a bad mood, sullen with his pint, which he downed in a minute or two, then got up and left. Ewan said he'd been like that for a while, grumpy, depressed, but I felt like it was more personal than that. More to do with me. That look made me nothing.

★

'I mean, the guy has a fucking Union Jack shaved into his hair, Ewan!' I said, afterwards, when we were back home.

'That doesn't mean he's racist,' he said. He didn't sound that convinced.

'Are you kidding me? It's pretty much guaranteed, trust me.'

Then Nathan, the blind one, went cold on me. He could hardly speak to me the next time we met. Turned from flirty to cold. And that, Ewan did seem pissed off about.

Eventually he told me. They'd been at the pub a few nights after meeting me, and Nathan had practically choked on his pint when he'd realised, from something Ewan said, that I wasn't white. He had got angry. Ewan came home with a black eye because Nathan had got into a random fight with someone at the bar after that, and he'd had to wade in after him, and got hit by the other guy.

'What the fuck can race mean to a blind man, Ewan?' I said, holding the ice-filled cloth to his eye.

'He just felt humiliated, Su, because he didn't know,' he said.

'So bloody what? What does it actually matter that he didn't know?'

'I get that,' he said, 'I do, but from his perspective . . .'

'From his fucking perspective, Ewan, I'm scum.' There was a silence. 'From *my* perspective, Ewan, you're being fucking crap standing up for him at all.'

'We were away together,' he said quietly. 'Squaddies stick together.'

'That squaddie is a racist bastard.'

'No, he's not,' he said, shaking his head. I could see his hands shaking too. Nathan and the others, they mean a lot. 'He's just had a hard time, Su,' he said, trying to reach his arms around me. 'And now he's back, and trying to find work, and he's blind, and there's just so many people from other countries, and they're trying to find work too, and it's tough. He's all worked up.'

The way he said it, as if Nathan wasn't staining me with his blind look.

'Don't mind them,' said Ewan. 'It's only a way of getting on.'

It took us a long time to get over that. It hurt like hell that it didn't initially make him as angry and sore as it did me. And he was pissed off with me too, that I didn't get it, the way the lot of them were his. He belonged to them and they belonged to him, like family.

I found out much later from Darren that Ewan didn't leave it there though.

I'd gone round to Darren's when Ewan was going through a bad patch. It was after the whole argument between the uni and the benefit people about who was supposed to pay his note-taker for the three hours a week of lectures he needs her. The funding for those things has been cut back, like for everything else, and the uni and the local authority couldn't agree who should pay. It's a lifeline to him, and no one seemed to give a shit. He'd not been right all week. The course is everything for him. Fucking everything.

Ewan hadn't met me when he was meant to, and I'd got a

bad feeling. So it was a relief when Darren's door opened and his rough face nodded.

'He's asleep upstairs,' Darren said under his voice, and opened the door to let me into his dark hallway. 'I gave him some of my pills.'

'What the fuck?' I whispered.

'Only sleeping tablets,' he said. 'Double dose. The guy needed it, Su.'

We walked through to his kitchen. There was a pile of plates and cups to be washed. Empty packets of food, and jars of pasta sauce left open. The others had kept up army discipline – their flats were super neat, ordered, sparse. But Darren's Darren. And he's let things go. He put on the kettle, though, and gave me an awkward kind of hug.

'He'll be OK, Su.' He leaned against the counter.

'You're sure, are you?'

Silence.

'He told Giles where to get off, you know,' he said then. 'Should bloody well think so too,' with a grin. 'You're our girl, Su.'

I felt something steadying then, a kind of anchor going down again, into Bay's Mouth. I was there again. Standing in Darren's flat. All there.

Nathan forgot about it all too, once he'd got some proper rehab, got on a back-to-work scheme, and got support from the Blind Veterans. But I haven't forgotten that he can only put it out of his mind because he can't see. And even Mum would've known what that Union Jack in Giles' hair meant. It meant that although he had twenty-twenty vision, he couldn't see me properly.

Ewan took Nathan up to the rehab centre, a massive old Victorian building that's been used for that for years. He said it was like being back in the army, all Union Jacks and rank and paraphernalia. The place was brilliant, had everything state of the art, and it was a place you could belong to, as an ex-serviceman.

Darren was pissed off about it. 'If you're blind or an amputee or have PTSD, you get taken care of OK by the charities, but if you're just a bit fucked up like me, you're on your fucking own.' By fucked up, he meant unemployed and a drinker.

'Nathan likes it,' said Ewan, shrugging. 'It'll get him sorted.'

To me, later, he admitted, 'It was like going back home or something.'

We sat in silence.

'But it's not a home I want, Su,' he said.

Ewan wouldn't go to them for help, not to the military charities.

He had less to do with Nathan for a while, and neither of us mentioned Giles till I asked, one day when we were walking down the seafront at Bay's Mouth, in the winter sun.

'We're just different people,' he said.

I nodded, disappointed that he put it that way, when what Giles was, was completely messed up.

'And to be honest,' he added, 'I'll never get over all that bullshit with you.'

I heard it, the ache of it, hurt that dries your mouth, makes you want to kick back against it, that way of seeing that makes you nothing worth speaking to, or acknowledging. And I was so bloody glad he shared it with me. We walked down the seafront, together.

★

Now, I pace along the promenade, frantic. Just me and what's in my belly. We've come completely loose from Bay's Mouth after visiting Magda's house, and I've got it, that vertigo, free floating without an anchor. I try to throw up into one of the drains, retching again and again. But nothing comes up. No one fucking stops. No one asks if I'm OK.

When I arrive at the hospital to see her, with the bank book still not opened in my pocket, I'm feeling so hot and sick I have to run to the toilet in the foyer. Afterwards I sit on the pan. Breathing. Letting the waves of it settle. I don't move for about ten minutes till someone knocks on the door.

'You all right in there?'

'Yep, sorry,' I say. 'I'm fine,' leaning against the cubicle wall.

I flush and then leave. I don't look at the woman who was waiting, but I can feel her following me with her eyes.

I walk through the ward, passing several bays of beds before I get to Magda's. I can hear her ages before she comes into view. She's busy giving one of the nurses precise instructions for what she wants for dinner.

'But I don't make the food, love,' says the girl. 'That's canteen.'

'Don't call me love,' says Magda, pointed as a dart. 'Have you taken note of my instructions?'

'Yes,' lies the girl. 'Got it.' She walks off, rolling her eyes at me as she goes.

Magda looks up, sees me, looks down and starts carefully arranging her blankets.

'This place isn't what it should be,' she says. 'Whatever

happened to proper nursing?' She snorts, then lies back again, weary.

'What's wrong,' she's asking me now. 'What's wrong, you silly girl? Why are you loitering? Come and sit down, at least, instead of gawping at me like that. Haven't you ever seen an old woman before?'

Damned stupid Indian. These acrid green walls. I can hear the visitors from the next bay laughing, and it echoes between the four walls of my head. And then I can hear the monitor of the old lady opposite, bleeping, bleeping, bleeping. And the edges of it all are curling inwards, turning black, until all I can see is Magda's face in the middle of the page, saying, 'Susheela, Susheela.' And then, 'Help! Someone. Help her!'

There's an arm around me and I'm sitting down next to Magda's bed in the easy chair. When my head clears enough to think, I recognise that the nurse is busy propping up my feet on some kind of a stool.

'It's the patients who are meant to be sick, you know, not the visitors,' she's saying. She smiles. She has a round, tired face. Freckles.

'Sorry.'

She grins. 'It's all right. She says you're pregnant,' motioning to Magda who's sitting on her bed, next to us, reading a paper. *Cool as a cucumber.* My mum's voice says that in my head. *Cool as a cucumber.*

I nod.

'How far gone?'

'I can't remember.' This is true. The doctor had said

something about twelve weeks, but I've tried not to think about it. I don't want to know how old this thing is.

'You should get yourself checked out.'

'Yes,' I say. 'I will.'

'Now just sit tight here for a bit and let it wear off. When the doctor comes round she'll take a look at you probably. She's one of the nice ones.'

'I'll be OK,' I say. 'It was just hot.' And then I remember it, the reason why I came. I look at Magda, sitting under her neat blankets with the newspaper on her lap. Prim as anything, as if nothing's happening, as if she hadn't just been shocked by her carer fainting all over her. And I decide not to say anything about going to her house. Not today. I don't want to look at that bank book with her and see its good news or its bad news. I carry it, a dead weight, like the deadening feeling of knowing those photos and the handwriting on them: *The Natives*.

When I get to Dad's, the book still in my pocket, I'm feeling awful. He takes one look at me, switches off his blaring music, and makes me sit down.

'Good grief, girl,' he says. 'What's up? What on earth's wrong?' shaking his head at me with wide eyes. 'You look awful. You look bloody awful, girl. Are you ill?'

'No, no. Leave me a minute, Dad, I just need some quiet, and some food, and maybe a cup of tea.' I sit down heavily in the blue armchair, Mum's favourite seat.

'You know, you could be anaemic,' he says, getting up to run some water into the kettle. 'Your mother was anaemic, if she didn't take those tablets. Without them she'd get so pale and ill.' He puts the kettle back on its rest and switches it on. 'Just like you now.'

'No, Dad, I'm not anaemic.'

'B12 injections. That's what you need,' he mutters to himself, opening the fridge and getting the milk out ready. 'B12.'

'I don't need injections, Dad. I just need a cup of tea and a bit of a sit-down.'

The kettle boils slowly, and the pressure in the room seems to grow. He gets the cups, brews the tea, adds just the right amount of milk, and sets it in front of me. Then he grabs the sugar bowl and adds a sugar.

'Looks like you need it,' he says.

It's nice. Strong and sweet. I don't usually take sugar, but this will be good today. Sugar. I take a hot sip, and feel instantly better. I feel strong enough to take the newspaper Dad's pushing at me across the table. Young faces, angry and ugly, crowding the front page.

'They're all getting into politics,' I say. 'At college all the students are. They're fed up.'

'Politics is for liars,' says Dad, batting it all away with his hand. He strokes my hair away from my face. 'Are you sure you're OK?'

When I look up at him, his face has that drawn expression he'd get with Mum.

'I'm fine,' I say. It's a funny thing, telling lies. Kills off little cells in your heart. Sitting here, pretending to read the paper, I have this unsteady feeling, like I'm all a lie – not just the course, or Ewan, or the baby. I'm play-acting my life. How can you let someone love you when you're doing that? I think of

Magda's fuck-off eyes and her don't-give-a-shit attitude.

'Dad,' I say, looking at the empty bottom of the cup.

He looks up at me.

'I'm pregnant.'

The tea he's holding spills onto Mum's perfect carpet.

'Oh good grief,' he says. 'Good grief.'

Chapter Eighteen

Twenty satyagrahists sink down to their haunches and begin to scrape the mud with fragments of bamboo. They work to the singing of a hymn. Their mud is collected by a few others and is dumped into a round mud-filter three feet high.

A yellow liquid stuff – water from the lake – floats in.

The men hope that the water will settle down, dissolve the salt crystals in the mud, and then trickle out through a bamboo spout from the filter's side into earthen pots.

Some of it does, and the earthen pots are then carried off to a bamboo shelter – beflagged as before – where the water is boiled on fires made in mud ovens. In the process the salt undissolves itself once more, and there you are: The whole band's labours produced in three hours enough dirty and probably dangerous salt to cover a shilling.

'The Salt of Politics', the *Manchester Guardian*, 12 April 1930

There is trouble in India. And there is trouble with hatred in my house.

I have turned in on myself. At first I wanted B to stay with me as often as he could, despite the small meannesses that crept into our life, the little ways in which he forbade me

153

suddenly, to be myself. But then the big things happened. Like the time he locked me in.

Although she made me furious with hatred at first, I'd grown a restrained affection for Mrs McPherson. I could see now how she had become what she was, as I was becoming not unlike her myself. The same hankering for Home. The same bitterness in the face of other people's spontaneity. The same carefully guarded body. The same unfaithful husband.

Once, when we were sitting on our lawn, I saw her laugh because two of the kittens came rolling over each other, playing across the grass. She stifled it, but I could see how she must once have been fresher, less dried and pickled and strung out by British India.

From then on, I tried to make that laugh come more often. I made her little gifts. Just lace and flowers and such things, but I knew how they were valued when her husband was so negligent and left her here alone. I also had her sit for a portrait, and made her as pretty as I could, smoothed out her brow, and had her downturned mouth turned slightly up. She smiled at herself, and hung the picture in their sitting room, though her husband wouldn't even look at it when he finally came for a visit.

I also found a man who could tune pianos and I was able to teach her some small minuets on theirs, though it had languished so many years in the sitting room, sweating in the heat and silence, that middle C was never quite tuned to perfection.

We were playing a simple duet one day when she suddenly stopped. Her hands fell to her lap, and her head bowed.

'Anna?' I said.

She remained silent a second.

'We're moving to Nagpur,' she said, looking at me with a heavy, passive expression. 'They're posting George to work on the new railway line there.'

Indian life is transitory, so this was to be expected – people were moved, no one put roots down, but twirled on like blown dandelion clocks; but despite this, we had the beginnings of a friendship. She and I both knew it. I was beginning to get to her, to Anna, beneath all that haughtiness.

She got up, brushed herself down.

'We shall have no use for this there,' she said abruptly, motioning to the piano. 'You can have it,' and she walked out of the door, in her haste almost colliding with one of the servants who had, after a long delay, finally brought in our tea. He was left standing redundantly there with his full tray when I also swept past him, crying, out of the house.

'What use can we have for one?' asked B, as if I had asked for a trampoline, or my own car.

'I would play it,' I say.

He snorted. B didn't like Anna, calling her *that drab woman,* and had grown scathing of my affection for her.

'I might teach the child,' I said.

He considered this.

'Useless skill,' he said after a long pause. 'Have him learn something more practical.' B is determined that it is a boy. 'Engineering,' he said.

So, when her servants turned up carrying it between them, like some kind of revered corpse, he was unprepared.

They did what the best servants will do, and pretended not to understand him. They brought it in anyway, and placed it in the corner with a great clanging.

'Why didn't you stop them!' he shouted at me. 'Stupid woman.'

Those kinds of insults were becoming common, even then. I ignored them.

I had already made my way over to it, and had sat down. I started to play Schubert's seventh, as well as I could.

It was sheer chance that Burrows arrived just then.

'Beautiful! Beautiful, Evelyn. I didn't know you played!' he said delightedly. 'You could play at one of our dinners some-time. What a boon to have a wife who plays the piano,' he said. And I think perhaps it was that, the notion that B could be envied for me again, that made him soften, for the piano stayed, though he didn't let me get away with it entirely.

As a farewell gift to Anna, I had prepared a parcel of some of my best dresses (which I'd had altered especially for her, a book or two, and a new picture of her standing in her best dress which I'd been working on for several days. I was in my room, assembling the parcel, ready to be taken down to the station to say goodbye. I packed a few extra items, including a photograph of the two of us sitting on her pristine lawn with our dogs, as English as can be, and, picking up the parcel, I walked to the door.

Turning the handle, I found myself locked in. I frantically felt for the latch of the door, then kicked at it. Then, when nothing gave, I shouted for B. For B and then for Benedict. No response. Only, somewhere far away in the house, the sound of servants chatting in Bengali. I shouted for Anwar, Madan. But although I knew they were there, no one answered. Scream and shout and kick as I might, no one answered.

That day B became Benedict completely, and Benedict made my imprisonment in India clear.

It was after that I got my first dose of the Indian flu, and they really feared I might lose the baby, though I didn't. Thankfully I didn't, or I don't know what I might have done.

I never saw Anna again, save for in the stiff, formal postcards she sent, signed Mrs McPherson. I couldn't bring myself to write to her of what he had done.

We move of course, with each shift of season, as is proper and correct in India. Shortly after Mrs McPherson leaves the hills, it is time for us also to go back down to the plains. This time we travel to our new 'permanent' house in the perfectly contained little England that is the European quarter at Kharagpur Junction, with its long flat avenue of English homes, its impeccable church and dull humped horizons, its tidy verandas and neat lawns, its rose bushes, tennis courts and bowling club, its bandstand and bustling maidan, its other well-to-do railway families, with their pageants and dances, its long days of gossip, its absent children and often absent men, its railway line like a precisely stitched scar, which neatly segregates us from the Indian districts, its nearby prison where steadily more rebels are kept, and the waiting servants who stand at its doors, lay its tables, make its beds, service its kitchens and stand awaiting Memsahib's orders, watchful, coiled, ready to spring.

Chapter Nineteen

Poisoning by Narcotics, such as Opium, Datura, &c. *Empty the stomach with the first emetic at hand — salt and water, if there is nothing else to be had; give strong coffee, some stimulant, and rouse the patient with smelling salts.*

The Complete Indian Housekeeper and Cook,
Flora Annie Steel & Grace Gardiner

When the doctor comes, I have difficulty distinguishing him against the other shapes in the ward, the other people, present and past, who crowd in.

'How are you feeling today, Mrs . . . ?' he says, looking for my full name in my notes. Behind him there is something being beaten out, clouds of dust springing from it into the sunlight. The ward is broken into pieces by dust-glittered rays of Indian sun.

'Ms,' I say to the sun, to the doctor. 'Ms Roberts.' I know very little of the present day, but I know that this is now my name. I name myself after my mother.

'Ah, on your notes it says—'

I am my mother. We look from my eyes over his shoulder,

we scowl with our mouth at the notes he holds.

'I know,' we snap. 'They're wrong.'

'No problem, Ms Roberts,' making a note in his file. The scratch of his pen is a mosquito itch.

'Oh, just call me Magda.' I swat my hand in the air, to kill him, this mosquito.

It is Anwar and Madan behind him, beating out the rug, they beat it until dust eclipses the shapes of the other beds, golden and beautiful. It settles around us. But still, the doctor.

'Magda. How *are* you?'

'That's for you to tell me.' Under the circumstances I am proud that I hit the right pitch of peevishness.

I make a determined effort to focus on him, because, I suppose, he is real, relatively speaking.

Indian, or Pakistani, or Bangladeshi, as they are sometimes now – the ones from the north of my India. He is young, but not too young to be effective as a doctor. A lot of stubble. Black glasses. A clever mouth.

He is sighing and raising an eyebrow. Good.

He looks at my notes. 'Are you still having hallucinations, Magda?' he asks, quite gently. His English is clipped, perfect. He could be from Bengal himself. They get everywhere. They even get into my house.

'What do you mean *still*?' pulling myself up in the bed.

'The nurses say you speak to people who aren't there,' gently again, coming to sit down beside me so that the bed gives, and everything begins to pour towards him. I look around for them, the servants, so they can shoo him away. But of course now, there's no one. They've been emptied into the realness of him.

'And who are *they* to judge?' I say, as evenly as I can. *They* are the nurses, who watch and spy, and treat me with a practised kindness I find artificial.

'There's no judgement.' He's holding my look. He doesn't flinch. The dust has now entirely gone and the ward is coming into crisp focus. A medicinal smell, and under it something bodily and vile. Me, perhaps.

'Who are *they* to say one way or the other then?' I insist.

'They've seen you,' he says, his eyes unwavering.

'Yes, but who are they to say they aren't there? The people I'm speaking to?'

His eyebrow lifts again. He nods, says, 'OK,' under his breath. Looks down at his notes again, considering.

A change of tack. 'We believe there's a deterioration in your liver tissue, Magda.'

Finally? I give a dry laugh. Which makes me cough. Damned malaria. Damned typhoid. Damned Indian diseases that made me so damned weak. I always thought it'd be the paralysis that'd take me. Not that liver of mine. It's followed me for three-quarters of a century and more, and halfway across the globe. The only other thing that's been so persistently constant is the guilt.

'Have you ever overdosed on diazepam?' he asks, trying to work out if I'm upset by the news. They always find me unfathomable, these doctors. I am so undisturbed by my state of mind.

I shake my head. Then I shrug. Finally I say, 'It's the malaria, the typhoid, not the tablets.'

'How long have you been taking it?' As if what I have just said is pure rubbish.

'As long as I can remember.' I smile brightly, for I must put on a performance to get him off this track. He is becoming heavier and heavier, sitting on my bed, I shall tip into him and disappear.

'I've had so many sicknesses, Doctor – they take their toll. Malaria. Typhoid. Diphtheria. The common cold. Did you know that a small dose of opium can cure the common cold?'

He smiles slightly too. 'Where did you contract all those?'

Ha! 'Bengal.'

He nods again.

'I was born there. My father was an engineer. I lived there as a child.' It's the first time in a while I've given anyone such reference points. The ward balances back into an ordered sequence, his weight no longer pulls so drastically at me, and the depression he makes in the bed becomes shallower, more reasonable. He looks at me, looks out of the window.

I follow his eyes. The hugeness of the landscape fills me, for I had been so preoccupied with interiors before, and with mother, Aashi, Anwar and the others, that somehow I had not been able to process that there was any kind of beyond to the windows. The hospital's perched on a hill, on the outskirts of the town, looking inland, away from the sea. The ward has a view across a broad stretch of fields, and then beyond them, to the hills. The hills are sugared lightly by snow.

'It's cold,' he says suddenly. And turns back to me.

He means out there. In here it's stiflingly hot. I find myself shivering suddenly despite this, drawing my cardigan – which the girl must have brought – around my shoulders. 'Yes,' I say, as huffily as possible. 'Yes, it certainly is.'

A moment.

'I expect you know that we can treat this liver problem, but we can't cure it. And if you continue to take diazepam in such quantities, it could be fatal.' His voice is flat and frank.

I nod, pressing my lips together against my familiar rage.

'Both the withdrawal and the drug itself will be affecting your perception. You may see things, even in waking life, that aren't there.'

I like this doctor. He is intelligent, and treats me as intelligent also.

'Do you not think, Doctor, that everyone sees things in waking life that are not there?'

He laughs. 'Fair point, Ms Roberts. But not everyone talks to apparitions.'

'Not everyone has the sense to.'

Silence. He's not going to entertain me much longer. He has a ward round to finish. I read impatience, anticipation maybe, on his face. Perhaps his shift's at an end. Perhaps he has a sweetheart to meet. Love. Or perhaps just a cold bed and dinner made in one of those terrible microwave ovens.

'We could give you other medication.'

'What kind?'

'Calmatives – they would dampen the pain, and possibly the hallucinations too.'

'Anti-psychotics, you mean?' It's an effort to be sharp. But I must be.

He nods. Smiles. 'You're too quick for me, Ms Roberts.'

I smile. 'I'm too addicted to my apparitions, as you call them.' I feel suddenly very leaden. 'I'd rather you left them alone, Doctor,' meeting his gaze as squarely as I can from the bed.

He shrugs. 'We'll give you a small dose of diazepam for now anyway,' he says.

'Valium?' Thank god.

'Yes, basically. It won't do any good to take you off it entirely right now.'

'Perfect.' That *is* good. 'When can I go home?'

He says nothing for a few moments. 'Ms Roberts,' he says, finally, 'you have signs of liver failure. I would rather keep you here, or in the community hospital, where the care is accessible and close.'

I just sniff. 'Care? And what do I care for care?' I close my eyes and lie my head back on the pillow, spent with all this logical talk.

'We can talk about it again tomorrow,' he says, suppressing a sigh.

As he leaves, I hear a voice. It is 'one of my apparitions'.

That's my girl, he says. *That's my girl. Give them hell.*

My husband.

It was always between us, Michael and I. My wanting. We tried for a child for ten years. Ten years of unwanted blood and a bellyful of emptiness, ten years of watching the mothers of babies grow slowly younger and younger and feeling myself dry and age. I'd marvel at their bodies, fresh and unlined, how their pregnancies rose and fell effortlessly, and how their children grew into bloom. It was a ten-year war between my body and its own emptiness, of anger at myself, at Michael, of wondering every day whether I perhaps felt nauseous enough today to allow myself to dream myself pregnant, whether my bleeding might be just late enough yet for that addictive hope. It pervaded our whole relationship with its absence. Our home became a kind of tomb. A place where the child was not. I scrubbed and polished it, aligned its ornaments perfectly. I made it just perfectly right. I wanted a child with a kind of sickness that made me mad.

Motherhood was to be a return to love, a return to Kharagpur, to Aashi, and perhaps, yes, perhaps to Mother.

I haven't felt Michael's presence for many years.

I discharge myself. I am within my rights to do so, they say reluctantly. I demand a taxi home. I have, as always, a quantity of notes beneath the insole of my shoe. The carers always find it a joke that I make them put them there, but it's a travelling habit I've never shaken. If you have money you have a way Home.

After a certain amount of argument, they phone the care company and it is, at length, agreed that I will be allowed back to my house.

'On a trial basis,' says the sister. She means out of pity, *as this old bird is on her way out!* Annette comes to keep me company in the taxi, to push me into my house again. Good, placid girl.

'They're not sure about this, Magda,' she says uncomfortably. 'Are you certain you can't just stay a few more days, let the doctors keep an eye on you?'

'I don't need eyes, thank you. I need Home.'

★

When we arrive at the house, I can tell instantly. The house has betrayed me. The house has been showing its guts to someone else. Its spilled secrets are in the unsettled dust that rises as Annette opens the door. From the shut wing where I no longer go, I can hear the secrets whispering. Someone has let the past out. I can hear servants padding up and down stairs. Yes. I can hear them walking. I know, without seeing her, that my mother is busying herself making a certain kind of floor polish and is telling some servants, who I cannot quite decipher, how to apply it. I can't see the servants precisely, but I can hear them kneeling, and dragging their cloths across the woodblock floor, my mother's chiding following their every move.

When I look at the white wall of the dining room, it is suddenly covered by diagrams of the railway. Tracings appear wherever I look. And I see a compass in the middle of the table, poised to draw a perfect circle.

Someone has been here. Someone has let the house know about itself. I am wheeled to the lavatory.

Father's broken body is lying on the floor. His blood seeps slowly out onto the tiles.

'Stop!' I hear my frayed voice shout as we arrive at the door. 'I can't go in there. No! I won't go in.' My voice is breaking, and I don't care.

'Why not, Magda? C'mon now. You need to go.'

I refuse. I sit there for I don't know how long with Annette's pleading ringing in my ears. I sit there until the urine soaks my legs, the chair. And she has to mop it all up.

'This is unfair, Magda,' she says. 'You mustn't be like this. I'll have to call it in. You need to go back to hospital. You're not right.'

I think of what Susheela said. *They'll put you in a home, Magda. They'll put you in a home.* I'm crying. I'm crying into my useless hands. I'm a child, crying.

'Please, Annette,' I whisper from between my fingers. 'Please don't,' and then I take a breath in. Wrench my head from my hands, face her, and hold her eyes. 'I just need time to settle, and I'll be right as rain.' My voice is as strong and hard as I can manage.

Annette looks at me with her brown, soft eyes, considering.

'You've really got to go to the bathroom next time.'

She strokes my arm. The imprint of her touch. Her heart. Pity. She's one of the good ones. The ones who don't calculate eventualities, who can be persuaded to do silly things.

'I will,' I say, thinking of Father's body. Over my own dead body will I be wheeled into that bathroom.

Annette stays and settles me in bed, giving me supper there on a little bed table. I feel grateful to her suddenly, Annette, whose life I find unintelligible. Her rather naive care is more valuable than I had realised.

I feel tired, and weak, and I almost fall asleep midway through the small meal she's cooked, of chicken and potatoes.

Later, though, I can hear them talking downstairs. They're sleeping in now. Two of them at a time, since I have signed to say I will, somehow, pay for it for the first few days. These tiresome women. My house will never be free of them, even in darkness. I need loneliness. Company closes around me like a net in the bed, and I dream that I am a sea creature, a porpoise or a whale, caught in a great mesh, thrashing and thrashing for dear, dear life, caught in my own deep sea.

Chapter Twenty

[A] child can never be as well nursed by a lady of rank and nervous and refined temperament — for the less feeling and more like an animal the wet nurse is, the better for the child.

Queen Victoria, in a letter to her daughter Alice

I am pushing to turn myself inside out. We are all — two nurses, the midwife, the two maids and I — focused on what will happen between my legs. The black pain is a fault line I tight-rope along, trying to stop it splitting me in two. A downward inevitable pressure, something deep, deep, trying to come up for air. And my body, holding itself in from a lifetime of habit. My legs are open. They have been placed in stirrups. My belly is pressing downwards like a straining cloth, towards the split, opened now by a knife. I make a sound like nails down a blackboard.

And then lie back, panting, the baby still inside and only one inch closer to oxygen they say. I will have to strain many more times before we break through the boundary of life between my legs, and make today a birthday.

Push. She says. Breathe. Push. I ask for more medicine. The

one they gave me is useless. She doesn't answer. They have nothing else. I ask for my father's bible.

'Don't be silly,' says the midwife. But I only want to see it, for strength, a small piece of Home to hang on to.

The burning pressure comes down my spine, from my hips, my legs. It tries to set my weight behind the baby. To brace all of me against it. But we're still one body. My cells, my womb, are still holding on, and the baby sinks back into me.

I make the noise again. *This is no longer your Home.* There are imperatives written into my muscles, my womb, my thighs, and I follow them, until I'm a thousand pieces on the bed. Endlessly. Endlessly.

And as it continues, I'm sunk back into the nothing else. It goes on, and I am aware, somewhere I am aware, but I'm drifted away, or sunk deep in an ocean. Perhaps I'm dying. There's only the pain, my distant screams, far-off voices.

Through my screams, its cries come, birds on a distant beach. Seagulls perhaps, on a grey Punch-and-Judy seaside. She takes it away to wash.

When it's returned to me, it smells of British India. Unnaturally clean. Disinfected. Soapy. A faint tinge of turpentine. No one tells me the sex, and it doesn't seem important. At the tip of its head, I can smell a solitary daisy. I hold its little, spent body, swaddled in a pillowcase. I hold it weakly. We are together, sunk into our deep ocean. My whole body hurts. Its whole body is perfect.

I hold it. I can't hear what they're saying. Around me, they speak and give instructions, but I can only hear their voices blend and mesh into flat notes, like the sound of a ship's engine chugging. I'm in the sea again, rising and falling on the deep sea, and holding it. My my my my.

She's a girl. My girl is to be called Magda and to be loved. Her eyes are screwed tightly shut. Her legs and hands are beginning to punch and kick against the unhomeliness of the Raj. Despite our marathon, she still has fight. She has been born only to find herself lost, so far from Home. She punches and kicks against it.

I don't. I sleep.

When I wake it's because Benedict is in the room. A predator. My whole body reacts to him.

'What's wrong with you now?' he asks me, as I reach out to stop him lifting my baby. What is wrong with me?

Benedict is delighted. He lifts my baby in the air, forgetting to support her head, so that I cry out. He spins her, although she is far too new and disorientated to enjoy it, rocks her twice, and then gives her back to the nurse. She is as yet too uninteresting as something to play with. That's a blessing.

The nurse is watching me; she's wondering.

That is the last we see of him for a week. He's off to Calcutta to discuss plans for the new embankment. This is a good thing because it means that for a few days, without his supervision, I can nurse and be mother myself. Of the many coldnesses, the first is that I am not allowed to feed her at my own breast. It is infrequently done here, Benedict said, as it makes Englishwomen seem *too animal*, and *too undignified*, and so we are to give her a bottle. Benedict himself was never fed at his mother's breast of course. Indeed, from what he says of her, for she died of typhoid years ago so I cannot know her directly, she did very little mothering at all, but spent her time being a fine society woman. There is one of those plate photographs of Benedict as a small child. He is still, still, and done up like a lord in white frills. From the side of the plate a brown arm is extended to hold him firmly in place. A child of the Raj. His childhood would have been full of small powers.

Benedict has sourced army-issue feed for my girl. It sits in its dull packaging in the kitchen. I don't trust it. For the week that he's gone, I feed her furtively. I hold her warm body to my sore breast, and feel the sure, stinging suck of my child. The midwife says nothing, for she's a cold, bland creature, capable only of the kind of clinical supervision that's tantamount to surveillance.

'When your husband comes back, you'll only have yourself to blame,' she says. I hate her, and ignore her expertly. To think we were told she was the best English midwife in Kharagpur. Even an Indian one might have had more compassion.

I sleep only in snatches, feeding Magda, and being fed by Anwar.

He brings me great mounds of food, and smiles at me as I nurse her.

'Memsahib makes a very good mama,' he says. And when my little girl sleeps, he frequently strokes the soft down on her head. 'Beautiful girl. Beautiful girl.' And, although I am unable to walk or pass water without severe pain after the birth, I feel perilously contented. There are moments when I can almost make myself forget the discomfort, and enjoy these days of Home before Benedict returns. I write to Helen, or into the silence that she's become. *She is beautiful*, I write. *Oh Helen, she is so beautiful.*

★

The seven milky, sleep-blurred days pass too quickly, and Benedict comes back cruelly early, blustering into the house in his big boots on the morning of the seventh day (I think). It's only now, when I have someone else so dear, that I realise how unlike love what I feel for him has become. It is ugly.

I use what strength I still have to fight for her to be nursed. Not by me, as that is beyond question, but, as Anna McPherson advised, by an Indian girl. This is not customary advice these days, but Anna told me privately that an Indian nursemaid, if we can procure one, will give protection against diseases.

Aashi, the nursemaid Benedict has brought in, arrives after only three days, during which time I am permitted to nurse, for otherwise Magda will be used to the bottle and won't latch. I feed her when she wants for those days, despite everyone's disapproval, for it should all be done according to the manual. I secretly hope that, as the nurse warned, she will refuse another woman's breast if she becomes too used to mine, and that by some miracle, I will be able to keep nursing her in secret.

There is something strange in Aashi's appointment. She is not of the caste that would usually offer the service. She is the young wife of one of Benedict's new Indian colleagues. We are to keep her secret.

Benedict objects strongly to the growing incursion of Indians into the upper ranks of the railway service, but has no choice in the matter, for the crown is sure of itself in allowing at least that measure of competency to be fostered. So Benedict puts up with his new brown colleagues with a degree of contained resentment, and seems to relish the chance to pull rank. Aashi's appointment is one such chance.

Aashi, though she is only just eighteen she says, has a baby of her own who must now be weaned off his mother's milk so that mine can take the breast. I feel unhappy at the thought, as I hear from her that he is only a few weeks old, but, as I understand it, Benedict has rewarded her husband famously for allowing it. And indeed her husband has been more than usually flexible. Benedict is adamant that it should be a high-caste girl. And I agree, for they *are* cleaner, and tend to be free of disease. The thought that there might be coercion involved doesn't cross my mind until I hear Benedict on our new telephone, bargaining.

'You're lucky to have a job at all, my man,' he's saying. 'Don't you forget that. Indians aren't generally promoted, as you've been. There's many a damned sight worse off that'd jump at the chance, and then where would you and your wife and your baby girl be?' Here, the other person evidently corrects him, for he says, 'Boy, then. Boy. Whatever you please. It's his future at stake, and your own. Are you telling me no?' He's silent a moment. 'Are you telling me no?' he says again.

We have told everyone that Aashi is simply to be an ayah, and a maidservant for me, partly as having a native wet nurse is lately disapproved of by society, and partly as her husband would be shunned, and so he made it a condition of her service. There is great pressure now, from Benedict, from the doctor and nurses, for us to make the transition from me to her as quickly as possible, or the baby will not feed with her, so I have the girl brought up straight away. I watch my baby's pale mouth around the girl's dark breast and feel Home sinking away from us all. Aashi and I both have tears in our eyes when they meet.

Anna McPherson told me to follow the manual, which stipulates that the baby should be fed every four hours, on a strict rotation, and so I focus on this timetable, and on making the servants change her and rub her with lotion to a regular schedule too. I make a chart of her stools and the yield of her bladder. I make Aashi eat what I would eat myself, although I can tell that she balks at the strangeness of the English food, and I have to allow her, as a Hindoo, to forgo eating beef, though the iron would do the baby good. I especially forbid her to eat spices, for fear of giving my baby colic, and I sit awake with her as she feeds for half an hour every four hours at night, which I time assiduously by the little carriage clock that belonged to Benedict's mother.

My breasts grow terribly sore and I must cover them in a poultice and cool cloths. This is the only time that I let my child and the girl out of my sight. Aashi can't meet my eye when I return, which leads me to guess that she knows what I have to do, and perhaps knows also how much I hate it, letting myself and my milk go sour so.

Helen never replied to my letter, and now, I cannot believe I ever sent it. That I had such joy to share. Over the following weeks, as I am not allowed to feed, to change, to mother my baby, I become toughened like old meat into a kind of sergeant major, and, when I look at myself in the glass, I become, day by day, more like the hard-faced Englishwomen who have surrounded me since I arrived, my brow creased by resentment of him, the man I came to India to love.

All love lost now, except for the tiny, gentle flutter of her sweet lashes, her shallow breathing, and the pulse at her soft, soft throat as she feeds quietly on the breast of the girl. Aashi looks at me fearfully, and, I believe, with a mixture of anger and terrible pity.

Chapter Twenty-One

But it will be asked, How are we to punish our servants when we have no
hold either on their minds or bodies? — When cutting their pay is illegal, and
few, if any, have any real sense of shame. The answer is obvious. Make a hold.

The Complete Indian Housekeeper and Cook,

Flora Annie Steel & Grace Gardiner

Dad sits, head in hands.

I sit next to him. All the mod cons Mum bought sit around us in the kitchen: the mixer, the rice cooker, the slow cooker, the cappuccino machine in pride of place with her last incense and offerings still beside it. There's the whirr outside, of a bus passing. A blackbird sings.

I don't say I'm sorry. I know it won't be enough. He says nothing for the longest time. When he looks up his eyes are two stones. He's the butler, at the British Hotel. Businesslike, professional, slightly cold.

'I suppose you'll get rid of it,' he says. His tone of voice is detached, ironic.

Absence. The sore word comes into my head. *Absence.* Mum's abandoned us completely.

'Yes,' I say quickly. 'I think so,' I add, in a tiny, child's voice.

'Right,' he says, in his own voice again. 'All right.' Dad doesn't look at me. He's not himself. He's not Dad.

It's only when he wipes his eyes, I know he's still in there. I make another cup of tea.

'Does he know?' he asks, as I hand it to him. 'The boy?' As if he's some kind of fourteen-year-old bad lot.

'Yes,' I say, 'I told him.' I stop, and then I say it. 'He left.'

He swears in Bangla. His fists are clenched. 'I told you about that boy,' he says. 'I told you.'

Then he sits, the silence stiffening around him.

I push his cup of tea across the table towards him, waiting.

'D'you think we can make it work, Dad?' I say it into the echo of the kitchen. By 'we' I mean Dad and me. Not Ewan.

He looks up at me. I notice then; his lip is trembling. And I feel a sensation in my belly. A feeling that's like the feeling of falling.

'Su,' he says, 'there's something you need to know.'

I'd known things were tight since Dad lost his job, but the debt he sets out, at our kitchen table, is a kind of tumour. The knots and tangles of Dad's lies, to Mum, to me, make inky webs around us as we sit in her perfectly neat, perfectly dusted, perfectly polished house. He brings out the statements, one by one, and shows me, page by page, item by item, how nothing that we own is ours. Our walls and windows, our garden, our TV, my computer, practically our bodies, fingernails, our hair, our whole lives have been mortgaged. At the end of it, we sit, at the darkening table, my hand over my mouth, his head in his hands.

'I'm sorry,' he says, his voice breaking.

'How long? How long until we have to move out of the house?' Mum's house.

'They say next month,' he murmurs. 'They say, unless I pay up, they'll repossess next month.'

I don't say it. I don't say any of the obvious things. Not, *Dad, how could you?* Not *Dad, what were you thinking?* I know full well. He was thinking he could keep Mum alive with his borrowed money. She always said we couldn't afford those extra treatments. The trip to America. The expensive injections he kept her in at the end. I don't need to ask him why he did it. When I think of her thin, thin body, how her hair came out in clumps, the translucent skin under her eyes, I know.

We've lied to each other. That's all that seems to matter now. We've sat at this table together. And he's lied. And so have I.

'I can't afford to keep you and this baby,' he says then, looking up at me with red eyes.

'No,' I say. He can't. There's a long silence before we both swear, me in English, and him, again, in Bangla.

'Where the fuck will we live?' Asking him, asking Mum's kitchen.

There's a silence. He tries to make a joke.

'We could start a band,' he says.

Neither of us can raise a smile.

'Hopefully you'll be a better businessman than I've been,' he says, his voice flat again.

I can feel the build-up of salt. My belly begins to quake, small tremor of tears.

When I tell him about college, he barely flinches.

'Oh god,' he says, sitting at the kitchen table, his tea cold in his hands. 'What a bloody mess.'

I sit in my room and dial the number on the leaflet the doctor gave me. The flat, empty tone. Engaged.

It feels impossible that anyone else could be in my situation right now, phoning the clinic, keeping the line busy. Phoning to get rid of a baby.

I sit and listen to the engaged tone for a while. The sound of being on my own but one of many.

As soon as I hang up, my phone buzzes. It's Ewan.

I can't speak to him now. He leaves a message.

'Su. I shouldn't have hung up like that,' he says. His voice sounds stripped bare. 'It was just a shock,' he sighs. He sounds so weary. 'I wasn't expecting it. Look, I hope you're OK. Can you let me know you're OK? Just call me. Please.'

The walls of my room are tight round me, sitting listening to Ewan's voice. I hurt so much. I hurt so much. I want my mum's company. It's like a thirst.

I get to the student canteen just in time for dinner. I don't usually eat there, but today I just need some space from Dad, so I spend some of the cash the office slips me for extra shifts. While I collect my food from the self-service counter, the other students are all on about a protest against fees.

'It's been on the news,' says a blonde girl with bright eyes, standing in front of me in the queue. She turns to her friend. 'It's on Facebook, look.' Holding out her phone.

I scrawl through my phone to read about it online as I stand in the queue. Everyone's posting videos and memes of it. Having Magda's bank book in my pocket makes me feel separate from it, like I'm suddenly immune to debt.

From all the food on offer, the only thing I can stomach is a baked potato and butter. I sit with Magda's bank book in my pocket. I can't face it. I ignore its beckoning, and look up to the news on the telly again. Three of the women from the canteen are watching it too, in their pinnies, shaking their heads. All that anger. There's a still image of a boy who's just broken a window and holds the chair he broke it with as the glass slowly falls away, the shutter speed lightning fast and his face abstract and still with it, the fucking fury that keeps all these kids from sleeping.

The news is all bloody rubbish, says Ewan in my head.

He'd said it from under the van he was fixing.

'They just tell stories,' he said, 'bad bloody stories,' wheeling back under the van. He was good at mending stuff: engines, beaten-in car doors, windscreens. He'd finish work happy at the garage. That'd been his job in the army too. Mechanic. Mechanical engineer. He kept the tanks and four-wheel drives running. And the guns, he kept them in working order too. That was pretty much the only thing he told me about it. *Satisfying*, he'd say, whenever I asked him how work had gone at the garage. It cleaned him all up inside. Made him dirty as hell on the outside though. He had oil all over him every day.

We walked back from the garage, him still in his overalls. He held my hand in his big oily one. The light was July.

When we got back we had a bath together. He didn't have a shower, just an old green bathtub, so he had to have baths even when it was hot in summer. I kept telling him just to buy one of those showers that attaches to your taps, but he'd got used to it, I think, and anyway, this was lovelier. We opened the windows wide to let the steam and heat out, and just hung towels in front of them so the neighbours couldn't see us. I got out of my dress and slipped into the hot water, still a bit shy despite the months we'd been together.

When he got in, the black oil from the garage made the water smoky, and there wasn't really room for both of us, but I didn't care.

'They never say how it is really,' he said, running a sponge up my arm.

'What?' He always did this, started a conversation in the middle, as if I knew exactly where his head was, when actually that was a huge guessing game.

'On the news,' he said. 'Real news isn't a good story. Like war's not exciting or . . .' he shakes his fist 'fucking triumphant! Or brave. It's just dull. Brutal.'

I looked at him. I knew what he meant, but I didn't really feel that way then, so I said nothing, changed the subject. I love the news, actually, and I've started buying one of those real broadsheets, like older people do, and instead of just read-ing bits of stuff on my phone and what people post, I read my way through it, grappling with how to turn the awkward pages, getting to grips with the complicated stories. You'd think, majoring in journalism, that he'd be the one doing that. But he was studying journalism exactly because he couldn't fucking bear it, couldn't bear the way they told the stories so wrong. Ewan, like Dad, is full of contradictions. Maybe that's why I loved him so quickly, and so fucking much.

Since I'd been at college, and with Ewan, everything had been thrown up in the air, shaken up, or shaken out like an old, mothballed blanket. The edges of it all were endless. Reading on the course, and with Ewan, was knowing that the way I felt wasn't the only way to feel, was knowing that good and bad were all tied together in a way you'd not have thought. Now Bay's Mouth, with its old pier, its long high street, its chain stores out of town and its complicated, stupid road system was all part of a changing picture that might just, if I held on to the details of it, make some kind of electrifying sense.

He got up out of the bath, dried his hands, which weren't oily any more, and got a cigarette from the packet he'd left by the window. He lit one, and sat on the chair by the bath, smoking, watching me. Something about this bullshit with grants recently, making him grovel around to get funding for note-takers and extra recordings of lectures, had made Ewan darker, made him distant.

'Come back in,' I said. But he didn't hear. Despite the open windows, the steam had clogged up the air and muffled my voice, so he couldn't hear much of anything at all.

Ewan was miles away now, looking in my direction, but not really looking at me. Smoking and thinking and distant. He did this all the time. I hated it, and I felt sort of jealous of it. That he was there, and not with me. And it sapped him so badly. There was nothing left of him when he finished up thinking about it. And all the silence after it. He dreamed of it when he was asleep. He lived it when he was awake. It was something to do with me being here more. He'd not been sleeping before, been leaving the lights on all night, to stop him being so twitchy. Because I was there now, he couldn't, and all this shit was getting worse and worse. Sometimes it stopped him in his tracks right in the middle of the street. I didn't know what he was seeing or hearing, but I knew I had to get him moving again.

So I got out of the bath, and went to him. I took the cigarette from his hand and laid it on the side of the bath. I stood between his legs as he sat on the chair, so that my stomach was level with his face, and I tilted his chin up to me and bent down to kiss him on the lips until he went soft again and held me, pulling my bare body to the heat of his.

Now, sitting with my half-eaten jacket potato going cold on my plate and the sound of the other students seeping into my ears, laughing like hyenas, talking in loud, nervous voices and showing off to each other as they head out to town for their Friday night of two-for-one pints and drunk snogs, I look out of the window, over the plain car park, and the halls opposite emptying, the buildings faceless and dull, and I remember how he touched me then, in his quiet, gentle way. I remember how his bare body felt on mine.

It takes me a long time to realise I've been crying.

'Cheer up, love,' says one of the canteen ladies, who takes my plate away. 'Might never happen.'

In Magda's bank book, when I open it, there's nothing good. Nothing. Absolutely. Nothing.

I walk along the marina in a blur. The tannoy at the beach begs the tourists: 'Last call then folks, the final call of the day. We're leaving right away. Last call for the six-twenty, two pounds all seats ride.' Over and over. 'Last call of the day. Last call of the day.' It follows me, fading, all the way up Magda's hill and her drive, towards her solid house, which never changes.

'What're you doing here?' asks Annette when I walk into the kitchen. I stare at her. I hadn't considered that one of the others'd be in. 'Oh, bloody hell! Have they mixed up again?' shaking her head, hands on her wide hips. 'Could've done with more time with Henry, too. Had to rush off to get up here.' Her voice drops. 'She's being a bloody nightmare. Won't let me change her or anything. Won't eat. I've been at my wits' end with her. I managed to send Shannon away, to give Magda a chance to come round, so we didn't have to call it in yet.'

I nod. Magda doesn't realise it but Annette's saving her bacon.

'Why don't you just go to Henry?' I say to Annette. 'Leave her with me. I've not got classes today. I can stay for as long as it takes.'

She looks at me doubtfully. I'm not wearing my work pinny, and don't really look the part.

'One of them was sick on my uniform,' I say. 'Don't ask.' I roll my eyes.

Annette laughs. 'One of those days!' she says. And grabs her bag from the back of the chair. 'You sure?'

'Yup,' I say, brightly. 'One of those days.'

When I go through to the living room, Magda's sitting under the clock again, slumped in her chair. Tiny and white and fuzzy as hell.

'Hi, Magda.'

She looks up at me and I think I catch a kind of triumph in her eyes. The kind of high-up look Mum used to have when we played cards and she had a good hand. She looks away quickly.

'Oh good,' she says, through heavy breaths. 'Don't leave me . . .' breathing 'with that nitwit again,' although they all like Annette, even Magda. 'Now,' she says, 'make me an egg.' She stops for more breath. 'I want it fried, both sides.' A breath. 'In lard.' Another breath. 'None of that . . .' a deep breath 'wretched vegetable oil.' Several breaths. 'And plenty of salt and pepper.' She runs out of air, slumps back again.

'Righto,' I say.

'Actually, I'll have it poached.'

'OK,' I say flatly. 'Coffee?'

'Tea,' she says, contrary as always. 'Assam...' breathing 'loose leaf. And have a cup yourself' breathing 'and an egg come to that.' A couple of big breaths, looking me up and down. 'You look a fright.'

'Thanks,' I say.

'Good lord, girl,' she says. 'What do you want? Compliments?'

'No,' I say, which is true. I stand there for a few seconds.

'Go and cook my egg,' she says, smoothing down her skirt.

It takes three tries before I get her egg just perfect, so I do help myself to one of the practice eggs, and a cup of Assam tea. Mum always had loose leaf too. *None of that baggy rubbish,* she'd say, flicking her hand and wrinkling her nose.

Eating the egg makes me feel better. More whole again.

'You'd have liked my mum, Magda,' I say, sitting down opposite her, sipping from my cup. Then I feel stupid. Magda'll say I'm being ridiculous. She doesn't like anyone. And because it's Mum it'll hurt.

She looks at me, about to say something, but she doesn't.

'The egg looks good,' she says after a while. And then, suspiciously, 'Did you use vinegar?'

'No. No,' I say.

'Good.'

'Just salt in the water.'

'That's the way,' she says. 'Lots of salt.'

I cut it all up for her, but she insists on trying to eat it herself with a fork, so I sit back and do the same. She tries to hold the teacup's tiny handle, and can't, so I hold it for her while she takes a few prim sips. Finally she waves me away.

'Enough,' she says, although she still has half her toast and egg left. She sits back, eyeing me with those small grey eyes. 'Now then. What was it you wanted?'

'Nothing,' I say.

'It's the baby,' she says. 'Whether to get rid of it.'

I say nothing.

'Can't help you there,' she says, shaking her head. She goes quiet for a while. 'But I can tell you one thing,' she continues eventually, her hand on my arm, her grip surprisingly firm. She pauses, holding my eyes. 'You're going to be all right . . .' a deep breath 'either way.'

There's a silence. I'm not sure if I've been told off or complimented.

'Perspective,' she says. 'That's what you need. Perspective.'

'Like you, you mean?' It's out of my mouth before I can stop it.

She looks at me fiercely. 'Watch your tongue,' she says.

'Sorry.'

'Don't apologise either.'

'S—'

'Dignity,' she says. 'Dignity.' It's funny, her sitting there in the chair, about to have the last few mouthfuls of toast and egg spoon-fed to her, and saying that.

'I don't want to have a baby,' I say.

She nods again.

There's a silence.

'Not on my own,' I say.

She sighs. 'Loneliness,' she says, 'isn't all it's cracked up to be.'

There's a silence. I feel the pressure of her memories suddenly. The feeling that there are perhaps other people, standing at the corners of the room, like me ready to jump to, whenever she needs them. Perhaps Mum is here too, with me.

How the hell did you manage it? Annette asks when I text her to say Magda got off to bed for her morning rest all right. I reply saying, *Don't know.* But I think I do. I think I'm getting Magda, more and more, the way she keeps that house, like armour, the way she grabs at any power that comes her way, her funny kindness and the fact that underneath it all, she's grieving too.

Chapter Twenty-Two

Only the care of the home remains believable, still open for a certain time to legends, still full of shadows.

'Walking in the City', *The Practice of Everyday Life*,
Michel de Certeau

Everything is mottled by memories. While Susheela sits, opposite me, asking concrete questions with her quick, modern voice, and more liminal questions with her demerara eyes, the room dissipates around me, its fragments interspersed by fragments of another room, another time, in which Mother is busying herself polishing brass ornaments.

This house, she's saying, *is a complete shambles. Coming to bits, all of it.*

I ignore Mother and focus on the girl. But part of me knows she's right, Mother.

When Susheela leaves, Mother's gone too, though I can still feel her, rooting about the house, and at times I think I hear the sound of her commanding voice coming from the east wing, or from my own ribcage.

'Mother!' I call into the house. 'Mother!' But she doesn't

answer, sunk into the gaps between the floorboards in the basement, or slipped behind that loose skirting board I've been wanting them to fix for years, the servants.

'We don't do odd jobs like that,' said that awful woman they call 'the office'. 'Personal care only, Magda,' she said. 'And your washing-up. You'll need to get someone else in to do the rest.'

I ordered in a cleaner of sorts. She comes once a week. *Mrs M*, she calls me. Asks me how I am and storms out of the room with her blasted hoover before I have a chance to answer. Doesn't do a proper job. I used to keep these windows vinegar-clean. You could have eaten a banquet off my parquet.

No longer.

After Susheela leaves I spend hours distracted by a ball of dust that's snowballing in the corner of the bedroom. There's a cobweb in the right-hand corner above the window in the living room which has such longevity I almost feel affection for it. But oh so irritating to look at it and be unable to order anyone to do anything.

Looking at it, that galactic ball of dust, things seem to fade and then refocus, fade and refocus and I think, for the first time in a long while, properly, about Michael.

I rarely remember the early days. It is a cluster of things, which I tend to leave in their tangle, and not separate out into moments and particular things. There were, I know, long meals out and longer walks where we talked, mainly, of chemistry. There was a sense of people looking at us and seeing a happiness we didn't perhaps fully feel. There was the feeling I had for him, my tall, clever husband, a kind of heady, competitive love. He was a professor. Not as good as me at the work, but more successful, moving swiftly through the carefully delineated ranks at the university.

In those days I do believe he loved me. I can almost believe it fully. And he was more dutiful than most husbands. I could never quite allow myself to fully trust it, but there it was. We became engaged after a suitable period.

Within the tangle, unlikely things. A film out. A dance. Days by the sea. Kisses and touch that I can no longer feel the traces of. The way we made love, though, was rudimentary, perhaps slightly functional, but still it was as close to affection as I could bear, and suited me very well.

From the memories, galactic and barrelling, that are those early days, what emanates is a kinetic feeling, of momentum, our momentum together, and how, when I was with him, things progressed and fell into their allocated place. Our lives slowly blended as he lent his name to the papers I published, so that they would be quickly peer-reviewed, placed. We had our wedding reception at the university, and lived together at number three Victoria Drive, where that difficult thing failed to happen. A child. We finally became stuck.

The anger over it built slowly. He couldn't see what he was doing, messing up my house. Messing me up. The house became such a problem between us that, usually lacking in humour, he tried to make light of it.

'Oh Memsahib,' he said, poking me in the ribs after he walked dark footprints across my newly polished floor, 'will you ever forgive me?'

'Not sure,' I said. 'That'll take some scrubbing.'

I was expected to keep up with the work of a whole band of servants, or let standards drop. I could feel it, gathering at the walls of the house, pressing in towards us. Dirt, pollution, airlessness. You had to have standards against it. Our house in Kharagpur haunted me persistently even then, its million-times-polished floor, its bright cutlery, the way everything we ate was carefully weighed and measured by Anwar under Mother's beady eyes. It was only that level of meticulousness that could make me feel held. Pursuing it gave me a sense of momentum at Bay's Mouth. Though I never attained absolute control.

I come to, in my house, in my chair, and think that. I didn't manage it. Even now I haven't managed it. My house rebels against me. I can feel the chaos groaning beneath the floor-boards. The paint peels and makes patterns, which can be read. *Joy*, say the peeled bits in the paint, *hilarity*, they say, *do you remember?*

Things with Michael were bad before he left.

'You're making us into some kind of model,' he said one day, his voice tight and fierce, after I'd gone spare at him for leaving his shirt out. Not tucked in. 'It's not real, Magda. It's not bloody real.'

I remember the way he said it. Accusing. Bitter. I wasn't what he'd hoped. I couldn't be what he'd hoped.

The laboratory felt like a haven by that point – the perfect, assessable struggle of the months of long lab-work, that white-coated measuredness, late nights of painstaking testing and balancing, the slowly turning reactions of elements spliced together in a cooled environment of sulphur dioxide at -112°F. I took comfort in precision, the delicate aim of pipettes, the containedness of carefully corked bottles and test tubes, and the long days of hiding as I tried to prove a hypothesis. In the lab, the aim was always to click things slowly into place, like that puzzle the boy brought, cogs turning all to face one direction, all pleasing and logical as the results came in, and at the writing-up, to have language lined up obediently, without ambivalence or metaphor. I was perfectly suited to that kind of tirelessness and discipline. I fitted myself to it and it made me a regular shape. Distant. I can barely remember anything about Home during that period, except a faint anxiety, a sense of Michael as a receding satellite. The only reactive element left. He was to be contained and kept cooled behind glass.

My last few memories of him, before he left, are still unsolved in my head.

He was leaning against the kitchen counter, looking at me, perhaps searching for me. I try to look back at him, in memory, to see the shape of his scruffy jacket, his hair, which, from the years and years of trying and trying for a child, had greyed. I try to sense what it was to stand with him, here in our house. But there are only wisps of him, a few stray cells, a trace element left on the door handles, a sense of footprints in the hallway, and the shadows of his breathing. Michael is an old dream, a poorly recorded experiment, and I can't recover him from memory.

'Life can't be lived from a bloody manual, Magda,' he said, and walked out of the kitchen. Or I think that's what he said. It was under his breath. It was outside my exclusion zone. But it must have been that, because those words, though faded and almost illegible, never seem to balance away, and my mind returns to them, their unsolvable thereness.

That day we found an anomaly in the research; some leak, some trouble had crept into my lab-work, seeping perhaps through my protective clothing, out of my body and into the solutions we had painstakingly mixed. All the results were spoiled.

He died of a sudden heart attack last spring. They sent a card to tell me.

I come back to myself: my perfect English house as it rots around me. I sit held by the bed in a room filled with un-savoury dust. I'll soon be dust myself.

I think very hard of how I have ten rooms in all, and all have a plan made out for them.

They are to be swept and aired daily.

A cloth is to be wiped around the skirtings weekly.

Any patches of wear on the wooden floors must be rubbed with a preparation I found in my mother's old books.

The silver is to be moved from room to room according to the season (the dining room is too damp in the winter, the front bedroom too bright in summer, and the study a waste of silver, for what is silver for, except to be seen?).

The silver is to be shined monthly.

The books are to be rotated twice a year to ensure that no one volume is left all year in the light.

At this juncture each book is to be taken out and checked.

If any spines sink they are to be repaired and made to stand upright, held together like a real lady in a corset.

And the papers. The papers are kept. The letters and photographs, classified assiduously, and shut up.

To guard against all that silence, I have kept my mother's piano, which she'd had carted all the way back on the ship, and not disassembled like everything else. It did remain in tune for years thanks to Frank Matthews, a blind man with an ear for it. He passed away of some growth in his stomach so many years ago I've lost count. And since then the piano has sat, untuned and dusty, just a few yards away from me now, silent.

There was a woodworm crisis the autumn before Michael left. It had to be dealt with immediately. I could tell you, step by step, the manner in which it was got rid of, tell you the exact quantity of beeswax required in the preparation I used, but I couldn't be sure what it was that made Michael say to me that I was 'bloodless, cold, and not like a real wife'.

Chapter Twenty-Three

The rod of iron with which he rules her never appears in company — it is a private rod, and is always kept upstairs.

The Woman in White,
Wilkie Collins

Benedict insists that I go with him to the gala although I can't face the pomp of it, or their insincere questions, for all the society women will ask me endlessly about my baby, as if I were a real mother. They will ask me, 'Does she feed well? Does she have colic? Do you have to bounce her? Does she keep you up in the night?' although they know perfectly well that just as they themselves never had to deal with these things directly, neither do I. Our children are all to be brought up by proxy. I try to get out of it by telling him that I have no dress to wear as my figure is still so altered by the pregnancy, but he simply says that I am being ridiculous as I have any number of dresses that can be adjusted within the hour by the deft Indian seamstress I always use. Which, of course, is plainly true.

We go in by car. It's strange to pass through the streets again after my confinement. I am beginning not to notice the

Indians at all, and to take note only of fine Englishwomen. I catch myself wondering, as we pass a young girl with very pale skin, whether the hem and beading she wears is the latest fashion at Home. Although I have never been given to caring about fashions at all, catching that tracing of Home suddenly feels so compelling.

It's hot in the car. A pressurised heat. Especially as it is only Benedict and I together in the back. Especially as my baby is left at home in Aashi's care, and so I am desperate to be back to supervise. Without me, will the girl keep to our four-hourly schedule? More than once, when I have fallen asleep mid-feed, I have woken much later to find Aashi still feeding, long past the time limit I set. She claims the baby has not fed properly and needs more time, but although I know it may be true, I find myself ruling with an iron rod, and making her set my girl down hungry. I can't believe I do this, but I do. I'm failing, even at a distance, as a mother I'm failing. The baby cries forever.

We see Mr Burrows, who, like Benedict, has been posted to Kharagpur to work on the Kharagpur-Nagpur line, and Benedict has the driver, whose name I have decided not to learn, stop. I have decided not to make an effort with names or communication any more. It's too painful when all this wretched status makes us as distant as if we were two separate species, and makes me lonelier in the company of servants than I should be alone.

'Benedict!' says Mr Burrows. 'A sight for sore eyes you are. I hear there's good news?'

Benedict smiles. He is more pleased about the baby than you would think. Magda is a demonstration of his virility,

even if she is a girl. Why does a child confer such power on
him, and not on me?

'Eight pounds three,' he says. And he pats my leg, apprecia-
tively, with mock affection.

I don't smile. Mr Burrows only looks at me briefly. He
will see a pale, swelled creature. An empty, distended body.
Redundancy.

'Will you be back to the office next week?' asks Burrows,
bending to the open window of the car.

'I'm back already,' says Benedict. And, at Burrows' look of
surprise, 'There've been problems.' This is the first I've heard
of it. I glance swiftly at my husband. He's frowning and leaning towards the window. 'The new embankment,' he says.
'The farmers are upset. It's affected the harvest, they say. The
floodplain doesn't fill because of it. They claim the water table
is all out of whack.'

'Blast!' says Burrows. 'A pain. A pain.'

Benedict grunts. 'We've had to put down a few Indians
we'd promoted, to stop them stirring up a fuss.'

Burrows nods. 'It never really works giving them rank
anyway,' he says, shaking his head as if at ruined milk. 'They
have their own priorities, and lose sight of the long game.'

The long game, of course, is the Empire. I don't ask
Benedict why they built such a railway embankment in the
first place without considering water – which is, here in
this dry-mouthed region, like gold. I don't ask how bad the
harvests were, or whether anyone went without food. These
things used to worry me. They worried me because I believed
them uncommon. Now they're like summer and winter and
just a part of life.

When Benedict shuts the window, he turns to me angrily.

'You might at least smile when the baby's mentioned,' he says.

I nod. But he sits in stony silence for the rest of the journey. We sit hating each other all the way up the main boulevard, under the struggling trees.

We stop at the grand house of the Lennetts, and I'm helped out of the car by our driver, who is faultless in his attentions, unlike my husband. When I see Mrs Lennett, I know why Benedict was so anxious to come to her gala. She is as pretty a little thing as I have ever seen, and swoons all over my husband, ignoring me as young women are liable to ignore women whose bodies have been marked by use. It's only months since I was one of them, but the pregnancy and heat made me swell so, and I have a pallor that makes me seem drawn, and older than I would have thought possible.

She and Benedict go inside quickly, to where I can hear the peals of laughter and the ringing tones of the women of high rank and class. Oh how they grate on me, although I'm now an understudy, learning their ways. In the foyer is Burrows again. He takes my arm and leads me up the wide staircase, introducing me to people as we go. I am being led through a gallery of wasps.

I'm presented to around twenty new faces, who look at me uninterested until they're told whose wife I am, at which point they turn on their Sunday charm. We are at the top of the staircase when I meet William. His name makes me think of one of the children I taught. Affection. At first I don't look at him, and then when I do I wonder whether to give my hand, because this William is brown. Indian brown. Coffee and milk.

I hesitate, and then extend my hand. And he takes it, and says, 'Delighted to make your acquaintance,' impeccably.

He's a strange creature. I find myself turning back to look at him, and our eyes meet. And it's the strangest thing for him to be standing here amid all this pomp. I am reminded vividly of my own out-of-placeness, on that ship, among the unabashed snobbery of the upper decks, how I wanted to be down below and away from the society ladies, their censure and spite. I wonder if he feels that, this William. Does he want to be away from us all, and on the streets between his own kind? He will never really belong here, no matter how fault-less his 'how do you do?'s.

'They're gaining on us these days,' says Burrows, seeing my look. 'We're training them into better positions, and so the occasional high-flyer is let in, even here. That one's real name is something Bengali, but he's taken on William lately,' he chuckles.

'He must be a great talent.'

'Oh yes – as an engineer, there's none better.'

'An engineer!' I'm astounded. 'But how does he manage?'

'With a firm hand they make perfectly good students,' says Burrows with a smile.

I think of Benedict's complicated calculations and how they sit on those sheets of white white paper, the numbers marked around his meticulous drawings, which I still find beautiful and mysterious despite how I feel about the man who drafts them. Could an Indian? But then I think of how my cooks follow a recipe these days, so adroitly and to the letter, with not an ounce misplaced, how they've learned to preserve and make custard the English way and set out a table, in just the few months I've been in India. And I think of myself, of how wasted my mind is between the gossip and frippery of womanliness in India. Perhaps the Raj is pointless. Or perhaps I'm just ill.

'I feel unwell,' I say, and find myself leaning on Burrows' arm. Sickness.

Benedict's unhappy that we have to go home early. He'd been having a lovely time with Mrs Lennett and her glamorous friends.

When we arrive home he, for once, comes up to the nursery with me. Aashi is nursing, sitting with our child at her bare breast. She doesn't have anything close by to cover herself with properly when Benedict walks in. I give her a shawl.

'How is she?'

'Sleeping,' says the girl, draping the wrap over her. 'It was difficult to wake her for milk.' Aashi speaks good English. Her husband and she use it at home, she says. These up-and-comings make such an effort.

Although she smiles, I can feel the reproach. She doesn't like the rota, which means forcing the child to wake for food, and then forcing her to stop feeding. Even the Indians think I'm a poor mother.

'She looks strong,' says Benedict, smiling. 'She looks well.' And then he actually leans forward and pulls back the wrap slightly to stroke my baby's cheek as she lies at Aashi's breast. He says her name: 'Magda.'

And I know then, I know that whatever his faults, he will love Magda. He will love my daughter.

It's a few more days before we hear of the riots at Bombay.

When Magda is about to turn two, Benedict decides to contract a nanny. We need one, because Magda progresses at an unfathomable rate. She is so bright the servants don't know what to do with her. She learns to speak late, but in full sentences. She seems to watch and copy in a way that makes the ladies of the club uneasy. She has the makings of a career woman already.

Benedict seems rather proud of this. It will reflect well on him in these days when women can progress a little, to have a successful daughter, although he'd never countenance the idea of me working, of course. Still, 'She will be a clever child,' he says. 'We must bring her on,' he says. 'We must have her well educated.'

If Benedict were of lower rank, then I should simply avail myself of the help of one of the other women's girls. But Benedict says it is not done to allow servants of lower-ranked men and women into our home. It's like on the ship. I'm stuck within the snobbish confines of my class.

It all happens more quickly than I had anticipated.

Mrs Greenson takes it upon herself, at interview, to explain how she would first give the house a thorough spring clean according to the specifications of *The Complete*, and keeps repeating the fact that 'It will be a Home from Home. A Home from Home,' but saying it in the most stern way imaginable, so that I can't imagine any place being Home so long as she is within striking distance of it.

She had children herself, she says, though they were brought up by a sister in England, and it seems she has little to do with them.

'It is better,' she says crisply, 'to let them be sent home, because the climate, the language, the morals of India are so very inclement,' shaking her head and wrinkling her nose as if perusing cow dung.

When she said this, ice grew in my gut.

'I don't warm to her,' I tell Benedict.

'She seems a very sensible kind of a woman,' he says, in that closed way he has.

'I don't like her views on child-rearing.'

'Which parts?' He raises an eyebrow, looks at me as a teacher might, giving a test.

'Every part. But especially how she believes we should send her home.'

Benedict sighs. 'Burrows said this would be a source of strife. Women do get all silly around the issue. It's an inevitability, Evie. This place does them no good. Disease, bad manners, bad blood . . .' Benedict himself was sent home as a child of course, to be disinfected of India in a boarding school on the south coast, where I expect he learnt something of cruelty and spite. 'India's no place for a child to learn to be a young girl, or for a young girl to learn to be a lady,' he says now, with absolute conviction.

I say nothing, but simply leave the room.

I won't have it. Would he have me be like Anna McPherson, whose son George had been away at boarding school so long she had trouble recalling his age? She had none of the trappings of motherhood, nor any of its softenings. I couldn't bear to ask her about him. Three times she trotted out the same old anecdote, of how he loves to ride little ponies.

I am shocked to hear from Burrows' wife, Clarice, that Benedict has contracted Mrs Greenson after all. She tells me as we are taking one of our slow walks along Kharagpur Avenue, past the club and up towards the maidan. Clarice and I are acquaintances, since she finally came down from the hills, after her husband, but we will never be friends. She's an Indian veteran, has been out here for so long there are no cracks in the armour. She makes little attempt at a life with her husband, and as I understand it spends her time between bridge clubs, other people's weddings, galas and the Railway Institute. She has become entirely engineered by standards, class, and some idea of dignity which means simply coldness and pride. Talking to her is like speaking to a manual. About Mrs Greenson's appointment she says:

'You should know that I advised him to do so, as she is a sensible and conforming type,' while swatting away some flies and correcting the fall of her blouse, as if what she is saying is of very little importance.

I can't reply for anger, with her, with him. I keep walking, silently. I save my arguments and rage for my husband.

'I can't believe you'd go against my wishes so callously.'

'Evie, you raised no sensible objection.'

'No sensible objection? I disliked her completely, and made that perfectly clear!'

I can feel the anger, like spice on my tongue.

Benedict looks at me, puts his work to the side for once. He holds his arms out to me, sitting there with an appealing, friendly look.

'Come here, Evie,' he says.

I do so, because although I'm furious, it's been so long since he's called me to him like this.

He holds around me. It feels strange. Like returning to a town I once knew, only to find it altered. I try to graft the B I once knew onto this face, which now seems so hard-lined and rigid.

'We need her,' he says. 'She was the only woman of standing ready to do the job.'

'She'd have me abandon this child in no time.'

'We'll not let her. Or at least not for a few years.'

I step back. I've a sense that this is the time to make a bargain. I haven't many chips to put on the table, but I try.

'How old?'

'What do you mean?'

'How old can Magda be before she's sent Home?'

Benedict hesitates. 'It varies. It depends on her health, comportment, a myriad of factors.'

'How old if she's healthy?'

'Five, six, perhaps seven.'

'Seven,' I say it firmly. 'Give us seven years with this baby, and Mrs Greenson can come.'

On the day that Mrs Greenson arrives we also hear about the killing of Judge Beynon. It was brutal, so they say, and there is fear of more riots in celebration. Judge Beynon is a friend of Benedict's and he seems angry, more than upset, about it.

'Savages,' he says, looking up at Anwar from behind *The Times*.

'Why did they kill him?'

'Oh they hate the judges,' says Benedict.

'Why?'

Benedict stubs out his cigarette. 'They have some jumped-up idea that the system is prejudiced against them.'

I look at him blankly. There are moments when I think we are all fools.

I have Benedict's paper after him. Judge Beynon, it seems, presided over the trial where one of their so-called freedom fighters was put to death. The words 'freedom fighters' and 'put to death' – the whole debacle, in fact – seems surreal, here where our roses and dahlias are currently in full bloom.

I write of it to Helen, though I have never had a reply to a single letter. As I write I try to imagine her soft body as it works at the mill, bending, flexing capably. I long to see the callouses on her hands and to hear the timbre of her voice. But she is fading; the small details are blurred now. I can't remember whether that mole of hers was on the left or right wrist. Even Helen is not indelible. I try to write of the troubles here in a way that will thrill her into replying, so that she might come back into focus.

It's only when we hear of the shootings in the jail at Hilji, right here in Kharagpur, that I begin to worry that the whole Indian undertaking might come crashing down around our ears like a flattened bungalow. The inmates shot by our guards in the prison were celebrating Beynon's white blood, and so now Benedict and Burrows celebrate their spilled black blood with several brandies and bad jokes. In *The Times* it says that there is an Indian writer who causes trouble over the affair; some of their 'politicians' want to come to collect the bodies themselves. I wonder what my servants think of it all. I wonder whether the thought of letting our white blood excites them. It rather does me.

Mrs Greenson is not long here before she gets her way in most things. She convinces Benedict absolutely, within a matter of hours as far as I can tell, that the lion's share of my child's time should be spent with her, rather than with me.

'Evelyn should occupy herself like a lady,' she says, with heavy emphasis on the 'like'. 'She has plenty of embroidery, sketching, socialising to do. Her child's education should be left to a professional.'

'But it isn't all education,' I say to Benedict. 'It's showing her love.'

I'm not sure he knows what I mean. The way he responds to Mrs Greenson with such approval makes me suspect that his own mother, who died when he was a very young man, was cut from the same, rigid cloth. His father was already an old man when Benedict was born, and a colonel. Benedict himself had nannies. Three in total. When I asked what they were like, he spoke of them with varying degrees of approval, but little affection, as if affection were an irrelevance – and perhaps it is.

Magda's growing so big. I look at her often, and think, *where did it go?* Her babyhood. *Where did it go?* I feel it's passed me by. I've missed so much of it, although she's the sole reason that my time has not been wasted. Despite what I often feel, on the long, sweaty nights, when the sound of mosquitoes keeps me awake, my time has not been wasted.

'Oh Evelyn, you're so soft,' was all he had to say. 'You're soft, and it'll make your child as useless as you are yourself.'

I've learned to expect the words, but I didn't expect what happened in the library. I was getting over my second lost pregnancy since Magda. I'd stopped bleeding, but my breasts were still sore, and my body heavy. I was looking through the window, pretending to be taking a note down of the various jobs and alterations that needed to be done, a pen in my hand just hovering above the blank paper, with nothing to say. I'd been at it for a week, trying to find ways of putting our house back in order. Order, that was it. That was what was required.

It all seemed to sag around me. The decor and furniture looked tired and rough and imperfect and Indian. Looking at the garden, I couldn't fathom a single way to make it seem more real. More lifelike and English.

Then, suddenly, Benedict's hands were around my waist. It was so quick. His mouth at my throat. His teeth at my ear. His hands now reaching around my breasts.

I tried to say it. No. But I couldn't breathe. I tried to push him away. But he just gripped at me. Pushed me down against the table.

Afterwards, when I stood up, my dress was covered in blue ink, and the paper where I'd written the order of things was nowhere to be found.

Chapter Twenty-Four

Self is the wall which keeps the creatures from breaking in.
'The Doctrine of the Chhāndôgyas (Chhāndôgya-Upanishad)',
The Ten Principal Upanishads,
Translated by Shree Purohit Swāmi and W. B. Yeats

Because this is abortion, I expect there to be placards, protests. I expect there to be crazy bible-bashers screaming blue
murder. I expect this to be something. But this isn't America,
and isn't the films, the place is a clinic in a hospital department
that's just like any other one.

I pass nurses, porters, doctors, cleaners. I follow the signs
that say 'Gynaecology'. A poster on the corridor wall an-
nounces that herpes is on the increase again. Another talks
about diabetes. I check in at the desk that says 'Drop-in'.

'I don't have an appointment,' I say.

'That's fine, love,' says the nurse on reception. 'Just take a
seat.' She motions towards a half-empty waiting area.

I take a seat on my own on a row of four blue plastic chairs
that are clumped together on a metal frame. A couple sit
opposite. She's in work clothes, a smart suit, and has a name

badge; her ankles are neatly crossed underneath her seat. She looks at her partner next to her, and they try to smile at each other. He's in a suit too. He has kind eyes, and holds her hand, strokes her thumb with his own wide thumb. Perhaps they have kids already, and this was one too many, or perhaps there's something wrong with the one she has in her belly? Sometimes things like that happen, don't they? Another younger woman, maybe only my age, sits nearby too. She plays with her phone. When she looks up, her eyes are like a mirror, and I have to look away. At least the nausea's gone, these past two days.

There are a few magazines. *Homes & Gardens. Reader's Digest.* I could do with something else. Politics, or travel, something to remind me of how fucking big the world is.

They call the girl and she walks to the double doors where a nurse is standing, waiting to lead her off down the corridor.

'Hello, love,' says the nurse to her. 'Come through. Don't worry, we're not here to scare you,' she laughs. The girl hesitates, but the nurse gently presses a hand to her shoulder, and they turn into a doorway and disappear.

Like the girl had, I take my phone out. Four messages. Ewan. I switch it off without reading them, but the first words of the last message had flashed up on my phone. *Please please call me.*

'Susheela Gupta.'

I get up, walk towards the nurse.

'Don't worry,' she says. 'We're not here to scare you.' I hear myself laughing brittlely.

She points to a chair in the corridor, and reaches out to me with a clipboard, a form on it. 'Fill this in. Dr Stevens is just with another patient, he'll call you in when he's done.' She leaves me on a chair outside his office.

I sit and stare at more health posters. Keep Our Patients Healthy. WASH YOUR HANDS. I start blindly ticking the boxes on the form. They prove I'm still healthy. I'd score top marks, if there were marks. I leave the space where it says 'Reason for visit' until last. And then I write in it. *Abortion.*

After a few minutes, the doctor pops his balding head around the doorway.

'Come in,' he says, with a smile.

I walk into his pale green room. Just an examination couch, a desk, computer, a couple of those yellow hospital bins, and a chair for each of us. He takes the form on the clipboard. I sit down. Two minutes or so pass while he checks through it.

'How many weeks are you?'

'I don't know.'

'When did you have your last period?'

'I don't know.'

'OK,' he says, frowning slightly. 'Roughly, then.'

'Maybe two months, maybe three,' I say.

He nods. 'We'll need to do some tests,' he says in a flat, calm tone, 'just to work out where exactly you're at.'

'OK,' I say.

'Tell you what,' he says, looking at me carefully and smiling a bit, 'a couple of people have cancelled appointments today, so there's some space in the schedule for tests. I can send you for those now, and then we can talk through your options. Does that sound OK?'

'Yes,' I say.

'So,' he says, standing up and walking to the door, 'you just go and wait out there, and a nurse will call you in for an ultrasound.'

'Ultrasound?'

'Yes. We just need to take a look at the foetus and see about what stage you're at.'

Foetus. I hate the word suddenly. Foetus. 'OK,' I say numbly, and leave the room again.

They take a while to call me for the scan, but there are no thoughts in that time. Only that word. Foetus. Foetus. Foetus.

I have to walk with a nurse all along the corridors to the ultrasound unit.

'Sit down here,' she says, 'and we'll call you when it's your turn.'

Another waiting room. I'd forgotten this about outpatient treatments with Mum, how you bounce between one plastic chair and another for hours. One of the things no one tells you about terminal illness is the huge amount of precious time you waste, waiting.

This time the waiting area's full of couples. Some almost middle-aged, some young like me. Most of these look happy. Happy to be pregnant. Why are we sent to the same place? I sit, staring at my phone, my only portal to something else.

A feeling in my belly. A sudden movement.

I must have jumped, because the lady opposite me, whose pregnancy is pretty far along judging by her bump, smiles at me and strokes her own belly fondly. I just stare at her. And then stare down at my phone again. And Ewan's messages. I go on Facebook for the first time today. Pictures of Leah and

the others out last night. Blurred, too much flash. *Leathered.*
Pissed. Fucked. I put my phone down and stare straight ahead
until they finally call me.

'Just come in and lie on the couch here,' says an older-looking
nurse, motioning to a raised examination bed beside her, covered with a roll of blue hospital-issue paper. 'Have you got
anyone with you today?'

'No,' I say.

'That's fine,' she says. 'Plenty of girls come on their own.'
She sits down in front of a monitor. 'Now, I'll just tell you
what's going to happen,' she says. 'I'll need you to roll up your
top, and just open your trousers so they're low on your hips
and I can access the whole abdomen. I'll put a bit of gel on
your belly, which will feel a bit cold, and then I'll just press
this across the whole area.' She holds up a kind of torch. 'So
we can see what kind of shape the baby's in,' she smiles. 'OK?'

I nod.

I roll up my top, and open the top button of my trousers.

'That's fine,' she says. She rubs a bit of slimy gel on my belly,
and then pushes the torch around.

'OK.' she says, with a smile, turning the monitor towards
me. 'Here it is!'

'I don't want to see!'

Little thing, green on the screen, moving and moving like
a real human, or a small frog in water. I stare at you. I stare at
you.

'OK,' she says, turning the screen away from me. 'Seems
fine,' she says quickly. 'Has all the right bits. I'd say at least
fourteen weeks.'

I reach out and turn the monitor back towards me, stare at the screen.

I stand up suddenly, rolling down my top.

'Hang on!' she says, but I'm already out of the door, running along the corridor, through the double doors, towards the big turnstile entrance and out into the car park and life.

Book Two

Chapter Twenty-Five

She will be zealous in guarding her children from promiscuous intimacy with the native servants, whose propensity to worship at the shrine of the Baba-log is unhappily apt to demoralize the small gods and goddesses they serve.

The Englishwoman in India,

Maud Diver

Mummy hits me because of Daddy. Daddy's eyes are hot hot hot like chillies when they look at Aashi. But pretty Aashi is like yoghurt and cools right down, walking away from him and trying not to be in the same room, although he's the most important. Here Daddy is the most important of all and so I'm the most important child.

Mummy says I'm not to be mollycoddled. Mollycoddled means saying yes to the sweets when Anwar and Madan slip them under the table like a secret. On my tongue the sweets melt and pop, and are sometimes sour and spicy so I can pull my secret face and Anwar and Madan laugh like this. Huh. Trying not to make a noise.

Daddy's angry that they laugh because he's working. He's drawing the railway. Daddy's lines are all perfect and just right. He's clever like me. He uses the brass draughtsman's tools from his wooden box. They're pretty, his little tools, but they're sharp and too sly and so I'm not allowed to touch unless Daddy's hands are there too, showing me how to do it. One is a compass, which we use to draw a circle which is like the world with India on one side of it and Home on the other side.

Home is where there is no spicy food and no Indians and where Mummy says we are very happy. It's not so very far on my perfect circle from India to Home but Mummy says it takes weeks and she would be sick almost the whole way and so might I and so we won't go until the baby.

The doctor will come with his gloves and take the baby from Mummy's apple stomach and I shall have a little brother. Mummy says we don't know which we are having but Anwar says Daddy is a big strong man so it will be a boy. He tries to give Mummy lots of a sweet drink he makes with rice and almonds to make sure of it, but she bats him away like a fly and won't look at the drink. Why does Anwar want Mummy to have a boy? I'm a girl and I am just so.

Mummy is growing every day like a fruit that is being blown up and up by the sun, and while her stomach grows her eyes sink back and turn grey. Her hair is not often put up in the pretty way and Daddy doesn't notice her any more. Lucky that Aashi does my hair for me. Aashi's is always beautifully combed. Aashi combs my hair and sings a pretty song about the leaves and the trees and the sun in the morning. Sun is 'sūrya' and leaves are 'pātā'. Daddy and I both know this but Mummy does not, and if she knows I know then she will rap my knuckles. But how could I not know when I'm with

Aashi so much and she sings over and over the same songs? Singing them like the bluebirds in the morning in Mummy's book of British birds.

Every week we learn about different British birds. The great tit. The blackbird. The nightingale. The owl. I know them all. Here there are different birds which sing in the morning and the evening, and sometimes in the night, but I'm to learn the British birds for when I go Home. Mummy says we are like the white storks we see at the lagoon which live between many countries. We have come all the way from England to India to stay but our Home is not here. But I am here and so I'm singing like Aashi. Why not? Singing is good and it fills your arms and legs and head with the song. Why not turn and turn like this when I sing it, Aashi's song?

This time it's Anwar who stops me.

'Your mummy will rap your knuckles if she sees you doing that, little Magda,' he says, and he shakes a finger in the air like Mummy. When I stop and say 'I'm not little Magda any more,' he just laughs. 'Big girls sing too. Why not sing "Baa Baa Black Sheep", or another English song?'

All right. I'm singing and turning and turning until my thoughts and all the words spin up together. Sing a song of sixpence a pocket full of rye, four and twenty blackbirds baked in a pie.

When I fall and break Mummy's plant pots there is trouble anyway. While she shouts and cries at me I stand with the singing and singing in my head, watching the brown earth from the pots slip and slide onto Anwar's perfect floor. Anwar will not be angry. I will be mollycoddled with more sweets if I cry because of Mummy.

★

Mummy's angry. Mummy's angry because she has come a long way from Home on a ship to be here and have me and the new baby and be married to Daddy. She's angry with everything here because it's not hers and she cannot go Home. Except for Daddy we're all afraid of her – Anwar, Madan and me and all of the other servants – but most of all Aashi, because Mummy hates her. Perhaps it's because of Daddy's hot eyes. I think it may be. I think maybe Mummy is unhappy.

I ask several people. I ask Raja. Raja comes to the garden to play when Mummy and Daddy are away and I'm left with the servants. Aashi lets him. It's because she is his mother, Raja says. Raja likes my garden. He likes my little house in the garden. He says it is so big, he cannot believe it is only a playhouse.

'Gosh!' he says. 'Gosh, madam!' and I am proud. He teaches me a lot of Indian games, and I teach him English, although he's already very good because his mother works for us.

'My mother is a whore,' he says. I do not know what that means. Why don't I ask Raja? Because I think perhaps Raja is even more clever than me. This is the first time I have had a friend who is clever. All the children at the Sunday school, for example, are as dim as blown-out candles. I'm the best at everything, at reading and writing and even at the Bible and saying prayers.

Everyone tells me Raja is dirty. 'Raja is dirty and will make you sick,' Mummy says.

But Raja is still my friend. And Raja never touches me anyway. If my hand touches his hand by mistake, or if I brush against him, Raja jumps away. When he leaves I wash and wash my hands and my face so that I do not get sick. I do this every single time he comes and so far, so good.

I want to ask Raja what a whore is. But I don't. I ask him similar but different questions:

'Was Aashi always a whore?'

'No,' he says. 'She was respectable. And then she was a wet nurse.'

This time I do ask. 'What's that?'

'It's a woman who gives her breast to other women's babies. Her milk.'

'Whose babies?'

'That depends. Rich women. Englishwomen.' He grins. 'Your mother, perhaps.'

'Did I have a wet nurse?' I ask Mummy.

Mummy is a little shocked. She goes a little quiet.

Then, 'Yes,' she says, because she knows I am very clever, and will know if she lies. 'I did not have enough milk.' She looks at me, and she laughs because I am looking so surprised. It makes me feel strange inside to think of drinking milk from an Indian breast, even from Aashi who is marigolds and roses. And why did Mummy not have enough milk?

'Don't worry, Magda. Your wet nurse wasn't Indian,' she says, because sometimes like me Mummy can hear other people's thoughts.

I'm happy to hear this. I would not like to think I had Indian milk. Everyone says Indians are dirty and not as bright as I will be one day, and I should not think their milk would be so good for you.

★

'Do you think Mummy is unhappy?' I ask Raja one day when we're playing a slow crisses and crosses game on the dusty floor of my playhouse.

'No,' he says. He looks surprised. 'She is English. She has a big house and a rich husband.'

'Our house isn't that big,' I say. Because Elizabeth has a bigger house. Her father is a lord.

Raja looks at me. He shakes his head. 'Madam,' he says. 'You are stupid.'

'I am not!' I say. 'I am not stupid.'

'Madam,' he says, with a flick of his hand. 'You know nothing.'

'I do!' I say. 'I expect *you* don't know where England is on the globe.'

'What is a globe?' he says. And so I take him inside to show him. We are in the drawing room with Daddy's beautiful globe where all the countries are pictured and coloured so perfectly. I point it out to him.

'This is where I am from,' I tell him. 'England.'

He stares at the globe.

'This is India,' I say, pointing at it.

'It is much bigger,' he says proudly. And I have to nod. Because he is right.

'When did you come here?' he asks me.

'Where?'

'India.'

'I was born here.'

'When did you last go home?'

I hesitate. I do not want to tell him that I have never been. Luckily, Anwar comes in right at that moment, and oh how he shouts and shouts at Raja to leave the house.

'Indian boys are not allowed here,' he shouts. And then he tells him something strange. 'Don't you know that she is untouchable?' he says in Bengali, pointing at me. 'Don't you know that it will make you unclean to play with her?'

'Bye bye, madam,' says Raja, running out of the door. He grins at me on the way out.

She is making lace when I ask her. She is making lace and so has to keep track of all the threads and the wooden pegs and the pins and I can't even understand when I watch her doing it. It is like other things that are not for little girls. I sit and watch her and I don't touch the pegs or the lace in case she taps my fingers away.

'Mummy,' I ask, 'can we go Home?'

'We will,' she says. 'When it's time.'

'But Mummy, aren't you unhappy?'

She stops moving the pins and the pegs. She sits very very still. I don't know much but I do know that her answer is
Yes.

'Is it because of Daddy?' Mummy is very very still. She is trying to shake her head for no but her head will not say it.

'Is it because of Daddy and Aashi?'

Mummy gets up from her chair, and all the lace and the pegs fall from her knees and she hits me so hard across the face that the next thing I see is the floor and then her heels leaving. Her heels are leaving.

Mummy doesn't see my bruise and all its colours. Mummy doesn't stay to see what she has done. Mummy is gone for days. Every day Aashi and Anwar give me sweets. But it is

Raja, it is my friend Raja who tells me: she is in hospital. And then I listen to the servants talking. Aashi and Anwar say it.

Memsahib has lost the baby. She has lost the baby again.

Chapter Twenty-Six

What a wonderful opportunity this magical InterNet provides to get in touch with old friends, former neighbours and fellow members of that simple, happy life in which we all partook during the years of the 'RAJ' – and all at the speed of light – when one learns how to use it!

Kharagpur Diaspora website

You, me, and my mum, we're stacked one inside the other like matryoshka dolls. Or like the layers of an onion. You're the mysterious, tiny one inside me, and outside us both, my mum, the outmost layer, all familiar things and Fairy liquid. She walks in her slippered feet around me, as I pad around their house, Dad's house now, dusting, polishing, making everything just so, despite Dad not really speaking to me and sitting rigid at the kitchen table, waiting for me to leave. Or at least that's what I think he's doing.

I've dusted the hallway, the lounge, polished each ornament on the mantlepiece, cleaned the glass on their wedding photo where Mum stands in her red and gold sari, glimmering, and Dad shines like a different person. I've polished the frames on my school photos too, where I'm shy and eager to please as ever. I make my way up the stairs, checking for cobwebs. Occasionally I stop, place my hand on you, and listen with my palm. Nothing. You're all tidied away again, inside.

The house isn't as she would've liked it. Washing in piles, newspapers crowding the porch. I put everything back in its place. You back in my belly, Dad's newspapers on the newspaper rack, his socks paired and laid in the sock drawer like babies in a big crib. Slowly the house is put back in Mum's order.

At the hotel too, Mum had it all kept just so, making sure the girls hoovered deep, deep into every corner and wiped its skirtings until they were perfectly blank. She'd patrol the corridors, checking that every picture hung at the exact angle it should, inspecting the windows, making sure they'd been shined tirelessly with vinegar, that every bed was perfectly made. Her British Hotel was more a bastion of old glory than any other of the Bay's Mouth hotels, or the fair rides, the pier, the tearooms, the Victoria Day Parade, or the other British fictions the tourists promenaded through, snapped pictures of, and wanted and wanted and wanted. 'Tea' at the British Hotel meant cucumber sandwiches, plum pudding and loose leaves in a teapot with a strainer. Dinner was roast beef, or lamb with mint sauce; pudding was always warm and always with custard. The Union Jack flew high from the parapet. Everything was British-made, or at least made in the Commonwealth – even the radios in the bedrooms, which were now pretty much antique. Mum refused point-blank to update them.

'That's what people are after,' she said. 'And that's what they'll get.'

The British Hotel was the 'real deal', and so a perfectly executed lie. It was owned by an American chain.

Still, Mum was absolutely dedicated to it. She'd not even think about coming home until she was completely knackered, slipping her shoes off her swollen feet and falling asleep on the sofa.

For a long time, I found this whole obsession she had with Britishness pretty funny. Me and Leah used to laugh about it, specially at Mum's story of how Granny and Grandpa had stood up for the first few years whenever 'God Save the Queen' played on the radio. Granny and Grandpa'd come to Bay's Mouth thinking that the UK was everything the Raj in India had pretended to be. They were totally shocked when they met normal working people. Mum used to imitate them, saying in a strong Bengali accent, 'Uncouth! They are so uncouth!' But she felt their disappointment really. They were pretty unhappy when she married down. Compared to Mum, Dad was riff-raff. We've not seen much of her family, or his, over the years.

The whole thing at the hotel was so well done that the BNP tried to book their conference there. It was almost funny. And then I realised they were going to let them come.

'You can't have those racist bastards here!'

'They're paying customers, Su,' she said, looking worried for once. Mum was up for the whole cucumber sandwiches thing, but only in a hotel, not in politics.

The company that owned the hotel turned them down in the end. But another political party did come, who were pretty much as fucked up. When the conference was on, I sat in the office behind reception and listened to them all filing through the foyer, talking in loud, satisfied voices, laughing. They had this confidence: that they were the normal ones. All their publicity talked about 'The good people of this country', by which they meant themselves, not me, and specially not Mum.

Once they'd gone through the doors into the big function hall, and the sounds of their big, confident voices were muffled inside, I went through to the laundry room where all the sheets and towels are stacked in mini skyscrapers, each with their embroidered crown. From there you can look through the glass in the door into the hall. There was a guy on stage, giving a speech. His hands were making sharp shapes in the air; his body, in chinos and a summer shirt, was lit up bright against the purple PowerPoint behind him.

'People are really rather afraid that this country might be swamped by people with a different culture and, you know,' he said, 'the British character has done so much for democracy, for law and order, so much throughout the world, that if there is any fear that it might be swamped, people are going to react and be quite hostile to those coming in.'

Applause. It all sounded so fucking reasonable, like being beaten up in slow motion.

I went into the kitchen and spat into the perfect British gravy, stirred by Ravinda.

'What're you doing, Su?' he asked me.

'Adding flavour, Ra.'

'Very good,' he said, and started ladling it out onto the plates.

★

Now, when you go in from the seaside, into Bay's Mouth proper, there are anti-immigration slogans on the walls. They used to scrub any graffiti away within days, but now they don't bother, and I have to walk past a load of it every day, to college.

I always got pissed off about crap like this, in a way that Mum and Dad didn't. It was like they didn't really think they had a right to. It worried them, hurt them, but it didn't make them rage.

'You and your rights,' says Mum in my head. 'You and your sense of entitlement.' She was proud though. 'You stand your ground,' she said once, when I came home worked up about something someone had said. 'You've found your ground. Now keep standing.'

I can feel it slipping away slowly beneath my feet.

The reviews at the hotel nosedived as soon as Mum went off sick. I check them, sometimes, on TripAdvisor, like picking a scab. *Not what it used to be. Standards have dropped severely. Not the place it was.*

I heard a rumour they're thinking of selling it so someone can turn it into flats or student halls.

Everywhere changes. Sitting down in my old room at Mum and Dad's, taking a break from the cleaning, I search for Kharagpur, Magda's town, on the web. At first I find nothing, just the website of a technical college, businesses, pictures of a sprawling industrial town in India, regular and busy. Then, three pages down, there it is. *Kharagpur Reunited.* Magda herself would never use the internet and I can't quite believe that the Raj has made itself a place there either. But someone did. The web page is old, old. Hasn't been updated for years. On the first page, a plaintive note with an elderly, fuddy-duddy style: *Please can someone help me to sift material? There is far too much for me to manage with my failing health. And please will people not send present-day photographs. We want to remember Kharagpur as it was, in the days so dear to us.*

Not sprawling, industrial, real.

Photographs of pageants and Christmas fairs, tennis matches, poodles all made up. Looking through the website's like doing some kind of archaeology. There's a feeling that I'm the only person to visit in a long while. Like some dilapidated old house with only me left haunting it. The site's a relic, a record of somewhere more English than England, like Bay's Mouth. Shared photographs, shared anecdotes that pale and pale up there on the web. A copy of a copy of a copy. How fucking sad it all is. I turn it off. It's too close to the bone somehow. I get up with my rag to keep dusting.

Once all the house is spic and span, I go through to the kitchen, to Mum's shrine in the larder. At suppertime the goddesses had to have their meal before she'd sit down to her own. The little troupe of figures. She spruced them up every day, kept them as perfectly Hindu as she kept her hotel perfectly British – and didn't see that as any kind of contradiction.

We keep them now. They make a semi-circle on her little table in the larder. Lakshmi, Kali, Durga, Saraswati and the others, every one of them painted brightly by hand, sewn by hand, kept sari'd, bangled and bindi'd, painted, polished, garlanded with tiny garlands, powdered with spices and dyes, little bowls of petals set around them. I set out Mum's puja tray, ring the tiny bell, light her diva lamp, spoon a tiny spoonful of sweet clean water from the small brass bowl over Saraswati's feet, and mark her forehead with kum-kum. Mum would always mark her own forehead too, but I turn back to Dad, sitting at the table.

He sits in his dressing gown almost motionless. He says nothing. Just looks at me wearily. His eyes have that dusky expression they had for so long after Mum.

I turn away from him and put the kettle on.

'I'm more than three months gone,' I say, with my back turned to him.

He says nothing.

I turn around. 'So I'm not getting rid of it.'

Dad nods. He looks up, and he exhales.

Chapter Twenty-Seven

Nowhere is the English genius of domesticity more notably evident than in the festival of afternoon tea.

The Private Papers of Henry Ryecroft,
George Gissing

I am no longer Evelyn Roberts. I'm fully Mrs Benedict Worsal Compton, and she's cold, she's hard, and has no interests bar making lace and pretty things, gossiping of dress cuts and watching the season turn and heat so that she may uproot her garden in its big, elaborate pots and take it to the hills.

When Magda asks me, on her sixth birthday, if she might have a flute to play, like an Indian boy she's seen, Mrs Benedict Worsal Compton says *no*.

Don't be silly, she says. *Don't be a silly child*, and she turns back to her work, knotting and knotting the lace until it's as perfect as the lace made by those black women on the Suez Canal when I first made the passage over, back when there was love, and when I dreamed.

There are no dreams now. My sleep is oddly blank, while around me India churns.

★

'Aashi's husband is coming this evening,' says Benedict, not looking up from his paper.

'Good heavens. Why?'

'Because he's moved up in rank, again. They keep having me promote him. He's a bright chap. Trustworthy. They need to show willing.'

'Willing?'

'Willing for Indians of all castes to rise up through the ranks, gain in prestige.' He stops, I think simply because he can't be bothered to explain further. 'It'll come to nothing, of course,' he says.

'Of course,' I chime, all a loyal wife.

Aashi, of course, is not invited. I am having to keep her apart from many things these days. My husband, who watches her overmuch, and Magda, who I daresay cares for her more than for her own mother. For Aashi is a desirable girl, smiling, kind, and quite pretty, in an Indian way. Magda has learned far too much Bengali from the girl, and produces its clipped syllables at any opportunity. It makes Benedict fume, and so we must rap her knuckles for it, which makes her cry.

I want Aashi to leave, but Benedict is resistant.

'She's useful to have about,' he says. And it is true. She mends clothes, and makes balms and perfumes better than any of the other servants. So I put up with her, at least for the moment. But there is no question of her coming to tea even if her husband does. It would be crossing a line.

So I don't go either. We are to leave the men to it and keep to our own quarters.

I do spy Aashi's husband through the window when he arrives. The young man lets himself through the gate, walks across the front lawn towards our front door, upright and intruding. And familiar.

William.

His incongruous name rings through my head. A small child with skin like china, holding up his copybook. William. And then this troubling, tall, brown man.

He's ringing the bell.

His young wife is upstairs. She suckled my child.

I close the curtains.

An hour or so later, when they must be on cigars and drinks (Benedict keeps an immensely expensive supply of Cuban cigars, which seem to still be plentiful, despite the way everything is beginning to be rationed because of some kind of trouble with supply lines across Europe), I hear Benedict's raised voice.

'Are you threatening me?' he's saying. 'By god, are you threatening me?'

I find myself tiptoeing down the corridor.

The quieter tones of the man: 'I was merely pointing out an aberration in the plan, sir. A possible unwanted consequence. One that might cost lives.' His English is so perfect.

'Don't you think this has been taken into account?' says Benedict. His voice is unusually high.

'Evidently not, sir.'

Silence. The clinking, cut-glass sound of the drinks cabinet. Benedict is pouring a whisky. It must be serious.

'You know,' he says quietly, after a long while, 'that

hydroelectric plant is, to me, essential. Aashi, meanwhile — well, she's entirely expendable.'

A silence.

'In fact you both are,' says Benedict, laughing. The sound of his clicking fingers. 'Like that,' he says, 'you could be got rid of.'

Silence. And then, quietly, the man's voice.

'Things are changing, sir,' he says.

Just then Anwar comes along, dusting the corridor. And I have to walk on, as if I'm merely chasing my tail around the house as usual.

He is right, of course. Things *are* changing. There are, increasingly, Indians living in houses like ours, wearing clothes like mine, taking important office and holding grand parties. They hold their own, but have not the habit that we do, of imitation. They are an imitation of an imitation, and so rather watered down. Still, they do fairly well these days, and, as usual, want more.

There have been several frightful protests. We hear of them, on the wireless, and presumably Benedict gets an army briefing, though he doesn't share its contents with me — ostensibly out of disdain for my conversation, though I think what he feels for me is perhaps more spiteful than disdain. But I have heard of occasional violence, and the wireless does tend to reel off improbable statistics of the number of hungry living around us in Bengal. Improbable, or so I think, until the rationing begins and until I notice a distinct pallor in Anwar's face.

Anwar, bearer and head servant, is more spirited and far smarter than I first thought, and frequently runs rings around me, turning me out of the house 'for spring cleaning' if he is offended in any way by my tellings-off. Once I swear he nicked into my bicycle tyres with one of his sharp knives when I docked his pay for poor thrift because he procured at market only half of what he normally might for the same price in rupees. Benedict, I think, appreciates Anwar mainly for his ability to flatter him, but I secretly admire him his ways of turning the tables on his masters with such unshakeable elegance and poise.

So it is a shock when, standing beside the fan, he faints. We have to bring him round by putting a pinch of curry to his nose.

'What on earth is wrong with you?' I ask him. 'Tell me.' For if he is sick we will need to know. Truthfully, there is also some genuine concern, for I have grown to respect him and his wayward manner, his clever methods of having his own back. He's surprisingly intelligent.

'Food,' he says, honestly. 'We struggle to buy enough for the servants.'

'Good lord, Anwar,' I say. 'Is it so bad?'

'Terrible,' he says.

After that we request a few more rations, claiming that Mrs Greenson has a son staying. We manage to tell the fib so well it's unquestioned. We can't have servants passing out while serving us the tea.

I find out from Mrs Burrows that the government is coming under censure for the impact of some of our infrastructure on farming. The allegation is that railway embankments, roads, dams, have disrupted water tables and harvests. It sounds far-fetched, even to me.

'Of all the ungrateful . . . !' exclaims Mrs Burrows. 'India was nothing before the British.' And I must say that I do agree. For I have not seen a road or a train or a dam or a decent bridge here built by anyone else, though their grand palaces and temples are admittedly very impressive. But really, they aren't infrastructure, are they? Whereas we are.

William is once again invited to tea. This time I join them, briefly.

'It's very nice to meet you,' he says again.

'Ah, but we've already met,' I say. I don't take his hand this time. I've learned. Give them an inch, and they take a mile.

He looks confused. Of course he doesn't remember, for I was just one memsahib among a hundred at the gala. Gosh, to think that then he was one of the only Indians. How opportunist they all seem to have become. Now, whenever we have society gatherings, there are several among the gentlemen and ladies. At times you almost forget they are Indian at all.

'How are you enjoying the work?' I ask him.

'Very much,' he says with a smile.

'Is it not terribly difficult?'

He shakes his head, looks exasperated, and then seems to remember himself. 'It has its moments,' he says, looking at Benedict.

Benedict smiles, then does something strange. He calls Aashi in.

She stands awkwardly in the doorway. For a second her eyes meet her husband's. You get a sense they know that together they are being ambushed. I feel sorry for her suddenly, though I frequently ambush her myself.

'Come in, girl. Come and sit down,' says Benedict. 'Have a cup of tea like a *real* lady.'

She sits down beside her husband.

Benedict makes Anwar, who stands by the tea trolley presiding over the occasion, give her a cup of tea, and a slice of cake too. She bows her head to Anwar, for thank you, and sits, holding her cup and saucer, too afraid to drink the tea.

'Drink it,' says Benedict with his hard, cold voice, watching her intently.

'Sir!' William is on his feet.

'It's only a cup of tea,' says Benedict evenly without taking his eyes from Aashi.

William stands for a few moments, and then sits down again. His eyes meet mine for a second. We're both appalled.

'Drink it,' says William to Aashi in Bengali.

She does, she drinks a sip or two.

'Don't you want the cake?' asks Benedict. And then he watches as she eats it, one mouthful at a time, her hand shaking each time she raises it to her small mouth. None of us speak.

'Lovely,' says Benedict, when she's finished.

There's a long silence, during which Benedict simply continues to observe her, his eyes wandering at leisure as she sits, hers cast down. William is pale with rage. But he can do nothing. We still hold all the cards.

As for me, what do I do?

'*Nothing*,' I once told my pupils, all those years ago, 'is not a verb.'

Chapter Twenty-Eight

Ants have wonderful laws, obey their queen, and keep their cows, and pet beetles, their slaves, and their soldiers.

How Girls Can Help to Build up the Empire:
The Handbook for Girl Guides,
Miss Baden-Powell and Sir R. Baden-Powell

'Have you told him, the father?' Magda sits, under the clock. I've combed her hair into a blur of white. She's dressed. She's had tea, toast. She's ready for a fight.

I nod.

'Well? What did he say?'

'He hung up.' There's a sore, rough place in my voice.

She sighs. We sit. The hollow ticking of the clock. 'What's he like, this young man?'

'What d'you mean, what's he like? He hung up when I told him I was pregnant.' My voice is high. I taste dried lemons.

She bats at the air with a hand as if that's nothing, completely unfazed by how worked up I am. 'Is he kind, or generous?' She's looking at me like I'm some kind of specimen in a jar. Examining me and my bloody awful situation.

'I used to think he was.'

'Before he left you?'

I nod again.

'What's wrong with him? Hmm?'

A silence. How the fuck did she know? I try to think of clues I've given off, nightmares of his I've mentioned. But there's nothing, only her steady grey eyes, acute as a microscope.

'He's been in the army,' I say.

She nods instantly. A pleased expression. She's getting somewhere. 'Broken, is he?' As if she's got a tick list. As if this is all half expected.

'Deaf.' I say it flatly. 'Well, pretty much. And he gets bad dreams.'

She nods. Thinks for a bit. You can feel the thoughts clicking by methodically, second by second.

'Bring him,' she says, finally. It's a command, not a question. I don't tell her there's no way in hell he'll come. Magda won't take no way in hell as an answer.

Perhaps because of that conversation, or just because I need to hear something other than the thrum of blood in my ears and feel something other than this tightness in my chest, I answer Ewan's call tonight.

'Hi,' I say.

A delay.

'Oh!' says his voice. 'Is that really you? I thought it was voicemail again.'

'No,' I say, 'it really is me.' Although I don't actually feel that's true. Who the fuck am I?

'Su, are you OK? Can I come round? We need to talk.' He

sounds like he always does: clever, gentle, easy to break.

'No,' I say. Just no. My whole body is so heavy. My head's like lead.

Then I start to cry, holding the phone, holding it. The phone to my ear is the closest thing to a person I've got.

'Are you at your dad's?'

I say nothing.

'Su, are you at your dad's?'

I close the door of my phone on him finally, click it shut.

The doorbell rings. I look through the side window. He stands there, in the dark and rain, his coat shining under the streetlights. When he sees my face in the window, he's like someone shut in who suddenly feels the touch of fresh air. His eyes go wide, frank.

'Who's there?' calls my dad from upstairs.

'Salesman!' I say, and slip out.

His body, standing there, tall and warm against the cool night.

'Su,' he says, as I grab his arm to move us both away from the house. The words come tumbling, 'It was a mistake. I shouldn't have finished it. I've been sick. In the head . . . hang on, where are we going?' as I drag him down the road, gripping the warmth of his arm through the raincoat.

'Anywhere,' I say. 'To the sea.'

We walk fast.

'Are you OK?' he keeps asking. 'Su, are you OK?'

Eventually I stop. I want to smack him across the face, but that'd be too easy.

'No,' I say. I look at him, his vulnerable, beautiful face, dark circles under his eyes from not sleeping, from the repeating dreams. 'I'm not fucking OK, at all. I'm not OK, Ewan.'

We walk along the seafront, whipped by the wind and sea spray, and I tell him: Dad's debts.

'Fuck,' he says. 'Fuck.'

'Don't you start.'

'Sorry.'

We walk again in silence. We walk past the arcades and their plinkety sounds, of coins falling.

'I told Dad about college too,' I say.

'Really?' he says, stopping. 'Well done.'

He's almost smiling, and I'm not ready for his smile. He must sense that, because it fades like a lowering sun.

'You don't have to get rid of it, Su,' he says quietly, turning to me. 'We can do this, you know?'

'No we bloody can't. But I can't get rid of it anyway. It's too late, Ewan.'

A space opens between us as we stare at each other. I look into his soft, lost eyes.

When he opens the door of his flat, I think for a second that thieves have been in. The pictures are skewed on the walls, two pot plants have been upset on the floor. There's a smell of gone-off things.

'Sorry,' he says. 'I've been in a weird place.'

'How bad?'

'Bad,' he says, and sighs. Standing there, in the middle of the kitchen, he looks out of the window, takes a deep breath. 'I can't study, too jittery. And it happened at the garage the other day. Someone came up when I was under a car, and when I saw their feet there, I fucking screamed.' He starts trying to clear a space to make food on the kitchen worktop. 'I'll be all right now you're here,' he says, throwing empty tins and old packets of cheese from the counter into the bin.

We make pasta, silently. We sit down at our plates, at the table. Ewan looks at me and puts his warm hand on mine. His hand has a slight tremor. We sit, bracketed by each other. Unsafe.

Chapter Twenty-Nine

Look where we will, the inevitable law of revelation is one of the laws of nature.

No Name,
Wilkie Collins

Aashi is starting to show. I hate her for it, that easy pregnancy. She hides it well, under the pleats of her white serving sari, but even if I did not notice the new weight she carries around her middle, I would have known by the heaviness of her face, her air of torpor, and the way she is so quiet when they're preparing food, as if overtaken by disgust as the smells waft through the open doors of our house. Apart from these subtleties, she carries on as before.

It only occurs to me that there is anything untoward about it when Magda comes with her strange question.

'Mummy,' she says. 'What is a whore?'

I'm shocked to hear such a word from her, since she is home-schooled so far, and rarely hears expletives of any kind. It is like seeing a real weapon in her hand, that word, 'whore'.

'Magda!' I say.

She looks shocked, having evidently no idea what she's said.

'Is it a bad word, Mummy?'

'Very bad, Magda. You mustn't repeat it.'

'I'm sorry,' she says, looking veritably unhappy, for she does like to please, my little girl.

'Where did you learn it?'

At first she will not tell me, and I have to shake her hard for an answer.

'Raja,' she says, crying.

This friendship has been trouble from the very start.

'And where did he learn it?'

She shakes her head, at a loss.

There's a silence. And then.

'He said his mother was one. His father said so.'

I'm taken aback. William didn't seem the type to throw insults around. So polite and charming. And as for Aashi? The epitome of propriety, except for that day with Benedict and the cake.

'Well it's a terrible thing to say, Magda. Next time, you must tell him that.'

She nods, and goes back to setting her flowers in the press, her tongue in the corner of her mouth. They are buttercups and daisies we have grown with such care you would think they were made of glass. Now they are flat to the pages of the press, like a frozen alphabet. They spell meadow. Outside it's red dry.

That was the first indication, and perhaps I might have been more prescient, but I didn't really begin to realise that

Aashi was in trouble until I saw her crying.

When I looked out of the door across the veranda and the parched garden that day, I saw Aashi, sitting alone on the edge wall of our valiant little pond.

Aloneness is not something they seek out, on the whole, our servants. Partly, presumably, because I keep them so busy. As anyone, and any manual will tell you, idle hands make idle minds; and idle minds, tongues; and tongues gossip.

But Aashi is sitting alone, and, by the way her shoulders move up and down and up, she's weeping.

'What's she doing?' I ask Anwar, who is sweeping the veranda.

He looks out at her. 'Nothing, Memsahib,' he says, as densely as he can.

I'm not taken in by him.

'*Nothing* isn't a verb,' I say.

He smiles. Looks troubled, and gives up his denseness.

'She's crying, madam,' he says.

I nod. 'Any idea why?'

'No, madam, not really,' he says. When I turn to him, I see that he looks genuinely perturbed.

'What's wrong?' I say. I look him straight in the eye. He doesn't avert his gaze.

'I don't know,' he says, and starts sweeping the corner with vehemence.

'For goodness' sake, Anwar. You clearly do. I can tell by your manner.'

'Must go, Memsahib. Must get the shopping,' he says quickly, diving out of the door.

'Come back here,' I say furiously after him, but I don't want to raise my voice and alert Aashi that we're watching her. Anwar ignores me. Usually he is more polite than this, though the other servants do often neglect to obey me these days, as they see how Benedict is with me and so judge me inconsequential.

Today Anwar leaves me there, looking out across the veranda to Aashi, sitting beside the pond.

I open the door, step out and tread gently towards her. She must hear my feet on our grass, which despite constant watering has turned as crisp as straw in this heat, for she turns around.

'Memsahib. So sorry. I'm coming directly,' she says, jumping to her feet. Her face is swollen and there are tears in her eyes. Over one eye, a bruise.

'Good lord, Aashi. What have you done?'

'I fell, Memsahib,' she says quickly. 'So foolish.'

It's a lie.

'What's wrong? You'd better tell me.'

'Nothing, madam.' A second lie.

'Do you think I'm stupid?'

'No, madam.'

'Then tell me what's wrong.'

'Nothing, a small fight. My husband . . . nothing.'

'You're pregnant.'

She stares at me, her eyes dry now. She looks terrified.

'It's all right,' I say. 'It's not a crime, woman!' She's still speechless.

'Isn't your husband happy?' I ask.

That starts her off all over again, crying.

I feel impatient with her. She shouldn't come to our house in such a state, and to sit in the garden where the Burrows next door might see and think our servants have free rein to lounge around. It's unforgivable. Only ... I've come to care for her a little, over the years, despite the small and huge resentments. Something like tenderness.

'Take the week off,' I tell her. 'I'll explain to Sahib.'

Her eyes well up again.

'Only, take care to come back in a fit state to work. There'll be no more allowances.'

She nods, trying to wipe her eyes.

'Go!' I say.

She jumps up, scuttles through the garden and into the house to get her things.

Midway through the following week, I'm about to enter the dining room when I hear Magda talking to Benedict.

'Why is Aashi sick, Daddy?' she asks, simply.

'How should I know?' he says.

'Raja said it was your fault,' says Magda. 'He said you did something dirty to her to make her sick.' Her words make me think of her father's cruel hands on my body.

Benedict is silent a moment. And then, 'That boy deserves a whipping,' he says.

Magda gasps. There's a small kerfuffle, and I hear her cry out, 'Let me go, Daddy!'

I'm about to spring into the room, to her defence, when I hear him say, 'Don't you dare mention this to Mummy, Magda. Do you hear me? Never mention this to anyone.' He says it with the hard voice he usually reserves only for me or the servants. 'If you breathe a word of it you'll be in terrible trouble, do you hear me?'

Then Magda runs out of the room like a wild animal released, not seeing me as she runs up the stairs saying, 'I'm sorry, Daddy. I'm sorry,' and crying her little eyes out. She will have to learn as I have.

I go to her room secretly that night, for I am forbidden by Benedict ordinarily, and I get into her bed, and I hold her. When Mrs Greenson has long gone to bed, when Benedict is sleeping soundly, either in his quarters or elsewhere, with some other poor woman, I hold my child, and Evelyn Roberts shares with Magda then, she shares quietly a few rare tears of her heart.

When Aashi comes back to work the following Tuesday afternoon, arriving at my bedroom ready to help with my bath, I make short shrift of her dismissal. I take her by the arm and march her up the corridor to the kitchen.

'Go away,' I say to her in Bengali once we're at the back door. It's the only thing we all know how to say to them in their own tongue: Go away, shoo. We call it to the children, the beggars and the dogs. And now I say it to her. And then in English: 'Get out of here, you little bitch.'

She gasps. And turns to run. I stand in the doorway and watch her, stumbling her way across the garden and out onto the road, her feet kicking up dust. I watch her white sari, her sandaled feet, her black hair turn the corner and disappear.

Oh, Aashi. What have we done to you?

Chapter Thirty

The chief function of the child – his business in the world during the first six or seven years of his life – is to find out all he can, about whatever comes under his notice, by means of his five senses . . .

Home Education,
Charlotte M. Mason

Oh, they're all so angry when they see us leave. And I'm not listening. And Raja is not listening. And we are just running away and away from them as if it did not matter at all that they are shouting at us, are shouting, 'Magda, child. Come back!' And shouting to Raja in Bengali that he's in trouble. Deep, deep trouble. We are in deep trouble together, Raja and me. And oh! It is such good fun.

We are running, splashing through the big silly monsoon puddles and all along the street, and then, would you believe it, across the railway line, and down another street where I have never been and which is oh, would you believe it, so dirty.

It's what I have always wanted to do. To go to the other side of the railway line! I'm with Raja holding his hand and we're running. And he is running faster than I am, and holding my hand and so I trip and I fall and oh it is so dirty, so dirty on my poor knees.

'Ugh,' I say.

'C'mon, madam,' he says.

'I am not *madam*, I am Magda,' I say to him again, but it's as though he's not playing the game, for he just says, 'There is no time for that now,' and he grabs my hand and begins to run again.

'Are you afraid, are you afraid, Raja are you afraid of them?'

'No. No! Come along, madam, run!'

'Magda!' I say, stopping sulkily.

'All right, come along, Magda, run. Run!'

'I'm tired,' I say, beginning to slow.

'They will catch us, madam!' He looks truly frightened.

'So what? It's only a silly, silly game.'

And now Raja has stopped and has turned and is facing me. He looks afraid. He looks afraid and serious.

'It is not just a game, Magda,' he says. 'I have to show you something.'

'Why? I'm only here to play.' I'm here to play a funny game and to run and hide from the servants so that they should chase and chase me through the whole of India.

'You want to see the real India?' he says, as if, like Mummy, he can hear me think.

'Yes, Raja. Oh yes.'

'Very well, Magda. I will show you,' he says.

And there is an angry look in his eye. There is the look of someone furious.

'What is wrong, Raja, what is wrong?' For he is my friend,

but he looks different. Ever since he came to the garden this morning to find me he has looked different.

'Come with me.'

He is reaching for my hand.

'I don't want to come.'

'Come with me, Magda.'

But I have no choice anyway, for his hand is holding mine so tightly, so tightly and he is running, and it's as if my body is nothing but a kite being dragged behind him along the alley and then out into an open road that has no paving. Along the road there are small houses like the ones we see from the train to Darjeeling, but I'm not on the train and so they are more real. They're funny, they're like pretend houses put up only for a day or two, like the one Daddy has had made for me in the garden.

I am afraid, looking at the men and the women in the houses. Is it all right for them to be in these little houses with so little room? Is it all right?

'Do these people really live here all the time?' I ask him. We're walking now, for even Raja needs to catch his breath. 'What about in the heat? Do they go somewhere to cool down?'

He looks at me. And he says nothing, he shakes his head.

'I am not!' I say. 'I am not stupid!'

We come to a real street eventually, one with small houses, but at least proper ones. I'm surprised when Raja stops at a house that is just a bit bigger than the other houses. A house that has its own proper windows and its own proper door instead of just holes. He makes me take off my shoes.

'Come inside, Magda. Come after me.'

'No,' I say. 'I'll stay outside. I'm not playing any more.'

But I can't remember how to return, how to return to our nice white house on our paved road, for it seems so very far away that it might be impossible ever to return. I'm so far away from Mummy and Daddy and the servants. And again Raja's hand is holding mine, and I have no choice but to go in.

The room smells of clean washing and spicy food, and also slightly of something else, a strange smell that reminds me of the times when I finally awake after the bright, fearful, angry dreams which Aashi calls malaria. I am awake and I am in my sickbed. The room smells like that.

Dust dances in the light that pokes in from the window. And in the line of yellow dust you can see a kind of bed. But it is on the floor. It is a bed on the floor, perhaps? And on it there must be a person, because you can see a heap in the middle of the bedclothes.

Raja speaks to it. In Bengali, he says, 'Mother, here is Magda.'

Aashi?

I run to the bed. But the person in there can't be Aashi, because there is only a slow whine. She does not jump from the bed to smile at me and say, 'Why hello, little ma'am.' So it cannot be her.

I step forward.

I extend my hand, for surely if it is Aashi, she will rise from the bed and call me little ma'am and offer me tea or perhaps lemonade?

She does not. She only turns over. But I see the mole on the side of her neck, and I know Raja is telling the truth.

'Does she have the dreams too?'

'It is not malaria,' says Raja. 'It is something given to her by your father.'

'Daddy says that is not true, and anyhow Aashi has not been at our house all week!'

I laugh, but then fall silent, thinking of the way Daddy hurt me.

Raja laughs. But his laugh is angry.

'And besides,' I say, 'Papa has not been ill, so how should he have given a sickness to your mother? Papa is perfectly well, and cannot be to blame.'

Papa cannot possibly be to blame.

Raja is looking at me. He just looks at me as if I am a strange creature he hates, and not his friend.

Then Raja leaves the room again – we leave the room, and are back on the street.

'Where shall we go now?' I ask Raja. But he has turned away from me, and is walking off.

'Where shall we go?' I ask him again.

'Nowhere, Magda. Nowhere.'

'But where are you going?'

He doesn't answer.

'Can you take me home?'

He stops.

'Don't you even know where you are?' he asks me.

I shake my head. 'No. No, I don't. I have only been to school and to the maidan, the bandstand, and to the parks and the riding school and the club,' I say.

He looks at me a long while.

He points a finger to the right and up, and I can see it now, the tall spire of the church, which is not so far from our house.

'But we are close to home!' I say, smiling. He nods. He doesn't smile. 'Only a couple of streets after all!' I say, looking at the church spire.

'Yes, madam,' he says. He says it like one of the servants and not like my friend at all. 'Yes, it is ever so close, madam.' And then he is gone. Then he is gone, and I only see the back of him, leaving. That is the last I see of Raja for a long while. So I do not get to ask him, where is his papa?

Of course I do not believe what Raja says. Of course I do not believe that it was my daddy, but when I asked Daddy the first time he got so angry that it makes me think of Raja, of my friend Raja every day. And you would never think my daddy could be so angry and so upset. I am sorry. I am sorry, Daddy. I did not mean it. I did not.

'If you mention this to anyone, you will be in terrible trouble,' he said. And he hurt my arm, holding it so tight.

Anwar tells me one day what it was. I have asked him so many times that he tells me.

'Perhaps Raja's mother got pregnant, Magda,' he tells me in Bengali. We are speaking Bangla because Mummy is in the next room. She is copying a picture from one of her botany books, copying the exact picture from the book out onto a new page. It is a poppy, it is a bright red poppy. She probably can't hear us. But I do not want her to hear me speaking of Raja. I would rather be slapped for speaking the wrong language.

'Perhaps she was going to have another baby, but it didn't live.'

'Why? Why?' I don't understand.

I do not understand, but when I ask there is no more information.

'Never mind, child,' says Anwar. 'Never you mind.'

But I do, I do mind. For Raja was my friend, and I saw Aashi, and Aashi does not come back to our house, and Mummy says that Raja will never be allowed to come again because we were so naughty. When I have dreams it is Aashi on the bed, and I wake smelling that room, and when I try to awake her in my hot, yellow dreams, Aashi will not be stirred. She will not wake and their small, impossible house is closing around me.

Chapter Thirty-One

In no circumstances whatever will the expression 'shell-shock' be used verbally or be recorded in any regimental or other casualty report, or in any hospital or other medical document.

British army General Routine Order No. 2384, 1917

Ewan and me get his flat cleared up together. Neither of us is going to college, and we don't talk about the future, but during our quiet, slow days, what's between us grows back into itself again, familiar.

Around the edges of these peaceful days, other kinds of times fizz. I can almost smell them. A chemical smell; burnt. He's walking across the room one time, when a plane flies over, quite low, and he cowers and cries out. He has a habit of suddenly turning around to look into the corner of the room, behind him, his pupils huge. When the postman comes to the door one morning, he jumps so much that he throws his tea all over himself. I notice that he's started going through doorways carefully, as if there could be anything, anything on the other side.

To begin with, I don't stay over. It feels like a risk. I'm

standing by a deep pool, wondering how the water'll be if I dive in. Will it be cold? Will it feel good?

But I've not really got any ground to stand on anyway. Me and Dad can't much bear being around each other at the moment. It all takes more facing than we can handle. I can't think of solutions to his problems and he can't think of any to mine. When I do hang out at his, we just move around each other in the kitchen like bloody robots, with nothing to say. We avoid talking about the things that matter because we've both told so many lies – the baby in my belly, the debts hanging over his head ... We can't find a good place to start unravelling it all from. Our conversations are short and tight.

'Are you still going to college?' he asks me once.

'Dad, I told you it isn't business,' I say.

'Yes, but are you going?'

He cares? His voice is tense with it, the hope.

With a practised reflex, I give it to him, the new lie he needs. 'Yes,' I lie. 'I'm still going.'

So I start staying over with Ewan every few nights, telling Dad I'm at Leah's because I don't want to talk to him about Ewan at all right now.

It's only then that I realise the nights are the worst. Ewan's dreams are violent, painful even to watch or hear. At night he seems to be trying to call out, over and over. To begin with, I nudge him. But there's no end to it, and at least if I leave him to the nightmare memories, he gets some kind of sleep. I find myself dreading our bedroom of nightmares. I can only sleep when he's awake. We have about fifty-fifty each of the night – half for him, half for me.

I wake one night to the sound of a heavy impact, and leave our warm bed to find Ewan standing in the kitchen, bleeding.

'Fuck, Ewan! What have you done?' On the wall is the dent his fist has left. He's hit the wall. He nurses his hand. I take it. An angry bruise is beginning to gather beneath the skin and his knuckles are inflating with hot blood, a small cut in his index knuckle bleeds down his arm.

'I don't know,' he says, looking at it as if it's someone else's. 'I don't know. Christ, Su, that could've been anyone.'

Between his episodes we go on all right. Neither Ewan nor me talk too much about his past and our future. We just slot back into some kind of sore love. He cooks for me, looks after me in a way, trying, trying. He strokes my shoulder while we sit, watching TV yet again because neither of us can concentrate to read, and he whispers *I love you*s which I do, I do believe. But he still hasn't touched my belly, hasn't listened in to the baby's movements, which have got more frequent in that distant and close world inside. At night, when I'm at his, I lie awake, listening to my heart drumming too fast.

He's beginning to plan. If he works more at the garage he says we can afford to do up the flat, make it suitable for the baby somehow.

'Isn't that the landlord's job?' I ask him.

He shrugs. 'He's pretty useless,' he says. 'And if we make him do anything he'll either put up the rent or make me move on.'

'But what about college?' I ask him. 'You'll not be able to keep up with the course if you work that much. And what about Dad? What the hell is he going to do?'

Dad's had a lot of letters threatening to repossess the house.

★

Magda's fierce when she finds out I've given up on college. We're in her long kitchen trying to make blancmange. I've never even eaten the stuff and it looks disgusting, and there's no way she'll eat it all on her own anyway, but she's determined. And when Magda's determined, there's no space for opinions. She's especially stubborn these days. I think it's because she's holding on so tight. You can feel them, her memories, skulking around the house, getting between her and these walls. Her days have the same sort of ghosted feeling as Ewan's nights. Physically she's weaker too, week by week. She rarely lifts her hands from her lap now. Her eyes, though, are as fierce as fucking ever.

We pour the sickly pink mixture into the mould, and put it in the fridge to set.

'How's college?' she asks me sharply.

'Not bad,' I lie, shutting the fridge on the geriatric weight-gain products she gets prescribed by the doctor, but won't touch.

'You're lying,' she says, quick as a flash. 'You haven't been going.'

'No.'

Neither Ewan nor I have even mentioned it to each other. We don't go in. Just the thought of that butterflying world makes me ache all over.

'Are you still feeling ill?'

'Nausea's gone. Just tired now.'

'Well then go,' she says. 'You're clever. You need to progress. Baby or no baby.'

I mutter it.

'What?' she says. 'Speak up, woman!'

'No point. We're not going to be able to afford the fees now anyway,' I say quietly. 'No bloody way. I don't want the debt hanging over the kid too.'

She looks at me hard. She leans forward suddenly.

'You young women don't realise how hard we had to fight for university education,' she says. 'It was terrible. You know the first time I said I wanted to be a chemist, they laughed.' She coughs a few times, after saying this. Her chest has been bad recently. Mucus, like memories, seems to stick to her more each day, dragging her down.

'You were a chemist?' I say when she's finished coughing.

'Yes, and not as in pharmacy,' she says tartly.

I must look at her like I think this is bullshit, because she says, 'Don't believe me? Go into the study – the door on the left from the hallway.' She has to clear her throat again. 'If you can get past the cobwebs, go to the second shelf along; all those journals are mine.' Through the thickness in her throat, there's something sharp and bright.

'Yours?'

'Well, I've papers published in them.' She smiles now, sweetly.

I jump up to find proof of this. I go through the door of the study, like I did before, switch on the light, look for the second shelf along . . . magazines. I leaf through one of them.

Sure enough, there it is on the dusty paper, under the bare bulb of the study light. Her name: Magda Compton, PhD.

I find many, many papers in those journals. Papers and articles on technical chemical processes I can't begin to understand. I find myself laughing out loud at them. What a bloody wonder she is. Smart as hell.

When I sit back down with her there's this edge of triumph to her look.

'You were a scientist?'

'Bloody good one too,' she says. She'd smack her thigh if she could. She leans forward in her chair, looking at me.

'Go to college,' she says. 'For now, just keep going.'

That night I tell Dad about me and Ewan.

'Dad,' I say. 'Ewan and me are back together.'

There's a long silence.

'Ewan and *I*,' he says, sounding like Mum, or Magda.

I laugh. And he bloody well laughs too.

I don't have to lie about that any more, at least. I take some more of my stuff over to Ewan's. It's almost like I'm really moving in, and we're going to settle down.

But that night, dreaming, he hits me. He fucking hits me. His hand, suddenly hard and sore on my face, him thrashing against me. I wake into the frenzy of it, and I'm halfway across the room, screaming, in a second. He puts the light on, sits up in bed and stares at me like an animal. We look into each other's eyes. And for a quick moment, I'm terrified. Scared he won't know me, won't stop looking at me like I'm some kind of predator and he's my prey. He looks petrified of me. And because of that my Ewan looks dangerous. We breathe quickly, we breathe.

'Oh god, Su,' he says, tears rolling down his face, holding the ice to my cheek in his strip-lit kitchen. 'I'm sorry. I thought you were . . .'

'I know,' I say, 'I know.'

'I'll work it out,' he says. 'Darren says it goes eventually.'

'It's been years, Ewan. And it's getting worse. You need help.' I feel cruel saying it, despite my hot, ice cheek, and despite the look of love I give him, immediately afterwards. In his eyes I can see it, that day when he lost his hearing, a swelled, blastingly loud day, saturated with colour and dry as desert sand. A hurting day.

He looks up at the impression his fist left that time when he hit the wall, and he nods once.

Chapter Thirty-Two

My heart is homesick to-day for the one sweet hour across the sea of time.

'Stray Birds',

Rabindranath Tagore

Benedict is barely ever here, as he is called to command new Indian recruits on the north-western border. He is upbeat about it. The hierarchical nature of military life has always appealed to him, I think. He is in his element when in absolute and mortal control. And it is a great relief to me, to be free of the danger of another bad pregnancy, at least for the next few months. On his desk are his plans for the railway strategy in case of another war in Europe. Many Indian trains would be commandeered to carry Indian produce to the ports as remedy for any lack in Europe. His plans will be meticulous and well thought out, just like his domestic cruelties.

I have focused on my needlework and on improving the level of service and authenticity in my house. By authenticity the books mean Britishness, and so I drive the servants hard. Forbid breaks. Make them pick weeds from the lawn daily.

Have them make flour from rice as we have no wheat flour these days.

Still. Since Aashi has left, and Benedict is so often absent, I have been able to mother my child a little, though I find myself wooden and the thought of real affection hits a discord in me. I tuck her in at night. I wake her in the morning. I sit with her on my knee. But I can't seem to mime other gestures of motherliness which I found so natural before. There is something wrong, something in that layer between skin and feeling, between body and self.

We throw a little tea party for the other small children in the community. We make it a fancy dress party; they are all rather thrilled. We have them come dressed up as their servants. Magda wears a small white sari, and has a red spot on her forehead, and her hair in a plait. She carries a broom, which is far too big for her. I put one of my bracelets around her ankle, and she looks very much the part.

I expect the servants to be quite delighted by the spectacle, but they are more than usually stiff. Perhaps we have caused offence? At any rate, Magda and her little friends are all smiles and cake. I am slowly growing to be in favour with my child.

It is to be short-lived. I knew something was afoot when I saw Mrs Greenson talking to Benedict in the library. He was nodding. *Yes, yes*, he was saying, *it is inevitable. She has always known it. It is pure silliness that it has not happened before. Stupidity.* Mrs Greenson was pressing some point, but her voice did not carry as Benedict's does.

'Evelyn will not have it,' he said. 'She will simply not put up with it, and will be as silly as possible.'

It was confirmed when Magda came running from her morning classes with Mrs Greenson. She ran straight into the dining room, and in front of Benedict, threw herself into my arms.

'Magda!' he shouted. And she drew away quickly, for she has learned from an early age that she cannot show me too much affection – it is disapproved of.

'I'm to be sent away!' she said, crying. 'Oh, Mummy! Mrs Greenson of all people! I am to be sent on a ship with only her, and sent away from you all to England.'

I sat, holding her, staring at Benedict.

'You didn't think to air it with me before telling her?'

He pretended to be reading.

'There was no need.'

'No need? She's my daughter as well as yours.'

'I thought you'd only turn her against the idea.'

'Mrs Greenson seems to have done a good enough job of that already,' I said, and, taking the child in my arms, I walked out. I walked out in such a stubborn way, and I knew that it would bring me trouble. There would be locked doors for it, and perhaps worse.

But Benedict came to my room after us, and he sat down a distance from us on the bed; he sat down calmly, and began, for once, to reason.

'I think it'll be better for her, Evelyn,' he said. 'She's becoming naughty and tricksy, and has made an unsuitable friendship with that boy. Children don't turn out well in India.'

Children don't turn out well when they have no love, no affection.
Children don't turn out well when their mothers are unhappy.

Magda said nothing. She was rigid with fear.

'Might I go with her?' I asked him.

He sighed, and there was a silence, a quiet filled with hope. Magda's, and mine, our hope swirled together.

'Good lord, no,' he said, and walked out.

I sit there, a long while. Magda sits too.

Anwar, who has been standing in the corner the entire time, eventually interrupts the quiet.

'May I please sit with you?' he asks.

I am so surprised that I assent. He sits beside me. He reaches across the table and strokes Magda's hair, and then he looks at me and smiles, gently.

'It will be all right, Memsahib,' he says. 'She will be all right.'

Magda has become very quiet and hides in the garden in her playhouse. I hear her sometimes, singing snippets of Bengali and English songs as she dresses and undresses her dolls. Sometimes she rehearses conversations between the dolls. They are never very nice to each other, but parody me and the other society ladies.

'Do you call that a dress?' I hear her have one of her dolls say to the other as I approach her in the garden.

'No,' says the other doll, 'don't be foolish. I call it a gown.' Magda at least will know how to hold her own in polite society.

'Magda,' I say, 'would you come in and pack with me?'

Silence.

'Magda?'

'We are having high tea,' she says, sulkily.

I bite my lip.

'And at what time will that be over?'

Silence again.

'By our real teatime.'

'All right,' I say. 'We can pack after tea.'

But we don't pack. And it is several days before I even think of the passage we have booked for her. Because of what happens to Benedict.

Chapter Thirty-Three

No Dogs, No Indians.

Sign at the Royal Simla Club

My papa shoots Meg the dog.

My papa bought Meg the dog for me for not talking about Raja and Aashi any more, or asking Mummy about it, and for being valiant about what Mrs Greenson says about going Home. He brought Meg the dog home with him from the railway and he said she might come Home with me, if we could get her a certificate. I made her a certificate myself, in case. It is a certificate that says NO RABIES. I stroke her soft ears and she leans against my legs, heavy. She looks at me with her brown eyes, as a damsel looks at a prince: with love.

Since Raja is gone, I play with Meg the dog. We play several games, over and over. The one with the ball and the one with the hoop and the one with the stick. She doesn't learn much English. Only *sit* and *lie* and *come*. She doesn't learn much Bangla either, except *go away* and *shoo*. I miss Raja, who used to tell me things about the real India and who learned everything so quickly he was like a magician. Meg can only learn the words for what she must do and what she must not, while Raja was clever in Bangla and Hindi and English and so made big stories of everything.

One day, I am on our lawn, playing with her with the hoop, and she suddenly stops. Meg the dog looks strange. She begins to have white spit around her mouth. She begins to whine. She falls over. She stands up again. She stands and begins to follow me. And then she begins to growl. She begins to growl, and the white spit is thicker and thicker around her mouth as if it is full of soap. She topples sideways, and it is as if her legs do not work well any more. Her legs are the stiff silly legs of a puppet. She gets up. She dances like a puppet. And then she falls again.

'Papa, Papa,' I shout. 'There is something wrong. There is something wrong with Meg the dog!' And I call him. I call him to come and see. And when he comes he sees her, and he shouts at me to 'Get away, Magda! Get away from her.' He pushes me hard, away from Meg the dog, so that I fall over, and then he takes her. He takes Meg the dog by the collar, and he drags her straight out into the yard, and ties her to the post, shouting to Anwar to get his gun. Meg the dog is crying. She is crying high. And when Anwar comes running with the gun, and gives it to Papa, Papa shoots her. My papa shoots Meg the dog. The sound is the air breaking. When the bullet hits her, something comes out of the back of her head. It is all her thoughts. It is *sit* and *lie* and *shoo*. It is our games over and over on the lawn. All the things that she knows come out of her head with the blood. There is a lot of quiet afterwards. Quiet except for my papa asking, 'Did she bite you, Magda? Did she bite you?'

271

★

'Why did he shoot her, why did he shoot her, Mummy?'

We are in the sitting room. I am cold all over.

'She was ill. She had rabies, Magda. There was no helping it.'

'But he did not even let me say goodbye.'

We are quiet. I am crying.

'Will she come back?'

'No, Magda. I'm sorry.' Mummy is stroking my head. She is like a real mother.

'And Raja? Will he?'

'No, Magda,' she says. She looks away. And then she says quietly, 'I'm sorry about that too.'

'Meg is dead?'

'Yes.'

'But Raja is still alive?' I am afraid, asking her.

'Yes, Magda, he is,' she says, and she puts an arm around me.

'So he can come back again?'

'No, Magda. You must stop thinking of him, child. He's gone now too.' Mummy is almost crying. 'He's gone.' Mummy is almost crying although I did not think she really knew about Raja. She is crying.

I do not believe her. I do not believe that Raja is gone, and gone forever.

Mummy says I can go to Meg the dog as long as I don't look under the handkerchief to see her head, and the blood where Papa shot her. I go and I stand above her, and I see her fur and her body all soft and the same as usual. She is lying so flat and her eyes when I peek under the handkerchief are oh so perfectly shut. And when I whisper to her quietly, so that no one will hear, 'Meg, Meg, oh Meg where is your little ball?' or 'Meg, Meg, fetch!' there's nothing. I hope that no one has heard me. *Madam*, says Raja in my head. *Madam, you are stupid*. And he is right, for Meg does not bark. She does not whine under the handkerchief.

I am not thinking about going Home. I am not thinking about it because I don't know what it can possibly mean.

We are doing the times tables again. Writing them all out in the schoolroom where the flies buzz. It is as if Meg the dog isn't dead, and as if there is nothing wrong. Daddy said to Mummy that she was not to make a fuss over me, that it is just a dog and I am being a baby.

Mrs Greenson has left me to write them out all on my own. She is watching over me. When I finish, and she reads my times tables in the copybook, she does not say well done, or good girl. Mrs Greenson does not ever think that I am at all good, not like Aashi and Anwar who think I am excellent. Mrs Greenson is always grumpy because her body is all shrivelled and hard like a lychee that has come off the tree. Mrs Greenson doesn't have a tree to hang from and belong to, so her brows knot together.

'Magda. You're to pack your things,' says Mrs Greenson now, closing my copybook after her inspection.

This is the way Mrs Greenson speaks. She says things with no warning. Mother says these things *come out of the blue*.

I feel cross. I will pretend not to understand her. 'What things?' I say, and look stupid.

'Your clothes, your books, and a few of your toys.'

'Why?'

She is watching me, in a strange way. She is not pleased. 'Don't be obtuse, Magda. We're to go Home,' she says, 'you know this.'

Obtuse is naughty.

Home is to come *out of the blue*. Home is not real.

So, I am obtuse again:

'To the hills?' I say. I like to go to the hills. It is cool and fresh like lemonade in the hills.

'No, to England. For goodness' sake, child!' she says.

'Why?' I am starting to shake. England is a long way and it is not a place that I have been in real life and without Meg the dog I shall be even lonelier.

Mrs Greenson says the next thing to herself, muttering: 'Because you've been out here long enough.'

Out here is India. People are always talking about it, saying, 'We have been *out here* for three years,' or 'We like it *out here*,' or 'You can't behave like that *out here*'.

'But what about Raja?' What about Raja? I can't look for him if I am in England. He will be completely lost.

It is all horrid and I hate her.

Mrs Greenson hates me too, and has turned her back with a huff through her nose. She is cleaning the numbers and the figures on the blackboard with a cloth, and ignoring me.

'You must stop talking about that little boy, Magda. It's tiresome, as I've told you before.'

'Will Mummy and Daddy and Anwar come too?'

Mrs Greenson has turned, and is holding the cloth, and looking down at her hands which are terribly firm and terribly thin. 'Your parents will visit you often.' What does she mean *visit*? And what about Anwar? I stare at her. 'You are to go to a proper school, and they will come Home in the summer sometimes to visit.' Her hands are fidgeting with the cloth, like two big insects eating something together.

I stand up. She is wrong. She is obtuse. We are not *out* here. We are *in*.

Home is something terrible, and I am afraid of it.

Chapter Thirty-Four

A very little key will open a very heavy door.

Hunted Down,

Charles Dickens

And this girl, Susheela. Her voice plays over and over. *I don't want a baby*, she says. *Not on my own.* And that comment of hers: *You'd have liked my mum, Magda.*

I'd know it anywhere: a child, in search of its mother. Perhaps she can grow love in her womb, where I grew only a house of shut rooms.

My house has a feeling of waiting, and, for once, I'm not quite sure who for. The windows look out hopefully towards Bay's Mouth. From the window of my bedroom I can see that the leaves from the trees on my drive have lain themselves down, prostrating themselves on the driveway in preparation for the tread of someone. Inside, my house is full of whispers, and I am a whisper too, my feet frequently invisible at the end of my legs, my throat stuffed full of something fuzzed. There's little difference now, between night and day, for both are full of spectres and hauntings. In the house in the early hours, there is the slow thunk of an old jacket being beaten out, a beating at my own back, and a lingering smell of incense hanging in my bedroom. I wake with the itch of an impossible mosquito bite on my upper thigh. It will swell to a welt, for they always do on me. Yesterday, when I looked in the glass of the vanity, my skin seemed to be brown leather, so perhaps I am rotting away? Certainly the house is in a poor state. I can no longer make out its seams at all, the line between skirting and floor, the trace of where the architraves are. Even where these forms are distinct, they make no sense and are all jumbled. The geometry of two walls and a floor is utterly impossible. When I try to work it out, the shape and form of my house, the rooms seem to curl at the edges like old parchment.

Although I have a lifetime's experience of summoning, calling to order, I don't really believe Susheela will bring him until she does. He stands beside her, entirely visible and whole, a tall young man (though older than she is, by a few years I'd say). He is poorly dressed, in awful, tattered jeans and a sweatshirt, but wears a look that means more to me than a good suit: he looks at me openly, his look not overlaid with prejudice, as many people's first appraisal is. My house softens for him, and for her, as they stand in my sitting room, together. Beside them stands Mother. Mother walks to him, and stops just a breath away from his shoulder. She looks him up and down, sniffs, and then, quite unexpectedly strokes his cheek before she leaves the room. I am so taken aback by the unfamiliar kindness of this sudden gesture that Susheela has to call to me several times before I rouse myself enough from it to answer.

They are unaware of Mother's prescence, or of the house's complete lack of integrity. They are always unaware.

'Ah,' I say. 'There you are.' I give them my best smile. For some reason Susheela laughs.

I make a great effort, and have them come entirely and beautifully into focus as they sit across from me. I am once again in my laboratory coat with twenty–twenty vision. I am making my assessment of what is here before me.

Yes, in this I can still excel. I have the ability to tell, within a few moments, a lot about a person from their stance, de-meanour, gestures, expression. Not to mention other, more superficial clues like shoes, trousers, shirts. And all that before they open their idiotic mouths to speak.

He is not an idiot. He is also not afraid of me. And he, like me, is in communion with his own bad ghosts.

'You've been away to war?' I say to him, with no introduction.

At that, he does look wary. Nods.

'Bad, was it? Bloody?'

He doesn't answer initially. One second, two. He nods again.

'You lost your hearing, I'm told?' My house has entirely dropped away, and we are in a blank white space. Me and him, and my questions.

Again, he nods.

'See things, do you? Hear things?'

He doesn't move.

'Won't stay in the past?' I ask. 'I know what that's like.'

'What d'you know about it?' he erupts.

Ah yes. Of course my house has laid me all out, for him to read. He will be judging me too. Susheela is looking at him in shock. This blurting out of thoughts isn't a common thing for him then? Good. I find him good.

'I saw my father killed,' I say. It rises, like bile, to my throat. The nameless thing. The incommensurable memory, unstoried.

Susheela gasps. Then they're both quiet.

'Shot,' I say into the house.

I have his attention now. I reach out a hand to him. And because he is good, he takes it, my old woman's hand.

'So you see, I know how the past can jab through, like a knife.'

Susheela stares at me.

I can feel the heat of uncried things at my eyes. My voice quakes with a built-up pressure when I say it: 'Don't you let it, do you hear? Don't you let it do that.'

Susheela's deep eyes, looking at him.

I am suddenly weighted and dull. I take a breath and then take my hand from his and say, 'Go to the damned doctor.' Then, 'I'm tired,' I say to her. 'Take me upstairs. Bring me a cup of tea.'

She nods. Her man springs to his feet.

'Wait here for her,' I say to him, as sternly as I can, though my breath shows ragged between the words. 'She'll need you to do that.'

On the way through the wide hallway, there is Aashi, dusting. I reach to stroke her shoulder as I pass, and, for once, she almost turns, I almost get to see her smile again.

Once she's wheeled me into the bedroom, Susheela sits down hard on the bed, determinedly present among the perhapsness of all my ghosts.

'I don't want to be a bad mother,' she says.

I laugh. 'You?' I say.

She nods. 'I'm not ready,' she says.

Mother in the corner is using one of Father's drawing implements to pick something from a hole in the wood panelling. I can hear her muttering to herself. *Dirt*, perhaps she says. *Dirt*.

'What type of a mother did *you* have?' I ask Susheela.

She looks at her feet, looks up again with full eyes.

'Kind,' she says, her voice splitting with the word. 'Funny,' she says, half laughing and wiping her nose with the back of her hand. 'Loving,' she says. These words, in her mouth, aren't lacking in form and precision as I would have assumed them to be in another's. They pulse with the presence of someone.

'Well then,' I say. 'You're a sight more prepared than I ever would have been.'

In the corner, Mother, with her back to me, stops, stiffens, but does not turn round.

That's when she does it, the girl. She bends down to me, and she takes me in her arms. I'm surprised to feel the first thaw of it, and the shiver of tears that come suddenly. When I look up, Mother stands facing us now. She is Mother and not Mother. She is some other unseen, homely thing. She wears only a pinny, plain flats on her feet, a scarf around her hair. She is not the person I knew who went from tea party to gala. The look in this woman's eye is open. And perhaps there is . . . love there beneath the empty dignity?

'Did that really happen?' the girl asks. 'Did you see your dad killed?'

I look at her, focusing again, slowly. I nod.

'Why?' she asks.

The question so simple. The answer so huge and so full of time.

Chapter Thirty-Five

A model of the doll's house presented to Princess Elizabeth by the Welsh people. Double-fronted, with four rooms, hall, staircase and landing. Opening metal windows. Imitation thatched roof. Four electric lights, less batteries. Front hinged in two parts. Length 30'. Height 23 ¾'.

Tri-Ang Catalogue, 1930s

Tonight I go along the dusty street, and I turn into the alley. I imagine that Raja is here, holding my hand and leading me down the street saying, *Come on, madam, come along.* And so I arrive at his dirty road with the pretend houses and I walk along with the people in the houses staring at me as I go, because I am a white girl. I am a proper little Englishwoman, and so I do not belong with these poor people who look so big in their little houses. On this street they do not have *drainage.* That is what Mummy says. On the other streets in India, they do not have *drainage* as they do on ours, and that is why it smells.

I have trouble finding Raja's because all the houses look alike to me, and how should I know which one is his?

Ah, but Aashi comes out of it, so I know! She is dressed in

282

a bright sari, and bangles, unlike the white one she wears at our house. I am about to say, *Hello, Aashi. How are you? I should like to see Raja if you please.* But then I see that she is talking to someone who is coming out of their house behind her. It is my papa! I jump when I see him, and I almost cry out with shock. Papa looks very tall and very yellow, coming out of their house. Papa should not be here! It is all wrong.

I hide. I am lucky that I did not cry out, and that my papa did not notice me, a little Englishwoman on this Indian road, or I might be in a great deal of trouble. Like hide and seek, I hide behind the big tin can, which is full of gasoline for the lamps in the houses, and I watch as Papa gives Aashi something. I think it is money.

What is he doing here? What is the money for? What is my tall, yellow papa doing in this place?

I watch from behind the tin can as my papa walks away down the road.

'You are a spy!' says the whisper behind me.

It is Raja. Oh! It is my friend! I am smiling because I am oh so pleased to see him.

But he is not smiling. Raja is serious. He is serious, and he is very, very thin. Perhaps they do not have food now that Aashi does not work for Daddy?

'You are a spy! Who sent you, was it your mother?'

'No. I am not a spy! I am here myself. Mummy and Daddy have no idea.'

Raja looks at me. I can't hear what he thinks by his look.

'Papa shot Meg the dog,' I say.

Raja looks up the street, then he takes a breath, then he looks at me.

'Your father has a gun?' he says.

I nod. 'He shot Meg the dog.'

'Is she dead?'

I nod.

'Where is his gun?' he says, as if he doesn't believe me that Papa has one at all.

'It is in his study, in the drawer,' I say, and then, because he still looks at me strangely, 'It is a small handgun. Papa has shown it to me and we have looked at the bullets and we have put it back in the drawer ready, just in case.'

'In case?' he asks.

'Yes, just in case.' I don't know in case of what. No one ever says. But the gun is for safety, and so Papa keeps it close.

Raja takes my hand, and he drags me into the house after him, just as he did last time we were here.

Aashi is there, cooking over a small fire. She looks up at us. 'Magda!' she says. 'What are you doing here?' and then she starts shouting at Raja in Bangla. She shouts so quickly that I can't understand. All I hear is 'English', 'dirt' and 'trouble'. Raja stands there; he ignores her. He ignores his mother. She shouts more loudly and then she hits him across the face. On his face the slap is red.

She comes towards me now.

'Magda,' she says. 'You must go home.'

'Why?' I ask her. 'And why don't you come with me?'

She shakes her head. 'I can't.'

'Why? Is it because of what Papa has done?'

She stares at me. And then she nods her head.

I hate my papa. I hate him. What he has done must be terrible. And he shot Meg the dog.

'Will you go home, Magda?' she asks me then. 'We need you to go Home.'

I stare at her. Aashi never speaks to me like this. She never speaks to me so honestly and with tears in her eyes.

'Yes,' I say. 'All right.'

'Raja, walk her to the end of the road,' she says in Bangla. Then she comes to me, and her arms are round me as tight as a bud. One seconds, two seconds. She pushes me, and says to Raja and me, 'Go.'

He runs out, and I follow him. Raja says nothing to me all the way up the road, and then he points.

'That way,' he says. 'Go that way.'

When I arrive at our house there is shouting inside. I can hear Mummy and Daddy shouting.

'I've given her money,' he's saying. 'What more do you want?'

I can't hear what she says back.

'For god's sake, Evelyn,' he says. 'This is ridiculous.'

Then I hear a great sound of hitting. I hear Mummy crying.

I go to the door of the study. I see Mummy and Daddy struggling. Daddy is struggling and has Mummy by the neck. He has Mummy by the neck, and he has pulled up her skirt. It is terrible, what he is doing to Mummy. What is he doing? He is like an animal with her. He is terrible. She makes a sound that I don't understand. And he makes sounds. Finally then, he's quiet.

I hear what she says then.

'I hate you. I hate you.' And she runs out of the room.

I hate him too. Mummy and I and Aashi all hate him together.

There is trouble in our house because something has gone missing. Something is missing and the servants are all in trouble. Mummy and Daddy are scared the servants are turning on us.

I look at Anwar and Madan, and I know they would not. But Daddy doesn't know that because he lines all the servants up in the garden, and shouts at them all. He has them turn out their pockets, and searches their quarters.

'It must have been someone from outside,' says Anwar. 'A thief.'

The police come. They put dust all over Papa's study, to look for fingerprints, but they don't find anything, only Anwar's fingerprints.

'Of course Anwar's fingerprints are in there,' says Mummy. 'He's the only servant allowed in to put that place in order.'

'Well he's the only one it could be,' says Daddy.

When the police are gone, Mummy says to Daddy, 'If you let them blame Anwar for this, I'll tell them about the money. I'll tell them you knew about the problems the hydroelectrics would cause and went ahead with them anyway. I'll tell everyone about Aashi.'

The servants and Mummy are busy upstairs preparing my things to go Home. I will have lots of trunks full of things and I will go on the ship with my cases and my clothes and Mrs Greenson.

I am in my little house in the garden having a tea party

with my dolls when I see Raja coming to our big house. He is sneaking into the house. He pushes the door and runs inside. I have just seated all of the dolls and have begun to serve the tea, but I stop, and I get up and out of my little house and I follow him. I don't call his name. There will be big big trouble when Papa sees that Raja is here. I run to our proper house through the sunny garden, I open the door and go in, just as Raja did. In the hallway it is so dark compared to outside, and it is cool. I can only hear Papa talking on the telephone. His voice comes through the hallway and entrance hall and into my ears.

'No,' he says. 'For god's sake, man, you have it all wrong.' Papa is angry. Papa is always angry on the telephone.

In the hallway, I can't see Raja. He must have gone up the stairs or to the kitchen. Anwar will box his ears. Papa will have him in deep trouble. Raja is a thief. Raja is a thief now in my house.

He must be in the kitchen and so I go there first. There is no Anwar. The kitchen is empty. And no Raja. Raja is some-where else. With Papa?

Then my head is full of the sound. It is the sound of a gun, like when Papa shot Meg the dog. I am frozen.

In the kitchen there is only the beans, soaking, and the smell of pickle simmering, and there is some meat, hanging.

I hear Raja's little feet. I hear Raja leaving the house.

I stand in the kitchen. Still.

There is the sound of a great many feet now, coming down the stairs. The sound of gasping and screaming. That is Mummy, screaming. She is screaming nothing. And then she is screaming my name. My name. 'Magda, Magda!'

'Yes,' I am saying. 'Yes.' And I am walking towards Daddy's study, and the door is open and Mummy is inside. She is silent. Mummy is standing.

'I'm here, Mummy,' I say. She turns.

'Oh thank god!' she says, and she runs to me, and she lifts me and hugs me.

Past Mummy, I see Daddy. Daddy is lying with all his blood, and his eyes closed oh so very, very shut oh so shut and quiet and flat. And it is terrible oh it is terrible.

It is because Raja is cleverer than me. It is because I told him, about the gun. And it is because Daddy is hated – even now, when he lies with his blood, Mummy looks at him, and he is hated.

Chapter Thirty-Six

Native teachers boast that not only can they tell a person's sex and age by their tracks, but also their character. They say that people who turn out their toes much are generally 'liars'.

How Girls Can Help to Build up the Empire:
The Handbook for Girl Guides,
Miss Baden-Powell and Sir R. Baden Powell

'Daddy shot,' Magda says over and over. *Daddy shot. Daddy was shot.* I send her off with Madan. This is no place for a child.

It is a frightful mess. Benedict has fallen forwards in his seat so that he lies across the desk and has bled out all over his latest draftings. The paper has curled red with the wet glimmer of it. And now, just now, the first drips begin to fall to the rug. The blue rug. That will take several washes. The bullet must have flown clear through Benedict's mind and into the wood panelling behind him, for it has split through the polished mahogany, and has left a small hole.

I walk over to the hole, and peer in. Yes, there it is. Despite its squalid journey, the bullet shines, glistens faintly, deep within the wood.

I turn round. Just the thing! In Benedict's hand, his brass compass. I remove it from his grip.

'Memsahib!' Anwar is standing behind me.

'What?' I say under my breath as I begin to pick and pick at the hole. But the bullet won't be brought out. We will have to undo the whole thing!

It is then that I realise my daughter is back again and crying. I turn round and she is standing there, and beside her is Mrs Greenson, who has the most stricken expression on her face.

I smile at Mrs Greenson.

'You'll be leaving tomorrow,' I say brightly.

She has the temerity to look slightly offended, amid the shock.

It's then that I look at Magda. She must have run up to her father, and touched him, for she has blood smears on her face, her hands, and on her pale blue dress.

'Child!' I say. 'You're dirty. Go with Anwar and have a wash. Anwar, what on earth are you doing? Clean her up. And tell all the other servants to stay in the house, until I say they can go home. Don't let anyone else in.'

Anwar is staring at Benedict. And then looking at me with wary eyes, but he does as I say, and takes her along the hallway to the kitchen where no doubt he will stand her in the sink and wash her right there where the food is prepared. Still, now is not the time to fuss.

When he has left with Magda, I ask Mrs Greenson to go up the road and report it to the police. She gets her bag directly, and positively dives out of the house. I stand, looking at Benedict's blood on the clean carpet, wondering what on earth will get the stain out.

★

Magda is, apparently, clean now, so I have her brought to me. Anwar passes her to me, wrapped in a big white towel. She is like a chrysalis in my arms. If they have bathed her well enough she will sprout wings. I dry her, rubbing furiously until she cries out.

'Oh, I'm sorry. I'm sorry, darling,' hugging her. What is wrong with me? Each task I do becomes frantic, overzealous, mad.

I carry her to my bed, pull a small nightdress over her limp body and tuck her in. She is asleep before I turn out the light. Terror does that to children. They run, they scream, but when the terror is over, they sleep like the dead. My small, porcelain daughter is the only live thing in me, here, at my chest, beneath all this starch and pomp and perfection, fluttering.

Anwar comes in, and puts a cup of something hot and sweet and spiced in my hand. He places my fingers round the handle. His hands are firm.

'Drink,' he says, steadily.

When I look up at him, we are two people, bare and alone.

The army investigators that come are faultlessly polite. They wipe their feet at the door.

'We had a report of a shooting?'

'Yes,' I say, nodding. 'My husband. You had better go up and see.'

They're staring at me, like Anwar did.

I nod. 'He's in the study,' I say. 'Dead.'

When they finally come down, they accept graciously my offer of tea. I have Anwar bring cake also. They look at him, and look at each other. My heart is beating, beating, but my hands, serving the tea, are steady. I am practised now. The perfect gentlewoman.

They sit down. Faultlessly correct. Polished shoes, army issue. Stiff collars. Slicked hair.

'Any idea who did this, ma'am?' The one with the moustache.

'None at all. I'm afraid to say the door was left open. They must have walked straight in, and then straight out.'

'Was he alone in the house at the time?'

'Good lord no, there were, what . . . two people . . . and at least three servants.'

He continues to ask questions tirelessly: where was I, where was Magda, where were the servants, who was first on the scene? They will need to speak to each of the servants in turn, and 'Can we speak to your daughter?'

I have Anwar bring Magda in. She is pale and sleepy. They ask her several questions, which make her cry, and establish that the poor girl is a terrible witness – who besides, they seem to accept, has seen nothing. I watch her face. There's an expression there I don't know. A grown-up, secret expression on my child's face.

'Gosh, how the army works its officers!' I say, when they seem to have given up with her. I give them some of Madan's cake, delicious, and impeccably English except for the butter, which is goat, not cow. Madan is a very obedient cook, at least on the face of it. I now have him fully trained. There's very little Indian about his cooking at all these days. They sit back, enjoying the cake, and we talk of the weather and the increasing heat, and they smile at me, and perhaps flirt a little even, though good lord I am out of practice and my stomach turns so at the thought of men.

'He'll be shot, most likely, madam – the man who did this.'

'Good,' I say. Although I feel indebted to him. Freedom fighter or fiend. 'Good.'

I look past the men on the armchairs, at Magda sitting in the window seat. Her face is white as bone. The men leave, and I go to her. She is holding a toy rabbit that was sewn and stuffed for her by Aashi. She is rocking and holding it and looking out over our garden, its careful lawn and tidy beds.

I sit with her in the window, and look out at all the pretence.

'Mummy,' she says. 'Daddy hurt you.'

It is so sudden, and not a question, but a simple statement.

She follows it with another: 'And now he's dead.' As if the one thing led, quite naturally, to the other.

My daughter knows something. The realisation is cold and heavy. If they find this out, my daughter and I will come apart completely.

'I should like to go Home,' she says, offering the solution.

Two, three seconds. And then I nod, once.

Chapter Thirty-Seven

Just now as I looked out of the window, I saw a big, perfectly round, red sun sinking behind the trees. I have told him to give you my love when he sees you in a few minutes.

One of the children of the Raj, in a letter to her mother in India

I remember the 'Return Home' clearly. Perhaps remember is the wrong word. I bear the shock of it as a fault line, just as a ripped continent bears the scars of a devastating earthquake that has islanded one part from the other and broken everything between. In my house, poised above Bay's Mouth, I often sit and feel the scarred ridges of these memories, tracing the break of them again, again.

The light at Home is dull and flat like when, in high wind, the dust in Kharagpur blows out the sun. I sit on my own, in the empty classroom. All the other children have gone to the dormitory but I stay, to read Mummy's long, long letter in which she says, again and again, nothing. The Colchester School is like a cage. The lights make an echoing sound. Thrum. Like when a person can't make up their mind, and you can hear their thoughts working. Past the lights there's only the clipping of heels up and down the corridors, the teacher's high voice next door, and feeling the years and years of children in that classroom, imagining their small writing scratching across lined paper in lines and lines of black, empty words. I am unloved again, in the school. One of the unloved ones.

They say it is a good school. They say we are still special, although there are only the old nuns to teach us and we are made to fold our own clothes, and even to put them in the washing pile ourselves. I am shown how to change my bed, and how to do my own hair each morning. The nun, as she shows me, tugs and pulls at my hair. 'Fearful idleness,' she mutters, twice, under her breath. By which she means that Mummy and I and the other society ladies, in Kharagpur and Calcutta and Darjeeling and all the other proper places in India, are lazy.

In her letter, Mummy says one thing of note. She says Grandpa will come to see me. Grandpa. This sounds as if I might belong to him now.

To begin with I am unkempt. The nun scowls when she sees me.

'Magda,' she says, 'you have become accustomed to an un-natural level of service, and must learn to stand on your own two feet.'

She means to survive without servants. But without Anwar and Madan, I am like a person who has no coat on in winter.

I learn slow as a snail, until the other children begin to

laugh at me. Then I am quick as a flash, for their mean words are like whips.

They call me Maharaja. They are stupid and do not know that a Maharaja is a boy and that I, if I am anything here, am a Maharani.

I wish there were other Indian children in my school – British Indian children, that is. But they are gone to another school which is even more expensive. Mummy said, in her letter, that we must be thrifty now Daddy is dead. She didn't send me to the original school, the one Daddy had reserved, but to this one, because we must be thrifty.

One day the girls have an idea that because I was born in India, I must smell, and after that they hold their noses at me. I ignore them. I imagine they are simply servants, to ignore. I imagine they are a different kind of person, untouchable, and so not to be taken into account.

It is several weeks of this before I make my first friend. She is called Hilda and is very ugly. She wears a thing called a brace on her teeth. It is a metal invention which, one day, will give her a beautiful smile but, at the moment, makes her mouth all black and shiny. She smiles at me as I cross the small yard towards her. She scratches her elbow, and smiles her smile, metal and kind. I imagine that she is half machine.

She agrees that we may play hopscotch in the correct way, and listens to my rules. We begin to play. Jumping in the correct way. Hop, skip, hop and land. I win, and we are friends. Hilda is dull. But she is someone at least. I tell her about India, about the servants, but I don't tell her about Papa, about Aashi and Raja, for Mummy said I must keep my mouth closed like a zip or It. Will. Be. Frightful.

Sometimes I sit in class, and imagine that the Indian sun is high above the fields outside, making them yellow like our dry lawn in Kharagpur – which Anwar said was grass with turmeric. That was his Indian joke. He said he was also with turmeric, and that was why he was so much more spiced-looking than me. 'You, little Memsahib,' he said, 'are all sour milk.' And he laughed, and patted me on the head.

I imagine all kinds of bright birds in the skies here, as in India, and then realise I never knew the names of any of them, any of those birds. Instead I learned the ones here. The black-bird. The blue tit. The owl.

Sister Latham says that I am *nostalgic*.

'You are terribly quiet, child. What do you think of?' she asks me one day when we are darning our socks together. Each week one girl goes to help the sister with her darning.

'Of India,' I say.

She nods. 'That's understandable,' she says. 'It has been your home.'

This is a strange, stupid thing to say. I think of Mother, in a corner of the sitting room, like a rabbit in its burrow. She is scowling over her lace, her belly swelling and then returning to flat over weeks and months and years. She was certain-ly not at Home. But then I think of Anwar. I think of the long, soft pleats of Aashi's sari, and I wonder if Sister Latham is right.

It is Sunday, and I am led to him, in the hallway of the school, and he wears trousers that are so old-fashioned they make the other girls laugh. How will they believe me, seeing him, that I am truly as grand as can be? How will they ever believe what I was in India? My teacher, with her high forehead, and her tight bun, tells me not to be conceited, and makes me sit with him in the school library.

'How is your schooling, love?' he asks me again, looking up at the tall, crooked shelves of books.

'It is well.'

'Do you like English best, or Mathematics?'

'I like Chemistry,' I say, for we have started to do it, and it is terrific and all magic.

He whistles in a terribly common fashion, his rucked face closing in on itself as he laughs, the laugh running through me with a slow shudder.

'Well,' he says, 'girls nowadays, they can do what they like. I should think that rich mother of yours could pay for your tuition if you'd like to be a chemist.'

That rich mother of yours.

It is the head teacher who makes the announcement one day after morning assembly, when the older children are preparing to marshal the younger ones out of the hall.

'Remain seated, girls,' she says. 'I have an important announcement to make.'

A general impatience rustles through the school. The girls shift on their chairs, play with the holes in their tights, scratch at the seats in front of them, send Chinese whispers ricocheting along the rows, stare at the ceiling, wriggle.

'We are at war,' she says, quietly.

I remember how her words dropped onto us, one by one,

and made a cold stillness. Faces froze, clothes emptied, hands stilled, hearts solidified. The word 'war' closed around my spine.

War? What did it really mean?

Chapter Thirty-Eight

Most people at one time or other of their lives get a feeling that they must kill themselves; as a rule they get over it in a day or two, and find that it comes from nothing worse than an attack of indigestion, bad liver or influenza . . .
How Girls Can Help to Build up the Empire:
The Handbook for Girl Guides,
Miss Baden-Powell and Sir R. Baden Powell

Bay's Mouth's doing a bloody brilliant job of representing this country, just not in the way it used to. Along the seafront there's rubbish blowing about, and black bags that haven't been collected on the promenade. The council's not taking as much care of the place these days. No money. No one has any money. It's not just Dad. Walking down here, we passed three newly closed shops.

Ewan's doctor's surgery is in one of the old B&Bs on the seafront, so while he's there, I sit on a bench on the promenade and watch the wind turbines turning like cogs, measuring out the time smoothly in their slow whirl as if there's nothing really changing and time just moves round and round, not forwards towards the time when I'll be due and there'll be a baby to push out and, somehow, to look after.

Two guys come out of one of the pubs on the seafront, shouting and shoving at each other. They fight on the ground for a while. No one comes to pull them apart. The smaller one manages to get away, and scarpers off round the corner into Bay's Mouth proper. The other man stands up, still looking angry. Lately you can feel it everywhere. Everyone's so pissed off. Angry and skint.

Still, when Ewan comes out, his smile feels like coming to land.

He grabs my hand.

'Let's walk, Su.'

We pace side by side against the wind. He has to shorten his stride a bit to match mine. The air rushes past and through us, clean and uncomplicated, although my body, against the wind, is still all mixed up. The sickness went for a while, and then it came back.

We walk along the promenade and onto the pier before Ewan says much. The slatted walkway passes under my feet like an old film reel. Looking down through the slats you can see the sea swill back and forth.

'He says it's PTSD, Su.'

I nod. We both knew that already.

'He's given me some pills and referred me. Says I'll be on a different list because of the army.'

I nod, and keep walking, pacing it out, this pier, three slats to each step. I don't say anything about what Darren told me. That *none of that shit works*.

At the end of the pier, the small pavilion's closed. We lean against the railings. The horizon's not saying anything.

'He says we get better, Su,' turning to me. 'He says we can crack this.'

The word 'crack' sounds.

'Course we can,' I say. But we're quiet then, both looking out to the unsteady sea, listening to the wash and wash of it.

Dad calls the next day with a weak, broken voice which carries the inevitable news that, 'The bailiffs are coming.'

They're going to ransack Mum's home. They'll take her furniture, her mod cons, the TV, everything.

'We have to get her stuff out of here,' he says.

Her stuff is her jewellery, her shrine, the photographs.

'We'll come round with some boxes,' I say, after a silence. 'We can store stuff at Ewan's for the minute.' Although where, I don't know. Ewan and I already manoeuvre around each other in his tiny flat like two climbers passing on a ledge. There's not really room for anything else on our ledge, but . . .

'You can stay here too,' I say.

There's a silence.

'You'll *have* to,' I say.

'I can get a room somewhere.'

'How?'

'I mean in a hostel,' he says. 'I called the council. They have a system . . . for people like me.'

'For god's sake, Dad. You're not homeless. You're coming here.'

But he doesn't answer.

When I tell Ewan, he bites his lip, asks for Dad's mobile number and calls him himself. I listen in from the kitchen as he speaks on the phone.

'Look,' he says, 'I know we've had our differences. But you're family. We're all family now.'

There's a silence. A sigh. And a couple of seconds later, Ewan comes through.

'What did he say?'

'Not much.'

At the door, two days later, his small suitcase in his hand, Dad looks old, and very alone.

'Can I come in?' he asks, when I look at the case.

I move aside to let him pass into the kitchen, where Ewan's filling the kettle. This is between them.

'Listen, s—' Dad starts.

'Don't,' says Ewan. 'Don't worry about any of it. Just put your stuff there. We'll make a bed up in the lounge.'

I do what Magda suggests, get my head down and start on a piece for the module Ewan and I take together. Ewan doesn't seem to be doing his. I don't ask. College is the least of his worries at the moment.

Ewan's not got broadband in the flat but I buy enough data on my phone for the research, and Leah lends me her laptop, so I get a lot of it written over the weekend. But when I look at it for any length of time, the writing feels unfamiliar again, like my body as it changes and changes with the baby. I go over the same paragraph in the article about twenty times, and it gets shorter and shorter until there's almost nothing on the page.

Dad, who's nervous about being here, and feels guilty, is in permanent, full-on butler mode; he spends his whole time trying to fix everything, clean everything. It's helpful, and it's great that the place shines like the bloody British Hotel when Mum was in charge, but it's a false shine. It doesn't feel like our place any more. Ewan seems to feel penned in by Dad. He's got a nervous tick with his leg; as he sits at the table, his heel bounces against the floor. I can feel how he's just balancing on his nerves, trying not to let any of it show.

'Shall I mend that cooker?' asks Dad, about a week in, pointing at the oven door, which has been hanging off at an angle for yonks. 'I can give it a good clean out tomorrow too.'

Ewan dives out of the room.

Later, when Ewan turns out the light, I lie in the dark listening to the sound of his breathing, and past it, Dad's steady snore in the lounge, marking time to the night. And I wonder, where on earth will we put *you*?

'Babies don't take up much space,' Leah said doubtfully yesterday, on the phone.

I looked at my swelling belly. Could have fooled me.

Despite the sedatives he's been prescribed, the flat, in the build-up to Ewan's psych assessment, is like a pressure cooker. It's like Ewan's charged. He practically gives off static, jumping with sudden movements or noises. The air crackles with it.

'Is he always like this?' snaps Dad when Ewan leaves the kitchen one day.

'He's having a bad week, Dad.'

I'm washing the dishes, my hands swilling in the hot water up to the wrists so that the sleeves of my jumper wick up the suds.

'Why? Aren't you? Aren't I? Isn't everyone having a bad week?' he says, putting the plate he's been drying away in the cupboard and shutting the door on it quick and hard.

'Oh for god's sake, Dad!' I splash a washed mug down in the water, and whirl round.

There's a long silence. I'm livid with him, and he's staring at me. The kitchen's very small and very bright.

We stand in silence. I take a deep breath. Two. I sit down slowly.

Then, the air's thin as I say it. The thing I've not wanted him to know:

'Ewan's got post-traumatic stress, Dad, from the army.'

Dad's looking at me. 'How long's he been like this?' he says, sitting down too.

'Two years, I don't know.'

Dad sits back. Inhales sharply. Exhales. Then, 'He's got symptoms?'

'Bad dreams. He sleepwalks. These sudden intense feelings from nowhere.' My throat is too full as I reel it all off, all the out-of-place feelings that come over him like storms in summer.

'You say he walks in his sleep?' says Dad.

'Only once or twice. It's more the hallucinations that are a problem.'

'Hallucinations?' Dad's voice is a cliff edge.

'Sort of; half-hallucinations. He'll think for a second he's seen something. Heard something. Smells. Blood. Gunshots. Stuff from the army.'

Some of the hurt Ewan's seen forces itself into the kitchen.

I look out of the window, to where between two buildings you can just see the edge of the big wheel on the seafront. I think it then, that his hallucinations are the dark, bleeding negative of the perfect British picture we all try to make in Bay's Mouth. Ewan just can't stop seeing it for what it is. Soon, if things keep getting worse in this country, we're all going to fucking see it that way too.

'He tells you?' Dad's voice is level now, under control.

'Not really. He can't really talk about it.'

We sit in silence.

After a long while, Dad gets up, and switches on the kettle.

'Yet,' he says. 'He can't talk about it yet.'

The next day Dad cooks, a new recipe: Thai curry with heaps of ginger and chilli. He doesn't put any music on, but he does cook. Just as we're finishing our plates, our eyes watering from the heat, he says this:

'My uncle came back from the war with shell shock.'

There's a silence. Ewan and Dad look at each other. Dad smiles a tight, sad smile.

'The war?' says Ewan, his pupils dilating slightly just at the word.

'Second World War,' nods Dad. 'He was a soldier. He came back to Kolkata pretty damaged. Had nerve damage in his right hand, but the worst was his mind. There weren't the treatments available then. You just went home and waited for it to go away. If it was bad enough they gave you sedatives.'

Ewan's staring at Dad, as if he's seeing him for the very first time.

'A lot of people in Bengal were sick with that kind of thing, after the war; Partition, and all that stuff.' Dad's lips close, grimly. 'You get yourself sorted out, Ewan. There are ways and means here, now.'

Later in bed, whispering so that Dad can't hear through the partition wall, Ewan says, 'I'd forgotten Indian soldiers were in the British army during the war.'

I nod. All I know about Dad's uncle is that he was ill, and that Dad always goes quiet whenever he's mentioned. He died when Dad was young. Dad kept a photograph of him tucked away in a drawer. A formal picture in his army clothes, poised and stiff for the camera, a far-off look in his eye as he fades away from us.

Ewan comes home from the assessment looking like empty clothes.

'How was it?' I ask him in the kitchen, my voice a bit too high and tight.

He stands, leaning against the sink, a half-felled tree.

'Intense.'

Intense. One of those words that's had too many airings to mean anything any more. It falls apart, blank.

'Is she nice?'

'He.'

'Is he?'

'I don't know,' he says, shrugging. 'I can't really tell. Says there's a couple of options. This thing called EMDR, which sounds fucking weird, or trauma CBT, which sounds a bit more normal.'

'Well, did it help?' I sound desperate. I feel fucking desper-ate. He raises a glass of water to his mouth, his hand shaking.

'Maybe. Maybe a bit.'

Chapter Thirty-Nine

Oh housebuilder! Now you are seen.

Siddhārtha Gautama

She left with Mrs Greenson. Her small case, and Mrs Greenson's dark, heavy one heaped into the boot of the car, and
then her climbing into the back seat, a pallid, shadowy
version of the child she used to be. I ran to her and bent
to the window, wanted to reach a hand in, but she had re-
ceded so far from me over the preceding weeks and months
and years of her life that she shrank now, from my touch,
and felt a thousand miles away already, withdrawn, turned
inwards.

'Be a good girl,' I said, more sternly than I intended. 'Don't
give the school any trouble.'

'No, Mother,' she said, with a kind of cold meekness.

'I'll follow as soon as I can.' Though they told me in no
uncertain terms that I should stay until someone is charged
at least.

'Yes, Mother.'

The engine started. That was it. I watched the black car as

it kicked up dust along the road, and finally turned into India and away. I was hollow, watching.

The Raj is unsettled. There are constant reports of war at Home, and I don't know whether it's that that fills me with this dread – the threat of another war trampling across Europe and towards Home – or whether it's the other reports, perhaps more insidiously worrying, and at any rate closer to us in this provisional world of ours, of native anger and constitutional reform. Benedict's murder, despite everything, is unsettling, even to Mrs Burrows, who looks at me with hooded eyes across the hedge, and when I look back, continues on her business with her small cutters saying nothing, acknowledging nothing.

The main thing, is freedom. We have few sources of news, and can't even ask the servants, as it would be horrid to discuss politics with them. Part of me hopes for it. The demise of Benedict's world. Although I know I'll sink with it like a stone.

When I asked Mrs Burrows what she knew of the political situation she simply said, 'Best not to think of it, my dear,' and carried on pruning her rose bush, muttering, 'Temporary. Temporary,' to herself.

But I'm not sure I believe her. The radio, which I listen to in my room, plays the anthem brittlely these days. And I can detect a hint of doubt creeping into the voices of almost all the British officers interviewed about The Situation.

There are food shortages, that much is clear. Even Anwar is unable to procure sufficient food from the market, and we must use the army supply lines, which are, as at Home, rationed ever more tightly.

They arrest Anwar first, when he is serving the tea. He sets down the pot, carefully, and offers his hands to be cuffed, but they still manhandle him carelessly out to the car. I beg them not to take him. It wasn't Anwar. It wasn't.

It takes Mrs Greenson three wretched days to come forward, and to acknowledge that he was waxing the floor under her supervision when the shots were heard. They take three further days to release him. I get the impression that they are disappointed. Or perhaps guilty. When Anwar returns half starved and with bruises around his eyes, I know the reason for the guilt. The Raj doesn't like its brutality witnessed. It is unseemly and coarse.

Early on Tuesday morning, two men come to arrest me. I am so shocked when it happens, so unprepared for the fact that there is no one, no one to defend me, not even a cruel and pompous husband, that I say nothing in my own defence. We are halfway to the army car before I begin screaming, 'It wasn't me! It wasn't me!' I'm drawn out between their hands like a hung garment flung about in the wind. 'It wasn't me!'

I hated him so. Perhaps I walked into his study. I imagine him, bent over the desk, his head ready for the shot. I imagine the punch-back of the gun's recoil. I imagine that I made that perfect hole in his mind and the wood panelling.

But I didn't. I am only Evelyn Roberts.

Chapter Forty

If you hear a policeman's whistle sounding, run and offer to help him; it is your duty, as he is a king's servant.

How Girls Can Help to Build up the Empire:
The Handbook for Girl Guides, Miss
Baden-Powell and Sir R. Baden-Powell

War, I learn, means that Mother cannot come. The days and weeks and months take India slowly further away. The other girls in the school begin to call me pale, and I am always cold. I miss my own big, red sun. We celebrate Christmas with turkey. The big bird, sitting on the long school table. We are each afforded a tiny portion of meat. One New Year passes, and we begin to head towards the next, and although I am accustomed now, to making my bed, washing and dressing, doing my own hair, even washing my own cutlery and darning socks, I always know: this isn't my life. This isn't my life. I try to tell the girls how grand I truly was, but only Hilda listens. The other girls look at me and whisper and giggle from behind their hands. Maharaja. Maharaja. Maharaja.

The Maharani writes long, angry letters to her mother. *Why?* she rages. *Why? Why? Why?*

Why have you left me here? You never loved me, you never loved me.

The girls begin to speak of boys. How they like so-and-so, who they have seen at church, how they would like to marry. I do not want to marry. Not ever. Why? To be like Mummy and Daddy? In a magazine Sister Latham gives me, I read about a woman who has become a great scientist.

'Women can do great things,' says Sister Latham.

I should like to be like that woman. A great scientist, with no need for a Home.

One day, Sister Latham comes into class and requests that I come to the office with her. The office is a tall room, with small high windows, and a big desk.

'Magda,' she says, from the other side of the desk, 'I have something to tell you. It is something a little frightening, but I want you to be brave.'

I nod. For I have been brave a long time now, without Anwar and without Aashi.

'Your mother is to appear in court, for the murder of your father.'

I look at her.

'Are you all right, child?' she asks. There is no air in the room and I cannot breathe.

Still, I do not say, about Raja.

★

The next time he comes, this man they call my grandfather, I ask if we might walk around the grounds, away from the other girls and their happy, respectable families. That is when he begins to tell me about mother's life before, before India. He is almost crying.

Mother was kind. She was a teacher. Mother was soft with her pupils. Mother didn't care for nice homes, for money or frocks.

In his stories he makes a person for me to like. It hurts. Mummy was never really soft with me. She was not really kind.

It hurts to hear the stories. I refuse to leave the dormitory to meet him the next time he comes, and the time after, although Sister Latham says I should because he is my grandfather.

Eventually he stops, and there is no one, only school and all this cold Home. And Mother's letters, all blacked out by the censor, which say nothing in reply to all my fear. There is only the chemistry book from the library, and the chemicals it speaks of. Helium, nitrogen, gold. I'm a witch with a book of spells.

War, it seems at first, means simply that we will be eating fewer eggs, and almost no sweets. I write to Mother to complain, hoping that she might respond, and I might feel a little better, but as is usual lately I get nothing back.

Then they make us hang pitch-black curtains in the dormitory, and stop up the classroom windows with cardboard each evening.

This is because of German bombers who circle above the school all night, silently like hawks. If you go outside during the night-time, one of them will pick you off and blow you to smithereens.

I don't fully learn that war means an emptying out, until they start leaving. School slowly empties. The girls are taken to the country to stay with family, one by one.

Sister Latham asks me one, two, four times if I will go to Bay's Mouth. To *them*, my mother's family. To him with his dirty, old clothes. But I shan't go. I shan't. Not to that strange, common man with the hands that are so big and so rough from what he called the ironworks.

Iron. Formula 'Fe', it says in my book of chemistry. *Latin name Ferrum. By mass the most common element on earth.*

At the end there are only two of us. Hilda, who as well as having bad teeth is an orphan, and I.

To look after us there is one elderly nun, Sister Josephine, who mainly sleeps.

We spend several weeks like that. It is very dull.

Hilda has an obsession with mice and is convinced we will all be eaten alive now the other children are gone. She has become very quiet. She is paler and paler and her legs turn to blotches at the slightest cold. I know several card games, which comes in handy since even I run out of imaginary things to tell us after a while and Sister Josephine doesn't really teach us, but sets us endless exercises from the book, telling us to work them out for ourselves.

'You're lucky to have a family to go to at all,' says Hilda as we sit, alone on the tarmac of the schoolyard. 'I'm going to a Barnardo's home in Scotland.'

'You haven't seen my grandfather,' I say to her. 'He's a brute. A savage. I'll be living like an animal.'

Hilda slaps me across the face.

'You're an idiot,' she says.

I carry that slap still. Burning and honest on my cheek.

I only hold out in my refusal to go to the people they call my family until Sister Josephine is taken ill. One day she simply does not wake. She is teaching us Geography, or rather she is sitting at the desk dozing and making her creaking breathing sounds while we attempt exercises from the book.

We have finished the exercises and she still doesn't wake.

Eventually Hilda says it.

'Excuse me, Sister Josephine,' she says. 'Can I go to the bathroom?'

There's no response.

'Sister Josephine?' she says.

Sister Josephine is very quiet and very still and very pale. Her body looks heavier and more solid now, as if it belongs to the ground, as if it has no light things in it, no liquids swarming, no breath, no thoughts to lift it from the chair.

Hilda and I prod her and poke her. We shake her. We shake her again. We shout in her ears. Then we're silent. We don't know what to do. It is like Papa, but there's no blood.

'She's dead.' It's quiet Hilda who says it. 'We had better phone a doctor,' she says, and Hilda is the one who goes to the office, who dials the number, who speaks to the operator and then to the police, the doctor.

I am frozen, thinking of that day, and Papa.

When they come, I tell them. I tell them everything.

316

Chapter Forty-One

Ni wnawn, wrth ffoi am byth o'n ffwdan ffôl,
Ond llithro i'r llonyddwch mawr yn ôl.

'Dychwelyd', T.H. Parry-Williams

Fleeing forever all our fuss and foolery,
Into the stillness our selves slip surely.

'Return', T.H. Parry-Williams

At Kharagpur police station there are two white officers, and one Anglo-Indian secretary, who looks at me, despite himself, with curiosity.

'I didn't do it,' I say, to him, to them, to the Raj. I think frantically of Magda.

'Tell us about the day your husband was killed.' It is the large man, with the small eyes.

We sit on opposite sides of a substantial wooden table, their hands hovering above their notes, mine still in my lap so that the table hides their shaking from view.

I pause, take a deep breath. There must be no room for doubt.

'Nothing,' I say. 'I was doing nothing, only sitting, and looking out of the window. Then I heard a shot. And when I went in, there he was.

'Were you shocked?'

'Of course.'

'Only Mrs . . .' he consults his papers, 'Mrs Greenson says that you were mainly concerned with the mess.'

'I am fairly particular,' I say.

They look at each other.

'He was killed with his own gun,' says the large one again. 'Army issue.'

I stare at them. 'Really?' I say.

They nod.

'You knew he had a gun?' asks the small one. He has a mean little moustache, which he plays with in a way I find unsavoury.

'Of course.' It was the quiet threat. The ultimate control. Benedict always gave off a lethal assurance. That was his power. His power sat in the drawer on the right-hand side of his desk.

'You knew where he kept it?'

I nod.

'Did you love your husband?' The moustache quivers as he leans forward.

I'm silent. I won't lie. I'll never lie about him again. 'He was a brute,' I say.

They look at each other.

He sits back again. 'He beat you?'

I silently acquiesce. Though the worst wasn't the beating.

'Did you kill him?' He leans towards me again, conspiratorial and preying.

I want to be able to answer yes. Yes. I killed him. I killed him.

But, 'No,' I say quietly. 'It wasn't me.'

The other one springs up. 'You expect us to believe that?' Fierce and booming.

'Yes,' I say. 'Yes, I do.'

They try another tack.

'Did he have many enemies?' The moustache is black, wired and slightly curved at its corners.

'Oh, plenty. He was that kind of man.'

'Servants?'

'They fear him.' Then I correct myself. 'Feared.' The past tense is delicious, even here.

The big one takes a deep breath in, inflating himself, ready to launch a question. 'And he didn't lock the drawer where the gun was kept?'

'No.' I say this steadily.

The fact seems surprising now. Why not? Why wouldn't he lock up a lethal weapon in a place where we fear mutiny daily? But perhaps *because* we fear mutiny daily. Benedict was always ready to draw it out, aim it, fire.

'Who else knew where the gun was kept?'

I think about it.

'No one,' I say.

Magda.

They nod. 'Madam, we're arresting you for the murder of your husband . . .' They begin their refrain. I listen to them numbly till the end.

Then I say, 'Can I possibly have some tea?'

They bring in tea and little sandwiches for the long wait.

★

That night they keep me in a small cell set apart from the ones where the Indians are. I barely sleep, I think, for there is such a din of coughing and so many mosquitoes. In the darkness I find myself unsure of who I am.

I feel perhaps I have gone native.

There is the sensation of my skin darkening overnight, and my mouth swelling with odd syllables which, the few times I do doze off, wake me as they spring from my lips unintelligibly. It is a great relief, when dawn comes, to see that I am still an Englishwoman.

I am released mid-morning. I get a talking-to by an army officer. Very grand he is too.

'We're releasing you . . . It just won't do.'

'Pardon?'

'We can't keep you here with the other prisoners. And this kind of thing causes such a furore. *Sahib killed by his wife.* Good lord. It won't do. Not this week. We have enough trouble,' he says gloomily. 'We'll put it on hold until things are more secure.'

He means they'll put charging me on hold, to save face, at least temporarily. Is this it? The best the Empire can do?

'But you still think I did it?'

He shrugs.

I get up. 'So I'm free to leave?' I say, haughtily.

'Yes, madam,' he says. 'But stay in Kharagpur.'

'Thank you, sir,' I say. And walk out into the heat and doubt.

★

Mr Burrows – who claims he always believed the whole thing to be 'poppycock' – says I 'should not under any circumstances live alone with the male servants'.

He says it sternly. 'Not in India,' he says. 'It won't do. Go and live with one of your friends.'

But I have given up on doing what is proper, and besides, Anwar and Madan, who I believe are also convinced of my innocence, are perfectly impeccable and loyal. I trust them more than I trust the house-proud vultures of the Raj.

The talk of war has become frequent, and indeed never lets up. Hitler is up to no good.

Talk of Free India raises the little hairs on our necks too. The main commercial ships are stopped. Magda feels infinitely far and I am very lonely, especially since no one ever drops round with a visiting card any more. I begin with a slight cough.

As the war progresses it becomes more common for other homes of the Raj to be without their man. Men are called up to command the Indian regiments, to prepare to go to Europe. Though a certain suspicion hangs over my situation, and I feel the cold shoulder of the other memsahibs rather intensely, I am, at least on the face of it, not in such an unusual position these days.

In the absence of some of our best men, the women are called to join more committees. Committees on neighbourhood order, examination boards, music schedules, committees on refuse collection and drainage, and even highway patrols. This is all terribly dull.

It is Mrs Burrows who asks me. We are clearing up at the town hall, after one of her pageants. I am stacking chairs, and she is clipping off the old dead flowers from the displays we have had made up. Things have been quiet recently, on the Independence front, and we are all beginning to hope for a return to normality after the war.

'The missionaries who taught at St Mary's have gone Home,' she says.

St Mary's is the church's mission school, which takes in little brown children and teaches them the rudiments of English and mathematics. They've done a fine job at turning out little Indian parodies of us for donkey's years.

'Really?' I'm surprised. They always seemed such a determined lot. Dogged in pursuit of Indian souls.

'Yes,' she said. 'Quite suddenly. The church has called them back to England as the war's likely to get worse.' She stands back to observe the flower display she's been pruning, frowns at it.

Things must be very bad.

'So,' she says, lifting the scissors to a wilting flowerhead, 'they're short a schoolmistress, several actually, and we wondered if you might . . .'

'Me?' I put my stack of chairs down, in surprise.

'You've taught before,' she says, reasonably, turning to me now.

Have I? That soft schoolteacher and this hardened lady are an ocean and a world apart.

'They'll provide materials. Slates and pencils and second-hand books from St Thomas's, and you can teach them English.'

'English?'

'Yes, they have great need of it.'

'What for?'

'Commerce, advancement . . .'

'Independence?'

'For god's sake, Evelyn. There's no need to be so bitter.'

She picks up two vases and carries them back to the sill, perfectly arranged, undying.

'Will you do it?' Her heels clipping against the parquet floor.

Walking towards the classroom on my first day, the blood throbs in my ears. The whole undertaking seems fantastical. That I should teach, and they might learn. It is only an hour, I say to myself, only an hour this first day.

I open the door. They're sitting on the floor in neat rows. The crackle of their chatter falls silent as I walk in. Their faces turn upwards like so many brown daisies. They're afraid. A cane is hung on the wall, at the ready. And perhaps I will be more that kind of teacher now.

'Stand,' I say. And they stand.

'The alphabet,' I say. And we begin together, our ABCs. After an hour of quiet copying and slow, accented reading aloud, we are done for today. They file out of the classroom, like shuffling corpses, but then break into a run. Glad to be away from me.

In the doorway I stand. My heart is too big.

The anticipation I feel, before the next lesson, seems dangerous. I try to keep it in its place, by meticulous housekeeping, but it won't stay. Somewhere I am coming alive again, and it terrifies me, thrills me and breaks me. Every bent head in my classroom is hers, each face focused in concentration, each set of dreamy eyes catching at a bird as it flits past the window, each high, piping voice is hers and hers and hers, and all this too late. I am very fierce with the children. I treat them as soldiers.

It is to be short-lived. The next day they come, with a date for court. It is to be public very shortly. I try to prepare myself, contract a lawyer. But I have no heart to fight it. For what if it was Magda who killed him? What if I should incriminate her? The thought of it sinks in me like a cold stone.

Within just two weeks, the crown's officers come round, and say that the case has been completely dropped. I am no longer a suspect.

'Why?' I say.

'Your daughter has given a statement,' they say.

My heart stops. Oh, Magda.

'She says it was her friend. She saw him go into the house immediately before.' The officer is blasé.

'Her friend?'

'Raja?' He reads the name from his notebook.

I stare at him.

'She didn't seem to know where the family had gone,' he said. 'They left Kharagpur after the incident.'

The incident.

I think of Aashi, his mother who I called a bitch.

I owe them quite a debt.

I'm silent.

'We'll keep looking for him,' he says. 'But there are so many people on the move these days.' He means the Mohammedans who have begun to relocate to the east.

That night I fall asleep on my bed fully clothed and wake under a thin sheet, placed over me by one of the servants.

Anwar brings in eggs, but I am unable to eat; for I think of her, Aashi, and her small son whose right to milk we stole.

I can't work out if Magda would be safer here, with all these freedom fighters about, or in Britain, so close to the Führer. Then we hear that some of the ships bringing the children of the Raj back to India are torpedoed, and the children returned to land in pieces, and it is clear that it must be me, not her, who will travel.

It's impossible to book a passage home for several weeks, for there are so few ships going because of the war. Father writes to say I should not come anyway. But I must see Magda. I must be with her. Then the passage I do book is cancelled. The next available is in a few months' time. India's fronds are all around me, tendrils gripping my shoulders, my ribs, my hips. My chest is heavy with catarrh that does not shift. Letters get through only occasionally, and then with half their thoughts blacked out by the censors. The blacked-out portions are like words you struggle to recall, places that remain shadowy in your memory, people whose faces only vaguely ring a bell. They make Home seem further still, and more impossible. It seems no part of me is now able to reach that place in Bay's Mouth where she, Mother, and Father, will one day sit with me again, around one table, and where I will not be cruel to the children I teach.

Finally, one day, as they are reciting their alphabet, fear in their eyes, I find the room is beginning to swirl. I wake up with one of the other teachers holding something sharp-smelling to my nose. Anwar takes me home and I take to my bed.

My body is beleaguered by feverish thoughts.

After that I give up all thought of teaching. My vocation has slipped away from me again. Of course it has.

I take to my bed after lunch each day, and sometimes don't emerge again until the evening.

Finally, the news comes: I am to travel on the fifteenth of next month. Home.

My body, in these liminal times, is drastically weakened, and I am frequently feverish. When I think of my parents' small house in Bay's Mouth, I cannot imagine what choreography of my parts could possibly make me fit back in.

Every day I spend a portion of the morning and afternoon in bed. I can eat only boiled rice. I am like their darling Gandhi, who they say languishes in a jail, fasting. I grow thinner, in parts, but other parts of me seem to swell. My ankles. My wrists. My body tries to change shape to fit into its new cast.

Magda's last letter tells me little news of her life, only that she has been studying independently: the chemical elements. How they blend and splice. How you can take salt from rock by submerging it and then drawing dirt from sodium chloride over a flame. That is very much what is hoped for by some fanatics for India; that the rock salt of this country might be dissolved, and then heated; so that some part of it, Mohammedan or Hindu, can rise neatly and be separated from the rest.

That's how it should happen they say, in an orderly fashion, but it isn't what I see. Last week one of the others stole Anwar's wages and though Anwar has always been the senior servant, he seemed to want no redress, and begged me not to make a scene over it. It is because he is a Mohammedan. There is talk of riots in Calcutta. Everyone has lost their composure. The women walk around in an undignified kerfuffle, whispering, 'We must leave.'

I have lost my composure too. Everything has taken on a strange yellow colour, and smells do not relate correctly to their sources. Rice, for example, smells peculiarly bitter. It is difficult to breathe. But I must pack.

Stopping for breath as I move things between my chest and my suitcase, I have a coughing fit which ends in blood.

I am one of the late ones. Our leaving, the leaving of the Raj, is executed with strict supervision by the Company, and every official I speak to seems to think I have been a little remiss in not leaving India sooner. Husbands, it seems, sent their wives home long ago. I had no one to send me, and have been languishing with my servants in our big house.

I am told there are quotas now, and so I cannot take most of the furniture. Mr Burrows is ingenious however, and instructs for most of ours to be made into packing cases so that I may keep them. Thus it is dismantled, the pieces of wood all over the sitting room, like strewn bones. At the end of our journey, the bones will be reassembled into furniture, and Home will be constructed piece by piece from the dismantled skeletons of Indian trees.

Though what I am to do with such paraphernalia at Home I don't know. Burrows says not to worry about booking a place on the usual passage for the great square cases made from our dressing tables and wardrobes, for he'll have it all put on a freight ship in a few weeks' time.

'Far cheaper, though far less salubrious for your furniture, and there may be some salt damage.' When people mention salt in India, the Raj shudders, because, ultimately, it seems that salt is what brought it to its knees.

'Still. We'll all need to watch our pennies now, Evelyn. What costs almost nothing in India will be an arm and a leg at home.' Burrows looks positively gloomy at that thought. He's one of the few who plan to stay, hoping against hope that there is a future for him here, when, quite plainly, there is not. Despite the years of dreaming of it, we are all poorly made now, for Home. We are somehow baggy and of poor design. False. I feel I should ask the deft joiners who come to remake the furniture as packing cases to remake me also. Like the furniture, I am to be taken apart, to be put back together at the other end.

I take just one servant for the journey to Bombay. Anwar, of course. He seems not himself. His hands shake as he drives, and twice I have to ask him to slow down. He was told to bring only one small bag and nothing of value because he will be coming back, but when he walked from the house to the car I could hear jangling and his clothing seemed lumpy. I feel he is also bidding Kharagpur his final farewell. We drive all the way to Bombay. The trains, even the private ones, are unsafe.

As we drive, we see reams of them, men and women, badly clothed, dragging their feet along the road towards Calcutta, clutching their emaciated children. It's like something from the Bible.

'Why don't they have any food?' I ask Anwar after a long silence.

'The rice . . .'Anwar says, and trails off. He is watching them too, a shocked expression on his face. 'So bad. So bad,' he mutters. And something about Allah, which has always been forbidden in our house.

The car comes to a halt. There is something on the road. It is a bundle of rags. Why doesn't Anwar just drive over it?

'Excuse me, ma'am,' he says to me, and opens his car door to get out. Several children are instantly at the door, their small, scabbed hands begging for food, money, voices like chirruping birds saying 'rice', 'food', and 'please'.

'Anwar!' I shout. I am afraid. Their hunger seeps through the open door.

But Anwar is lifting the bundle. He lifts it tenderly, and by the way he carries it, I see that it is a dead thing. Anwar walks to the side of the road, and bends to set it down, gently, in the dust. It is not as heavy as a grown one. It is not as big as an adult.

When Anwar sits again in the car, and the engine begins again, he is not the same reliable Anwar. His shoulders tremble with the engine.

We are silent the rest of the way.

At the port, there is a dining room, and scones.

When they call us to board, I take leave of him.

'Goodbye, Anwar,' I say, and am about to turn without ceremony, but I stop. I face him, and, for perhaps the first time, I look him full in the face. 'Good luck,' I say, my voice newly small against this India.

We are suddenly very heavy.

When our ship is moving away from land, moving out

steamily into the jewel sea on its cerulean journey, I turn back to watch the people milling on the dock. Anwar is there, in his white kurta.

He stands, unacknowledged and grey-haired, his back rounded, a small bag of possessions at his feet. When I close my eyes against it, he remains there, standing, his hands empty.

The cabin boy I am assigned is looking at me with trepidation, for I am beginning to fade, my legs uncertain, and a weight here, at my chest.

'Take it in,' I snap at him, motioning to my case. 'Just take it in and put it on my bed.'

It is to be only three weeks. Three weeks and a world until Home.

That I should fit back in, ever. The thought of seeing them again, my mother, my father. My body weakens against the impossibility. I think of her, with strange terror: Helen.

Who should I be? Who should I be now at Home?

My body is uncertain.

I sit, for hours on end in my cabin, sipping the bad tea brought by the boy, whose name I cannot ask, whose eyes I cannot look into. I am so hot I am cold, and so cold that I burn. My body is restless and unrested, has forgotten to abide by ordinary hours. I am sleepless, I am heavy and yet live-wired. I only go outside late at night, when there is no one else, to watch, through the cold sear of my fever, the slow cold play of the moon on the water, and the steam rising from the ship into the night as if it were a fevered body on ice as it slowly homes.

I think, each night, of Aashi.

When I return to my cabin, tonight, I take out my writing paper. I pen a confession, which I leave sealed, only to be opened in the event that they find Raja. The words done, I sleep.

It is the night, or the morning, and I have awoken coughing. I've dreamed of Benedict. His cruel hands. My lungs are aflood, their own ocean between me and Home. He smothers Home away into deep water. In the depths of my dream, Helen, sinking into the dark.

I awake again, and the sheets are wet with my sweat. Shadows move in and out of the cabin. Shadows dream across the walls.

I awake, surrounded by language.

I awake.
    'Open the window. Let her breathe some fresh air.'
    Volcanic coughing. India is breaking.

I awake.
    Aashi singing.

O troupe of little vagrants of the world leave your footprints in my words.

I awake.
    Through the window, the sound of something carrying across the sea? Church bells? A blackbird. Nightingale. Oh

smell of heather, oh clover. Oh the milk smell of my baby's soft hair.

I awake.
I awake.
I awake.

Chapter Forty-Two

Ar scáth a chéile a mhaireann na daoine.

It is in the shelter of each other that the people live.

Irish proverb

When I go to Magda on the Tuesday, she's in a bloody state, and mumbling to herself. I try to bring her round with tea. Eventually I give her a gentle slap across the cheek. That works, or I think it does.

'Impudence!' she says, looking at me furiously. And then, 'Is it you? Is it you, Aashi?'

'No, Magda. It's Susheela. It's me.'

But she doesn't seem to know me. She's crying, I think, her head in her hands. 'I'm so sorry,' she says, 'I'm so sorry, Aashi, oh Aashi.'

I sit with her, the house big and empty around us.

'It's not Aashi,' I say again, 'it's Susheela.' I reach out and squeeze her hand, feeling totally abandoned.

I'll have to phone the office.

She stops crying, and looks at me. Through the mist of

her grey eyes, something's surfacing.

'Don't,' she says. 'Don't call it in. I'll be all right. Just get me some sweet tea.'

When I come in with it, she tells me.

'I betrayed him,' she says. 'I betrayed Raja.'

When she's done with the long ache of telling it all, she sits back and her eyes close. I wheel her to the lift, and from there to the bedroom. She works with me silently to make the dangerous move between the chair and the bed.

Two days later, she's sitting up in bed, her hair in curlers, and I'm folding away her things, and telling her about Dad's debts.

'What was he thinking!'

A pale light comes in through the net curtains and seeps across her bed, an echo of the changing seasons outside.

'He wanted Mum to live, that's all,' I say. 'That can drive you pretty crazy.'

She nods quietly. 'What's he going to do?'

'He's staying with us,' I tell her, shaking out her nightdress before folding it in three.

'Good lord, but have you space?'

I shrug.

'Have you space?' she asks again.

'Not really!' I try to laugh.

'What a mess,' she says, like everyone else lately.

Then she's quiet. Tired again. Or thinking.

The next day I call in to the office to get my rota, hoping that they'll have given me lots of shifts. We need the money. But

I'm so bloody exhausted I can barely drag my body in there. On the rota I see that Magda isn't down for the next week. My chest goes tight.

'What happened?' I ask Glenda, who's tapping away at her computer. 'Did she get sick again?'

Glenda keeps typing.

'Where is she, what ward?'

'Nothing like that,' she says, finally looking up. 'Her friend's coming up this week and she asked for some time alone with her. Says the friend's a nurse so she can take care of her for a day or two. Her friend has to sign something for us to say so, mind.' She snorts at the ridiculousness of it. Over her shoulder I see she's on Facebook, a chat open on the right of the screen.

'Her friend?'

'I know,' says Glenda. 'Shocking, isn't it?'

What the hell is she up to? Up the overgrown driveway, pacing quickly, to the house. The key's in the usual place behind the flowerpots.

'Why've you cancelled the carers, Magda?' I ask her straight away, walking into the bedroom to find her propped up in bed, in her curlers again, not a hair out of place.

She looks up at me, smiles sweetly and says, 'Because I have the two of you to look after me.'

She's lost her mind.

I don't know what she means until I look at the piece of paper she hands me. In a shaky hand she's drawn a complete floor plan of the house, like an uneven chessboard. She's filled in the essentials of furniture, including the beds. Number three Victoria Drive reduced to shapes and lines. She looks proud of it, as if she's got the place under control.

It takes me a few seconds to realise the diagram's divided into two parts. Her own wing, marked 'ME', in capitals, and defined by a fierce, cross-hatched pattern, and then another part, made up of several rooms, including the kitchen, two bedrooms and the library, which she's marked 'Susheela' in small letters and covered meticulously in tiny dots.

'Just until you get yourselves sorted,' she says. 'Now go and toast us some hot cross buns.'

I'm so stunned, I do what she says without a word.

'Magda, it's so generous of you,' I say, bringing the tea and toasted buns back into the room. 'But we have the flat and anyhow there's no way they'll let me move in. They'll fire me!' I imagine the expression on Glenda's face.

'Your father can have the flat,' she says. 'And as for this terrible job . . . are you in line for maternity benefits from them?'

I shake my head. 'It's zero hours.'

Magda looks blank.

'I don't get stuff like that,' I say.

'Sharks!' she says. 'Well then, stop your panicking. We're awful work anyway,' she continues, motioning to her legs, listless in the chair. 'You don't want to be doing *this* forever.'

I don't know how to tell her what the rough kindness of it's come to mean. Old, proud Henry. Sweet Mrs Jenkins and the others. Her.

'It'll be a kind of holiday!' she says, her eyes shining. I've never seen her so excited. 'Like camping!' Underneath the pink curlers, her skin is unusually peach.

A holiday for you perhaps, I think. The twenty-four-seven of Magda's needs. I catch myself seriously considering the idea. The light in her bedroom's soft.

'No way, Magda,' I say, after a while. 'There's just no way.'
She looks cross.

'No way,' I say, again.

We drink tea in silence, her sitting up in bed in her night-dress and me on the yellow upholstered chair. I feel rooted here. It's like my belly's homing for the ground of the house. She sulks slightly, and I feel a bit sulky myself. I have to hold the silence until she knows I bloody well mean it.

'You won't tell them, will you? You'll keep coming?'

'As long as you restart the care package I will.'

She nods. I feel sorry for her suddenly, pale after all the effort she's made, and because of the disappointment.

'Susheela,' she asks me, 'tell me your full name.' And when I do, 'Spell it out for me?' taking up a notebook from beside her bed.

'Why?'

'I want it for my records. I need to make sure I keep everything in order. I tend to forget, lately, you know, who people are.'

She's never forgotten a face in her life.

But she looks at me with such a pathetic look, a different kind of Magda, vulnerable and old. I think *perhaps she is, perhaps she's losing it*. It scares me. I think of how she called me Aashi, again and again. A sad feeling rises to my throat. I try to swallow it away.

I begin to spell my name, patiently, as she writes it out with her tangling hand. She looks up afterwards, dog-tired, and waves me away. She'll need to sleep again. The sleeps are more frequent since she was in hospital. I find myself fighting back tears as I let myself out of her house. How long can we hold on to each other through all her ghosts?

Chapter Forty-Three

In these days, when we are all beginning to concern ourselves with essentials and to discard the things that do not matter, it is essential to remember these two facts:

1. What we can get is good for us.

2. A great deal of what we cannot get is quite unimportant.

Food Facts for the Kitchen Front,
author unknown

Mother is coming.

Having spent several weeks alone with Sister Latham in the echo and quiet of the school, refusing, and pointing out that we have paid fees and so I should be cared for, I am finally to go to Bay's Mouth to Grandmother and Grandfather's and to await her there.

When I arrive, at the end of my own long train ride, from Colchester, the sun is shining. I had not expected that, for the sun to shine.

My train arrives at the same time as another, smaller one, which comes in the opposite direction, carrying families for a sunny day at the seaside. Their apparel is terribly shabby, and there are no men, only women, as the fathers are away. Still, they are happy. A brass band comes onto the platform to meet them and there are several characters dressed up and doing mini pageants. The little children are absolutely agog with it all. And even I find it splendid and almost forget that I should be being met by someone. It's a long time since I've seen small children with their parents, and perhaps I have never seen them so at ease. The casual gestures of kinship between these people, the linked arms, the held hands, the pats on the head, are rather a sore sight. And there is a man, in army clothes, with strong, good shoulders. Oh, how he hoists his small son up onto his shoulders, and how the boy laughs. And there, a woman kisses her child's hair.

Aashi would stroke my hair as I fell asleep on her lap.

When I think of my mother, there are just recipes, needle-work, and a feeling of things shut away.

And yet I have chosen the one over the other. Raja will be in trouble, and Aashi will be broken-hearted.

'Magda?' It is a woman with grey hair, a round, comely figure, cheeks like red apples.

I extend my hand, but she grabs me and pulls me to her. I feel momentarily embarrassed. But when, after a few seconds, she doesn't let go, I find myself sinking into her. Her hair smells of rose soap, the same one Mother used. She holds me tight.

When she eventually lets me go, and pulls back to take a good look at me, her eyes are pooling.

She says, 'I knew it was you. He said you were the spit of her, but I hadn't imagined how much. Only . . .' she trails off, looking at me strangely, as if she suddenly realised something.

Then she grabs my arm and lifts my case in her other hand, and walks me down the platform. 'It's like having our Evie here.'

I only once heard her called Evie, by my father, I remember that he said it, and he stroked her face. Mummy winced as if his fingers were ice.

This woman, my grandmother, takes me to a bus. A bus! Which we board. The driver slings my bag into the luggage compartment. He speaks to the woman kindly, as if they were friends. A bus driver, and my grandmother. But it is nice that he smiles at me, honestly, not as a servant might. I try to smile back, though I'm out of the habit.

When the bus stops to let us off, we're in a broad street with meagre-looking red-brick houses. They are 'separates' at least, not a terrace or semi-detached. It reminds me a little, in fact, of Kharagpur, though in comparison Bay's Mouth is like a dinner gone cold.

I must lug my own suitcase to the door. Grandmother, who says I must call her Granny though I can't imagine doing so, pushes the door open and calls,

'Here we are!' into the hallway.

Upstairs, there's the sound of excited voices. A woman's, a man's, and I should think a great number of children by the din, though only two emerge, two boys with bits of chocolate all over their faces. Chocolate. I have not seen chocolate since the rationing started. I stand, silent. The house is not grand, but not shabby. It is these people. They are looking at me as if I belong to them.

'Jack and Henry, come here this instant,' says Grandmother. 'You'll have to have your faces cleaned before you can kiss your cousin.' She pats me on the shoulder. 'She's a lady, you know.' Her voice breaks. 'A real lady.'

I look at her sharply. Why is she crying?

It is only later that day, after I have begun to unpack, and after a good supper of pork chops and potatoes, that they tell me, of Mother.

Chapter Forty-Four

*. . . and they were so madly in love with the little house that they could not
bear to think they had finished it.*

Peter Pan in Kensington Gardens,

J. M. Barrie

The house is breaking into its tiny bones. It leaks dreams
everywhere.

At night, just before I fall asleep, I can see Raja. He is standing on a small dusty street in The Real India. He has no shoes.
He has a stick in his hand, and he's pointing it at something
that's behind me. I turn round, and there's nothing, and when
I turn back, Raja is gone. There are only two footprints in
the dust. Two small footprints and no Raja. He was pointing
at Papa who follows me everywhere too. In my dreams Papa
is angry. He makes Mummy scream again as he lifts her dress,
and as he does it death comes out of his head again, whirring
and blurred and red.

When I awake my hands are briefly numb, and my
chest.

★

343

I have always yearned towards completeness and so am urged to tie up loose threads. Susheela's situation bothers me. So messy. What I must do therefore becomes amply clear. *Deus ex machina*: I will make it all tidy. When Annette comes, I ask her to take me to the telephone, but first to go to the study and take out a file, marked accounts. In it there's the name Jeffers & Co, and the number. She agrees, because I myself agree to be co-operative, and don't even comment on the appalling state of the fried egg, which she serves me with a look of fear.

At the telephone, I ask Annette to use the wheel to call the number. She laughs at my old phone, with its proper dial.

'Haven't used one of these in years,' she says, passing me the receiver.

'You and me both,' I say between breaths.

I confess I feel a little intimidated, calling into the town, the world outside the house. I confess I feel the cogs of my house turning, setting the bricks all in disarray.

The phone is, incongruously, still functional.

'I need to make an appointment as soon as possible,' I say in my best memsahib. 'A pressing matter. I haven't much time. Today would be better, I'll pay double. Triple . . . Magda Roberts . . . anytime . . . yes, that will be fine . . . yes . . . number three, Victoria Drive. I'll order a taxi.'

Behind me, Annette gasps.

'You'll come with me,' I tell her, putting down the receiver.

No one says no to me. And besides, I have saved up a complaint against poor Annette, who I have been tipping several illegal little pounds a week for quite some time. She needs the money, and I was happy for her to have it in exchange for poached eggs, cinnamon butter, and now this outing. She hasn't got a leg to stand on.

When I put the phone down, the house shifts. There's a whole kerfuffle around it. The sense of old servants, stirring in preparation. What I am about to do is deliciously implausible, and yet, it is — it is possible in the way that unlikely scientific results sometimes are, and implausible is my favourite kind of possible.

In pursuit of my tenuous plan, I have broken my own hard and fast covenant. The house holds out when I try to leave it, tripping up the wheels of my chair and catching at Annette's knuckles as she pushes it through the porch. 'Damn,' she says, 'damn,' as it scrapes and judders. I think it is Anwar, behind us, who finally gives the chair a quick shove over the threshold of the world.

There is an awful lot of sky. I almost dissolve in brightness. My body, in cahoots with the house, protests against the fresh air, the openness, and wants to cough and seize like some rusted cog. I persevere against the cough quietly. Annette will take fright at the slightest sense of infirmity, and the house will have won. The ramp into the taxi is terror, the taxi driver and Annette panting and swearing. I am a tiny, quiet ship on a bad sea.

We drive through a devastated landscape. Behind us, in the taxi, my Victorian house stands firm in the shadow of high-rises. Rounding the bay in the taxi, the gruff driver thankfully silent now, we pass the closed art deco dance hall with its four green copper domes, a cherub balancing pointlessly on top of each one. At the foot of the big wheel, we are forced by roadworks to stop a long time, the wheel stopped too, like a broken clock. It stands unturning above my memories of the gardens that used to be here along the centre of the promenade. Now the promenade is an illegible road with junctions, traffic lights and signs, and the wheel stands in a traffic island, above the cars. I stare at it almost unable to breathe at its stillness, until, perhaps, it begins to turn again, above the remembered people in their bonnets and their Sunday best, above the little dogs on leads, above the patent shoes and best hats, and above the smartness of it all. Between its segments, the separated times. And as we begin to drive again, though the wheel has stopped again, I see that it still holds them, these segmented times, the parts of my life.

We pass them, the hotels, the British, the Imperial, the Palace, the Burlington, slowly crumbling, boarded up like empty promises. And between my bad, short breaths, I'm glad. I'm glad also that the tennis courts, where the covered games were played, are thrillingly overgrown with giant hogweed and that the King's Bowling Club, as we slow beside it, has a gaudy sign advertising mini golf. Real things have also sprung up in this place of memory. A technical college. Somewhere to buy phones. A shelter for the homeless. There are people of all shades, unholidaying and here to stay. They walk the pavements checking their phones. They are present and living. I feel suddenly very, very living too. Perhaps the homeless man we pass in our taxi, tripping in broken shoes, will tonight ignore the danger signs and break into the boarded-up pavilion to sleep. I hope so. I hope he will step out of his rightful place.

I will. The air as I'm wheeled out of the taxi is cold again, impossible to inhale. I'm wheeled out of my past and into

Jeffers & Co as I turn the cogs of my house, one last time. Turn them over.

They stop.

'Magda?' says Annette. 'Are you OK?'

I sit up. I must sit up and speak to her and to the fat little taxi driver who peers at me worriedly, and who is to come in with us too if he wants the full, rather generous, fee I have offered him.

'Absolutely, silly girl. I'm fine.'

The wheels keep turning.

It has been years since I've been here, in this cluttered legal office where I once filed for divorce, and where I also once dictated a letter to demand that Michael's name be removed from one of my papers. He put up no resistance once the threat was sent. Didn't want the fuss, the reputational damage of an academic furore.

'Hello, Magda,' says the clerk. I had entirely forgotten her, poor mousy little woman now, but I can tell by the servile tone of her voice that she has not forgotten me and my money.

Though everything is now becoming blurred, I continue with the procedure I have planned out. I am methodical. I dictate to the clerk the types of precise legal phrases needed, and the dishevelled solicitor, a new one at this firm, who is sweating away across the desk, suggests minor tweaks as she types it all up. I repeat the name, several times. Susheela. Su-shee-laa, for the clerk. I bring out the small piece of paper, shaking in my hands, where I wrote the name. I pass it to them and they look at it, frowning. They disbelieve in me; these nitwits are incredulous at the way such legal phrases and technical terms drip from my old tongue. But they cannot

347

rightly do anything, in view of my evidently sound mind and the wonderfully absolute, almost fairytale power of a last will and testament. I swear on the Bible through my heavy breaths – the last manual I will touch. And I sign a name with my unsteady hand – the legal one, which is, despite several deaths and a marriage, still Magda Worsal-Compton. God knows if it is legible, but a signature need not be. Annette tries to intervene, of course.

'Are you certain, Magda? I'm not sure you know what you're doing?'

'I do,' I say. 'Perfectly.' My voice is a stern whisper.

She's distressed, poor girl. 'I shouldn't have agreed to it. I shouldn't have brought you here.'

The clerk looks worried too. 'If she's not in her right mind, you can get an assessment to say so, and cancel it,' she whispers to Annette, as if I'm not there.

'Impudence!' I say. So the stupid woman shuts up.

The Bible sworn on, the papers signed, Annette a reluctant witness, and we're all done. And I'm done in.

With great effort, I reach my hand up and pat her arm, poor girl.

'Well,' I say, trying to sound brisk, 'you can take me Home directly.'

The ride home is unprocessed and quick. I shut it all out, focus on breathing.

My house, once I am deposited back within it, is all settled down and empty, a receptacle ready to be filled. Annette wheels me into the living room to be steadied by the ticking of the clock and busies herself with getting the kettle on while I attend to the outside life, which, over these few days, has seeped in. I look at the room. It is different and sprung, even the seconds as they pass seem irregular, impulsive. Life, with its rebellious fronds, curls around the recipe books, the manuals, the club rules, the travel passes, the unnamed servants, the unmothered children, the haughtiness, the distaste for bodies, the fear, the fear, the fear.

As Annette takes me to my room we pass the teak of the dressing table. I stroke it. Alive. Smooth and cool, like a young face, and I think of her. Of Mother.

Mother succumbed to typhoid fever a day from land. She came Home as a body in a casket. Dying meant that she never had to face Home after all. None of it ever came out in the cool grey wash of British daylight. She was one more to add to the repatriated corpses of the war.

Perhaps Mother would understand Susheela's young man and his shell shock. She knew how painful a Home is when you've become the wrong shape for it and can no longer fit back in.

In her things, a letter addressed to me. And, in brackets: *(to be opened only if they find him)*.

I opened it.

It was a kind lie. It was a tenderness I could not find, at the time, in any memory I had of her.

I think it again, how my packing-case dressing table is not the only thing that did not survive that journey intact.

We buried her in the cemetery at Bay's Mouth. Grandmother and Grandfather wept dismally. I was silent standing in that cemetery, far from Kharagpur, wanting Aashi.

★

And Raja, oh what of you, Raja?

I sit with the old guilt and mystery of it. The old never knowing. They didn't find him. In the archives there is nothing, no record of him, of his life, of his death. Perhaps Raja escaped them into The Real India? I hope it again. Again. Perhaps he was only ever a dream and so wouldn't feel my betrayal if he knew?

'Madam,' he says, in the gloom of my closed rooms, 'you are stupid.'

The Raj was too stupid to find him.

There is something wet on my face. I notice it without distaste.

Between the familiar grain of guilt and sorrow, a new ache now, for Susheela. Oh how I want her to have a dignity that's unlike this house. Perhaps she'll make a recipe of it, its stairs and hallways, its cobwebbed rooms.

Annette leaves me, settled in bed with Horlicks, a straw, and a book of British flora open to the middle pages of illustrations.

The species rising from my mother's book mingle around me in the semi-darkness as I sit in my bed. I watch them, watch their stems rise, their vines coil and their leaves gather and swell as they soothe the house and its resonant memories. Through the open windows, thrown wide, perhaps by Aashi, perhaps by Anwar, there's the smell of nut oil, jasmine mixed with exhaust fumes, and the distant sound of a tannoy announcing ship rides: *best ride of the day, leaving right away, two pounds all seats.* There's the sound of quick modern cars, and past them, of Bengali gasmen banging on canisters of butane. There's the smell of cardamom and wild figs, and the sweet sound of Aashi singing her now unintelligible words. There's the feeling of shifting ground, of a British seaside turning finally to dust, and of my house and its long-awaited homing.

Chapter Forty-Five

Solutions are just mixtures in which two or more substances are well mixed.
Culinary Reactions: The Everyday Chemistry of Cooking,
Simon Quellen Field

She bloody well thought she'd solved it all: my life.

'Who're you?' It's a small boy, standing in front of her closed door like some kind of old-fashioned doorman. He's got red hair, holds a football under one arm, and looks at me as if number three Victoria Drive belongs to him.

It's the day after the paperwork has finally come through, when the house has transferred to me officially, like some kind of unlikely adoption.

'Did she die?' He says it as if he's asking whether it'll rain later.

I nod.

He bites his lip. 'Can I still play here?'

'Did she let you?'

'Kind of,' he says. 'Are you going to live here?' he asks, looking at the house and wrinkling his nose.

'Why?' I say, not sure I want him to know we're thinking of selling, nor that it'll be empty for a while probably, either way.

'Spooky!' he says, with a grin.

'It is, isn't it?' I say. 'Really spooky.'

As Ewan and me let ourselves in to the dusty skeleton of number three Victoria Drive, I feel it brace itself against us. The door, from these past few months of being constantly closed, needs a good kick. We have to crack its ribcage to get in. We step through; Ewan feels reassuring and whole by my side. My body's as layered as an onion as I dare myself over its step.

Inside, the brollies and boots shuffle a bit when we brush past them. Magda could almost be here past the hallway, in the living room, sitting in her chair under the clock, which still ticks to the empty house. The hallway smells of polish and dust, a faint trailing memory of eau de cologne, and then something beneath it, gone off. The bins haven't been taken out. The light in the hall won't turn on, and I have this feeling of being underground with the roots and worms, buried.

Ewan gets a lightbulb from somewhere, screws it in, and switches it on. We sigh together: a choir of two. Everything's dirty and dusty and looks like bloody hard work. Slugs trail their way along the porch floor. Mould pixelates the walls. The kitchen's an empty womb. The house's staircase spine beckons.

The house had been holding out against change all these years, and instead of changing on the outside, it sort of wilted in its own skin. The house was something to keep Magda in before. Now it's our loot and our problem, with its diagnosis of dry rot in the attic, its old, slightly storm-damaged roof, the

dangerous wiring in the kitchen, the damp around the skirting boards and architraves, its doors which need rehanging,
and its long, slow ache. There's no subsidence at least, as far as
Ewan and I can tell. I was surprised about that. Magda's body,
which was so heavy when Annette and me tried to wake it
that last morning, seemed to pull the house to the ground
with a weight that was just impossible for it or us to bear
without buckling.

Magda tried to keep away from the cycle of it. Birth, death,
birth. In the end, she gave in. I still can't get my head around
it. Dying in her sleep. No fuss, no bother. Seriously? I knew
straight away there'd be some catch.

I didn't know about the house for a few weeks though. That
day when we found her dead, when her body was taken away,
I picked up the piece of paper from her bedside table, the neat
little floor plan she'd drawn, and slipped it into my pocket, her
crazy dream of how we were going to live together, her in
one wing, and Ewan and me in the other. Leaving hers that
day I felt like everything, everything, had come out of place.
That floor plan was the most perfect, ordered idea, and I'd
bloody well turned it down.

So, when I finally got the solicitor's letter and pulled the expensive, cream page from the watermarked envelope, my eyes
taking in the classy letterhead and following the print across
the page until I got to . . . *has bequeathed to you her property: 3,*
Victoria Drive . . . the first thing I felt was fucking guilty. Then
there was disbelief, the paper trembling as I took the words in
again and again and tried to find a hole in them, turned the
page over, looked to see if there was a note somewhere, some

small print that made this untrue. Maybe it was a scam?

It was impossible. But it wasn't a scam. There was no one to fight it either. No family. Both her cousins were long gone, her ex-husband too.

Only Glenda in the office made a fuss. It wasn't the first time, apparently. Not the first time a home carer's been cared for back by bequest. It's not illegal, just 'embarrassing for the company'. I smarted with the guilt of it. *You didn't even bloody know her that long,* said Glenda over and over again in my head. And that was true.

But past the guilt, the disbelief, and all the other abstract nouns I felt, there was something else. A kind of wild confidence in Magda, and in what had come to pass between us, that day, in the bathroom.

Indignity. The word kept coming into my head. And that's what it was. What we shared.

Sometimes I still find myself laughing at it. At all this. At the ridiculousness of sharing a toilet, and then, of sharing a house.

The bequest has been slowly ripening, like the baby, until here we are, facing her house down.

Inside me, you kick against the house.

The task of clearing the inside is a sad one. The furniture we can't shift. How on earth did she get it in here? Huge, square wardrobes and awkwardly shaped dressing tables. None of them will fit through the doors. Each one says their name on the back, 'Worsal-Compton', with a kind of brittle pride. A badge of honour that's irrelevant now.

We get a joiner in, with the idea of pulling them to bits to get them out and putting them back together afterwards, and he tells Ewan that they were packing cases once.

'But you won't find a modern joiner who can put that lot back together if you take them apart,' he says, running his wide thumb along their hinges and their tightly worked joints.

These pieces, although they've travelled so far, weigh the place down with a stuck feeling now. No wonder she struggled to walk. We think about it for a while: do we want to keep them? But they'd weigh us down too. In the end, Ewan takes out a door to get the damned things through and into the removal van to the auction. They bring in a decent price. People like things with a story. The wood is quality Indian mahogany and teak. There's a market for colonial relics. People want to fill their houses with the Empire. It weirds me out. It's like they want to be a copy of a copy of a copy. Like Bay's Mouth seafront, a kind of hall of mirrors.

I could swear Mum's shadowing us while we clean up, muttering, *spic and span, spic and span*, and Magda's own traces and her memories hang about here too, so that the house never seems empty. We throw out curlers, we throw out clothes, because none of those things mattered to her. But I keep the photographs and the journals she's published in. And I keep her mother's false confession.

She'd told me about it, but I didn't expect to find it in a small drawer in the desk, quiet and yellow with time, like suddenly feeling the ridge of a scar on someone's back. A reminder that the past is real and unsolved, like Ewan's hearing.

It took quite a few sessions with the counsellor before Ewan started talking to me.

We were walking down the pier together again, after his latest visit to her. The day was smooth and drizzly. We were the only ones out in the soft, still rain. Half the booths were shut but we bought strong tea in polystyrene cups from the tiny cafe in the kiosk halfway along. The sea stretched wide around us.

I don't know what made me look at Ewan then, at his face, his beautiful, tired face, or what made me touch his arm. Or what made him choose this moment, between two sips of tea, to talk. His voice, when it came, was a tight string vibrating against all that stillness, ready to break. What he said ripped Bay's Mouth open.

'They found out I was good with machines pretty quick. Had me repairing anything in sight.' He took a breath as if he was going underwater. 'There were never enough real mechanics to go round. I'd get taken out to fix anything broken in the field.' He stopped, and took another deep, shaking breath. 'We were heading out that day. A normal day. As far as days out there are normal, you know. Routine. We loaded up the kit. It was blisteringly hot, I remember, but apart from that it was just like right now, in a way. Normal. "Parklife" was playing on the radio. We were joking with each other, laughing as bloody usual, driving in a convoy of three trucks along the dust road, passing donkeys and people carrying their shopping from the market, leading their goats.'

He stopped. We breathed. The sea breathed too.

'There was this static in the air, just before it happened. Even the goats at the side of the road were kind of *taut*. I asked Shaun, who was driving, to stop, but the guy on the radio said we needed to get out of open country. It was quicker to go forward than to go back.'

The sea swilled. A seagull called.

'When it went off, shrapnel from the blast went straight through Shaun's eye and out of the back of his head. I just remember blood. Someone's mouth opening and closing, like they were screaming and screaming but there was no sound. It was Ian.'

The seagull was quiet. The sea too. He looked down as it swilled slowly under the slatted walkway of the pier.

'Half his body was gone. He bled out.'

I listened while he named it all, one word at a time. The other side of the Bay's Mouth postcard. The hurt that usually just sits out there on the seeping horizon, but that right now slowly tore a big rip through the whole bloody place.

After that lot of counselling was done, he'd gone for what we called 'the weird therapy' after all. Eye Movement De-sensitisation and Reprocessing. Something straight out of sci-fi. One of those things you can't believe will ever work. Ewan had to sit practising these relaxation techniques they taught him, and then he went to sessions where they got him to focus on awful things he'd felt and seen out there, and follow something with his eyes at the same time, moving it back and forth like in old-fashioned hypnosis. I imagine that, when his soft eyes shift and shift, it's like the shutter of an antique camera, making sepia pictures of his traumas till they behave more like bad memories usually do. Perhaps we won't live as much half in them and half out any more.

Perhaps. But they're still faded shadows, waiting in the wings, not completely programmed away. And the army's still a kind of *desh* for Ewan and the others; it's always got a place in him, in the way he works here, at the house, methodically, doing everything that needs to be done, labouring at it with Darren – and Nathan too when he comes down to lend a hand. They jibe at each other like brothers, constantly ripping the piss, but they keep moving till the job's done: one company, moving forward. They'll bloody well hold on to each other, and to that belonging, fitting themselves to its old patterns. I don't tell him that I'm wary of it, this *desh* of theirs, because although it holds them together, it sometimes holds me apart. I've learnt from Magda that *desh* can be an exclusion zone, like a home can be a fortress.

In the end the red-haired boy and Darren help me and Ewan tidy up the garden a bit, pulling up weeds, roughly chopping back the hedges, till you can see the shape of the place again, pick out its bones. We'd been clearing the last patch of brambles together, when the boy finds it there, between the thorns.

'Bloody hell,' says the boy, like a grown-up, lifting the cube for me to see.

'Bloody hell,' says Darren, taking his fag out of his mouth to stare.

A Rubik's Cube, all the sides turned perfectly. Blue. Yellow. Red. Green. Orange. White.

'She did it,' says the kid, pointing at the house, at Magda. 'I gave it to her, and she did it. She did it.' He looks confused for a second. 'Why did she throw it away?'

It's impossible, what he's saying. I can't imagine those old hands, turning it one millimetre at a time. Except that she was so, so stubborn and had so many long hours alone. What I *can* imagine, without any difficulty, is her flinging this cube into the garden from an upstairs window. Because making it perfect didn't make it live.

Ewan's been at the back of the house, surveying the state of it. He comes to where Darren, me and the kid are standing and looks around at the garden of brambles, long grasses, wild bushes and straggly old roses which probably haven't flowered for years.

'The grass needs properly mowing before we sell,' he says, like some kind of groundsman.

I look at him and shake my head.

I can imagine how much she'd relish it. The way we're putting everything perfectly back in order for her, polishing the floors, making the garden perfectly controlled again. But: *No.* I smile at her in my head, *I'm not going to dignify your bloody lawn.*

It's Dad who comes up with the idea of what to do with it, today when I meet him from his temporary job in the Colonial.

The place is all contemporary design and modern art, the punters mostly hip young couples doing Bay's Mouth in a tongue-in-cheek way, so Dad's butler routine'll be doubly ironic if he's got the guts to do it here. I've been hoping they'll give him a proper job, because it'd be such a boost, and part of me's expecting to see him in full butler mode when I turn up there. But he comes down the stairs behind reception carrying a mop and bucket and looking a bit awkward and out of place. The woman on reception, all asymmetrical hair and black lipstick, barely acknowledges his 'Right then, that's me done,' like he's not worth much. I'm so bloody relieved when he winks at me and rolls his eyes about the stupid cow.

I give him a hug to make up for her. He smells of jasmine air freshener and beeswax. My mum's favourite scents.

'How's my girl?' patting my shoulder and looking at my belly which is so big I can't do up any of my coats.

I shrug. Truth is I'm dog-tired after all the work at Magda's. My head's swimming.

'You OK, love?'

'I'm just a bit knackered; we've been doing stuff at the house.'

In the hotel lobby the guests mill around us and the sound of the tannoy seeps in from the beach.

'Dad, I don't know what the hell to do with that garden.'

He looks at me. He looks out of the big glass doors of the hotel, at the sea.

'I do,' he says.

He shows me the formula for what to do with it on a website.

To turn a difficult-to-maintain lawn into your very own wildflower meadow, first rake over it coarsely, sparing no pity for the green grass, then seed the lawn with yellow-rattle to choke it properly. You can now plant whatever wildflower seeds you like.

Dad and me scatter packets and packets of seeds like confetti all over the grass and the rude-looking soil that shows through it like a flash of knicker after the raking. We're whirling in circles and reciting the names on the packets like spells:

Ramsons, cow parsley, thrift, harebell.

By next summer there'll be tiger moths in the evenings, red admiral butterflies by day. I can already see them out of the corner of my eye, fluttering like sprites around the garden.

Dad whoops as he scatters the seeds. I'm laughing. It feels like we're writing some kind of wild epitaph for Magda, for Mum, for number three Victoria Drive, for the goddam British Hotel. I keep incanting them, the names:

Lily of the valley, lady's bedstraw, forget-me-not.

I stop, with my empty seed packet in my hand, and Dad stops too. I can feel it.

Future.

It billows out over Bay's Mouth, messy with loose ends, contradictions and different kinds of *desh,* full of birds from other places, odd moths, and incomplete lives.

Like a lady let out of her corset, or like the first inflation of a tiny baby's lungs, the garden starts to breathe.

Acknowledgements

During and before the writing, vital and vivid conversations were shared with friends, colleagues, ex-servicemen, carers, occupational therapists, psychologists, children of the Raj, ex-memsahibs and family. Your lives are not in the book, but your insights helped to shape it. Thank you.

Thank you to all the hoteliers, shopkeepers, librarians and museum guides (from West-Bengal to Weston-super-Mare to Llandudno) who made my writing visits valuable.

To writers and scholars Zoe Skoulding, Jodie Kim, Sampurna Chattarji, Laura Ellen Joyce, Kathryn Pallant, Kachi A. Ozumba, Neelam Srivastava, DeAnn Bell, Fiona Cameron, Maureen McCue, Tomos Owen and Holly Ringland, thank you for sharing drafts, embryonic ideas, books, or for encouraging me along the way.

With our colonial history largely publically inaccessible – like the British Empire and Commonwealth Museum which is largely out-of-bounds in storage – thanks to the Bristol Archive for making some of its material available to the public. Thank you to the British Library for access to invaluable audio and written materials, and to the British in

India Museum, in its suitably kitsch prefab in Hendon Mill, for giving a unique perspective, perhaps with unintentional nuance, on the legacy of the Raj.

Thank you to Bangor University and the AHRC for the grant that afforded me time to research and write this novel, and heartfelt thanks to Parthian Books, The Welsh Books Council, Literature Wales, and T. Newydd for your support of my writing until now.

To Jenny Hewson, for your incisive reading and work on my behalf, a big thank you. And to Federico Andornino, thank goodness for the rare combination of precision and openness that you brought to the process of editing *Dignity*. Thank you to everyone at Weidenfeld & Nicolson for taking care of this book and making others care for it.

Finally, to my Joe, for the gentleness, humour and affection of our home, which made it possible for me to see this book through. Diolch cariad, eto, o waelod calon.

Help us make the next generation of readers

We – both author and publisher – hope you enjoyed this book.
We believe that you can become a reader at any time in your life,
but we'd love your help to give the next generation a head start.

Did you know that 9% of children don't have a book of their
own in their home, rising to 13% in disadvantaged families*?
We'd like to try to change that by asking you to consider the role
you could play in helping to build readers of the future.

We'd love you to think of sharing, borrowing, reading, buying or talking
about a book with a child in your life and spreading the love of reading.
We want to make sure the next generation continue to have access
to books, wherever they come from.

And if you would like to consider donating to charities that help
fund literacy projects, find out more at www.literacytrust.org.uk
and www.booktrust.org.uk.

Thank you.

*As reported by the National Literacy Trust